"**ENTERTAINING**. . . produces all the euphoria of an actual musical; readers will be on their feet."
—*The Horn Book*

"**IRRESISTIBLY FUNNY**, insistently wise, and filled with the honest power of friendship."
—*Wichita Eagle*

"This may well be the **BEST NOVEL** that either John Green or David Levithan has ever written. Inventive and **INSIGHTFUL**."
—*Shelf Awareness*

"A **TERRIFIC** high-energy tale." —*Booklist*, starred review

"Powerful, thought-provoking, funny, moving and **UNIQUE**."
—*SLJ*, starred review

"Until now few LGBT titles became **blockbusters**. That changed with two boys named Will Grayson and a very large, very **GLEE-ful** linebacker named Tiny." —*The Associated Press*

grayson,
grayson,

will grayson

And the kid looks at me confused for a minute and finally says, "What's your name?"

This is freaking me out. Frenchy's isn't a place for *conversation*. So I just say to Piercings, "Can I have the magazine?" and Piercings hands it to me in an unmarked and thoroughly opaque black plastic bag for which I am very grateful, and he gives me my card and my receipt. I walk out the door, jog a half block down Clark, and then sit down on the curb and wait for my pulse to slow down.

Which it is just starting to do when my fellow underage Frenchy's pilgrim runs up to me and says, "Who *are* you?"

I stand up then and say, "Um, I'm Will Grayson."

"W-I-L-L G-R-A-Y-S-O-N?" he says, spelling impossibly fast.

"Ugh, yeah," I say. "Why do you ask?"

The kid looks at me for a second, his head turned like he thinks I might be putting him on, and then finally he says, "Because I am also Will Grayson."

OTHER BOOKS YOU MAY ENJOY

will grayson,

john green & david levithan

will grayson, will grayson

speak

An Imprint of Penguin Group (USA) Inc.

SPEAK
Published by the Penguin Group
Penguin Group (USA) Inc., 345 Hudson Street, New York, New York 10014, U.S.A.
Penguin Group (Canada), 90 Eglinton Avenue East, Suite 700, Toronto, Ontario, Canada M4P 2Y3
(a division of Pearson Penguin Canada Inc.)
Penguin Books Ltd, 80 Strand, London WC2R 0RL, England
Penguin Ireland, 25 St Stephen's Green, Dublin 2, Ireland (a division of Penguin Books Ltd)
Penguin Group (Australia), 250 Camberwell Road, Camberwell, Victoria 3124, Australia
(a division of Pearson Australia Group Pty Ltd)
Penguin Books India Pvt Ltd, 11 Community Centre, Panchsheel Park, New Delhi - 110 017, India
Penguin Group (NZ), 67 Apollo Drive, Rosedale, Auckland 0632, New Zealand
(a division of Pearson New Zealand Ltd.)
Penguin Books (South Africa) (Pty) Ltd, 24 Sturdee Avenue,
Rosebank, Johannesburg 2196, South Africa

Penguin Books Ltd, Registered Offices: 80 Strand, London WC2R 0RL, England

First published in the United States of America by Dutton Books,
a member of Penguin Group (USA) Inc., 2010
Published by Speak, an imprint of Penguin Group (USA) Inc., 2011

19 20 18

LIBRARY OF CONGRESS CATALOGING-IN-PUBLICATION DATA IS AVAILABLE

Speak ISBN 978-0-14-241847-5

Printed in the United States of America
Designed by Irene Vandervoort
Text set in Carre Noir

To David Leventhal
(for being so close)
– DL

To Tobias Huisman
–JG

will grayson,

chapter one

When I was little, my dad used to tell me, "Will, you can pick your friends, and you can pick your nose, but you can't pick your friend's nose." This seemed like a reasonably astute observation to me when I was eight, but it turns out to be incorrect on a few levels. To begin with, you cannot possibly pick your friends, or else I never would have ended up with Tiny Cooper.

Tiny Cooper is not the world's gayest person, and he is not the world's largest person, but I believe he may be the world's largest person who is really, really gay, and also the world's gayest person who is really, really large. Tiny has been my best friend since fifth grade, except for all last semester, when he was busy discovering the sheer scope of his own gayness, and I was busy having an actual honest-to-God Group of Friends for the first time in my life, who ended up Never Talking to Me Again due to two slight transgressions:

1. After some school-board member got all upset about gays in the locker room, I defended Tiny Cooper's right to be both gigantic (and, therefore,

the best member of our shitty football team's offensive line) and gay in a letter to the school newspaper that I, stupidly, signed.

2. This guy in the Group of Friends named Clint was talking about the letter at lunch, and in the process of talking about it, he called me a bitchsquealer, and I didn't know what a bitchsquealer was, so I was like, "What do you mean?" And then he called me a bitchsquealer again, at which point I told Clint to fuck off and then took my tray and left.

Which I guess means that technically *I* left the Group of Friends, although it felt the other way around. Honestly, none of them ever seemed to like me, but they were *around*, which isn't nothing. And now they aren't around, leaving me utterly bereft of social peers.

Unless you count Tiny, that is. Which I suppose I must.

Andbutso a few weeks after we get back from Christmas break our junior year, I'm sitting in my Assigned Seat in precalc when Tiny waltzes in wearing his jersey tucked into his chinos, even though football season is long over. Every day, Tiny miraculously manages to wedge himself into the chair-desk beside mine in precalc, and every day, I am amazed he can do it.

So Tiny squeezes into his chair, I am duly amazed, and then he turns to me and he whispers really loudly because secretly he wants other people to hear, "I'm in *love*." I roll my eyes, because he falls in love every hour on the hour with some poor new boy. They all look the same: skinny and sweaty and tan, the last an abomination, because all February tans in Chicago are fake, and boys who fake tan—I don't care whether they're gay—are ridiculous.

"You're so cynical," Tiny says, waving his hand at me.

"I'm not cynical, Tiny," I answer. "I'm practical."

"You're a robot," he says. Tiny thinks that I am incapable of what humans call emotion because I have not cried since my seventh birthday, when I saw the movie *All Dogs Go to Heaven*. I suppose I should have known from the title that it wouldn't end merrily, but in my defense, I was seven. Anyway, I haven't cried since then. I don't really understand the *point* of crying. Also, I feel that crying is almost—like, aside from deaths of relatives or whatever—totally avoidable if you follow two very simple rules: 1. Don't care too much. 2. Shut up. Everything unfortunate that has ever happened to me has stemmed from failure to follow one of the rules.

"I know love is real because I *feel* it," Tiny says.

Apparently, class has started without our knowing, because Mr. Applebaum, who is ostensibly teaching us precalculus but is mostly teaching me that pain and suffering must be endured stoically, says, "You feel what, Tiny?"

"Love!" says Tiny. "I feel love." And everyone turns around and either laughs or groans at Tiny, and because I'm sitting next to him and he's my best and only friend, they're laughing and groaning at me, too, which is precisely why I would not choose Tiny Cooper as my friend. He draws too much attention. Also, he has a pathological inability to follow either of my two rules. And so he waltzes around, caring too much and ceaselessly talking, and then he's baffled when the world craps on him. And, of course, due to sheer proximity, this means the world craps on me, too.

After class, I'm staring into my locker, wondering how I managed to leave *The Scarlet Letter* at home, when Tiny comes up with his Gay-Straight Alliance friends Gary (who is gay) and Jane (who may or may not be—I've never asked), and Tiny says to me, "Apparently, everyone thinks I professed my love for you in precalc. Me in love with Will Grayson. Isn't that the silliest crap you ever heard?"

"Great," I say.

"People are just such idiots," Tiny says. "As if there's something wrong with being in love."

Gary groans then. If you could pick your friends, I'd consider Gary. Tiny got close with Gary and Jane and Gary's boyfriend, Nick, when he joined the GSA during my tenure as a member of the Group of Friends. I barely know Gary, since I've only been hanging around Tiny again for about two weeks, but he seems like the normalest person Tiny has ever befriended.

"There's a difference," Gary points out, "between being in love and announcing it in precalc." Tiny starts to talk and Gary cuts him off. "I mean, don't get me wrong. You have every right to love Zach."

"Billy," says Tiny.

"Wait, what happened to Zach?" I ask, because I could have sworn Tiny was in love with a Zach during precalc. But forty-seven minutes have passed since his proclamation, so maybe he's changed gears. Tiny has had about 3,900 boyfriends—half of them Internet-only.

Gary, who seems as flummoxed by the emergence of Billy as I am, leans against the lockers and bangs his head softly against the steel. "Tiny, you being a makeout whore is *so* not good for the cause."

I look way up at Tiny and say, "Can we quell the rumors of our love? It hurts my chances with the ladies."

"Calling them 'the ladies' doesn't help either," Jane tells me.

Tiny laughs. "But seriously," I tell him, "I always catch shit about it." Tiny looks at me seriously for once and nods a little.

"Although for the record," Gary says, "you could do worse than Will Grayson."

"And he has," I note.

Tiny spins in a balletic pirouette out into the middle of the hallway and, laughing, shouts, "Dear World, I am not hot for Will Grayson. But world, there's something else you should know about Will Grayson." And then he begins to sing, a Broadway baritone as big as his waist, "I can't live without him!"

People laugh and whoop and clap as Tiny continues the serenade while I walk off to English. It's a long walk, and it only gets longer when someone stops you and asks how it feels to be sodomized by Tiny Cooper, and how you find Tiny Cooper's "gay little pencil prick" behind his fat belly. I respond the way I always do: by looking down and walking straight and fast. I know they're kidding. I know part of knowing someone is being mean to them or whatever. Tiny always has some brilliant thing to say back, like, "For someone who theoretically doesn't want me, you sure spend a lot of time thinking and talking about my penis." Maybe that works for Tiny, but it never works for me. Shutting up works. Following the rules works. So I shut up, and I don't care, and I keep walking, and soon it's over.

The last time I said anything of note was the time I wrote the fricking letter to the editor about fricking Tiny Cooper and his fricking right to be a fricking star on our horrible football team. I don't regret writing the letter in the least, but I regret signing it. Signing it was a clear violation of the rule about shutting up, and look where it got me: alone on a Tuesday afternoon, staring at my black Chuck Taylors.

That night, not long after I order pizza for me and my parents, who are—as always—late at the hospital, Tiny Cooper calls me and, real quiet and fast, he blurts out, "Neutral Milk Hotel is supposedly playing a reunion show at the Hideout and it's totally not advertised and no one even knows about it and holy shit, Grayson, holy shit!"

"Holy shit!" I shout. One thing you can say for Tiny: whenever something awesome happens, Tiny is always the first to hear.

Now, I am not generally given over to excitement, but Neutral Milk Hotel sort of changed my life. They released this absolutely fantastic album called *In the Aeroplane Over the Sea* in 1998 and haven't been heard from since, purportedly because their lead singer lives in a cave in New Zealand. But anyway, he's a genius. "When?"

"Dunno. I just heard. I'm gonna call Jane, too. She likes them almost as much as you do. Okay, so now. Now. Let's go to the Hideout now."

"I'm literally on my way," I answer, opening the door to the garage.

I call my mom from the car. I tell her Neutral Milk Hotel is playing at the Hideout and she says, "Who? What? You're hiding out?" And then I hum a few bars of one of their songs and Mom says, "Oh, I know that song. It's on the mix you made me," and I say, "Right," and she says, "Well you have to be back by eleven," and I say, "Mom this is a historical event. History doesn't have a curfew," and she says, "Back by eleven," and I say, "Fine. Jesus," and then she has to go cut cancer out of someone.

Tiny Cooper lives in a mansion with the world's richest parents. I don't think either of his parents have jobs, but they are so disgustingly rich that Tiny Cooper doesn't even live *in* the mansion; he lives in the mansion's *coach house*, all by himself. He has three bedrooms in that motherfucker and a fridge that always has beer in it and his parents never bother him, and so we can sit there all day and play video game football and drink Miller Lite, except in point of fact Tiny hates video games and I hate drinking beer, so mostly all we ever do is play darts (he has a dartboard) and listen to music and talk and study. I've just started to say the *T* in Tiny when he comes running out of his room, one black leather loafer on and the other in his hand, shouting, "Go, Grayson, go go."

And everything goes perfectly on the way there. Traffic's not too bad on Sheridan, and I'm cornering the car like it's the Indy 500, and we're listening to my favorite NMH song, "Holland, 1945," and then onto Lake Shore Drive, the waves of Lake Michigan crashing against the boulders by the Drive, the windows cracked to get the car to defrost, the dirty, bracing, cold air rushing in, and I love the way Chicago smells—Chicago is brackish lake water and soot and sweat and grease and I love it, and I love this song, and Tiny's saying *I love this song*, and he's got the visor down so he can muss up his hair a little more expertly. That gets me to thinking that Neutral Milk Hotel is going to *see me* just as surely as I'm going to see them, so I give myself a once-over in the rearview. My face seems too square and my eyes too big, like I'm perpetually surprised, but there's nothing wrong with me that I can fix.

The Hideout is a dive bar made of wooden planks that's nestled between a factory and some Department of Transportation building. There's nothing swank about it, but there's a line out the door even though it's only seven. So I huddle in line for a while with Tiny until Gary and Possibly Gay Jane show up.

Jane's wearing a hand-scrawled Neutral Milk Hotel v-neck T-shirt under her open coat. Jane showed up in Tiny's life around the time I dropped out of it, so we don't really know each other. Still, I'd say she's currently about my fourth-best friend, and apparently she has good taste in music.

Waiting outside the Hideout in the face-scrunching cold, she says hi without looking at me, and I say hi back, and then she says, "This band is so completely brilliant," and I say, "I know."

This marks possibly the longest conversation I've ever had with Jane. I kick at the gravelly dirt a little and watch a miniature dust cloud encircle my foot and then I tell Jane how much I like "Holland, 1945," and she says, "I like their less accessible stuff. The polyphonic, noisy stuff." I just nod, in hopes that it appears I know what *polyphonic* means.

One thing about Tiny Cooper is that you can't whisper in his ear, even if you're reasonably tall like myself, because the motherfucker is six six, and so you have to tap his giant shoulder and then sort of motion with your head that you'd like to whisper into his ear, and then he leans down and you say, "Hey, is Jane the gay part of the Gay-Straight Alliance or the straight part?"

And Tiny leans down to my ear and whispers back, "Dunno. I think she had a boyfriend freshman year." I point out that Tiny Cooper had about 11,542 girlfriends freshman year, and then Tiny punches me in the arm in a way that he thinks is playful but actually causes permanent nerve damage.

Gary is rubbing Jane's arms up and down to keep her warm when *finally* the line starts to move. Then about five seconds later, we see this kid looking heartbroken, and he's precisely the kind of small-blond-tan guy Tiny Cooper would like, and so Tiny says, "What's wrong?" And then the kid answers, "It's over twenty-one only."

"You," I tell Tiny, stammering. "You *bitchsquealer*." I still don't know what it means, but it seems appropriate.

Tiny Cooper purses his lips and furrows his brow. He turns to Jane. "You got a fake ID?" Jane nods. Gary pipes up, "Me too," and I'm tensing my fists, my jaw locked, and I just want to scream, but instead I say, "Whatever, I'm going home," because *I* don't have a fake ID.

But then Tiny says real fast and real quiet, "Gary, hit me as hard as you can in the face when I'm showing my ID, and then, Grayson, you just walk behind me like you belong in the joint," and then no one says anything for a while, until Gary says, too loud, "Um, I don't really know how to *hit*." We're getting close to the bouncer, who has a large tattoo on his bald head, so Tiny just mumbles, "Yes you do. Just hit me hard."

I lag back a little, watching. Jane gives her ID to the bouncer. He shines a flashlight on it, glances up at her, and hands it back. Then it's Tiny's turn. I take a series of very quick, short breaths, because I read once that people with a lot of oxygen in their blood look calmer, and then I watch as Gary gets on his tiptoes and rears his arm back and wallops Tiny in the right eye. Tiny's head jerks back, and Gary screams, "Oh my God, *ow ow*, shit my hand," and the bouncer jumps up to grab Gary, and then Tiny Cooper turns his body to block the bouncer's view of me, and as Tiny turns, I walk into the bar like Tiny Cooper is my revolving door.

Once inside, I look back and see the bouncer holding Gary by the shoulders, and Gary grimacing while staring at his hand. Then Tiny puts a hand on the bouncer and says, "Dude, we were just fucking around. Good one though, Dwight." It takes me a minute to figure out that Gary is Dwight. Or Dwight is Gary.

The bouncer says, "He fucking hit you in the eye," and

then Tiny says, "He owed me one," and then Tiny explains to the bouncer that both he and Gary/Dwight are members of the DePaul University football team, and that earlier in the weight room Tiny had spotted poorly or something. The bouncer says he played O-Line in high school, and then suddenly they're having a nice little chat while the bouncer glances at Gary's extrarordinarily fake ID, and then we are all four of us inside the Hideout, alone with Neutral Milk Hotel and a hundred strangers.

The people-sea surrounding the bar parts and Tiny gets a couple of beers and offers me one. I decline. "Why Dwight?" I ask. And Tiny says, "On his ID, he's Dwight David Eisenhower IV." And I say, "Where the frak did everyone get a fake ID anyway?" and then Tiny says, "There are places." I resolve to get one.

I say, "Actually, I will have a beer," mostly because I want something in my hand. Tiny hands me the one he's already started in on, and then I make my way up close to the stage without Tiny and without Gary and without Possibly Gay Jane. It's just me and the stage, which is only raised up about two feet in this joint, so if the lead singer of Neutral Milk Hotel is particularly short—like if he is three feet ten inches tall—I will soon be looking him straight in the eye. Other people move up to the stage, and soon the place is packed. I've been here before for all-ages shows, but it's never been like this—the beer that I haven't sipped and don't intend to sweating in my hand, the well-pierced, tattooed strangers all around me. Every last soul in the Hideout right now is cooler than anyone in the Group of Friends. These people don't think there's anything wrong with me—they don't even *notice* me. They assume I am one of them, which feels like the very summit of my high school career. Here I am, standing on an over-twenty-one night at the best bar in America's second city, getting ready to be among a couple hundred people who see the reunion show of the greatest no-name band of the last decade.

These four guys come out onstage, and while they don't bear a *striking* resemblance to the members of Neutral Milk Hotel, I tell myself that, whatever, I've only seen pictures on the web. But then they start playing. I'm not quite sure how to describe this band's music, except to say that it sounds like a hundred thousand weasels being dropped into a boiling ocean. And then the guy starts singing:

> *She used to love me, yeah*
> *But now she hates*
> *She used to screw me, bro*
> *But now she dates*
> *Other guys*
> *Other guys*

Barring a prefrontal lobotomy, there's absolutely no way that the lead singer of Neutral Milk Hotel would ever *think*, let alone *write*, let alone *sing*, such lyrics. And then I realize: I have waited outside in the cold gray-lit car-exhausted frigidity and caused the possible broken bones in Gary's hand to hear a band that is, manifestly, *not* Neutral Milk Hotel. And although he is nowhere amid the crowd of hushed and stunned NMH fans surrounding me, I immediately shout, "Damn you, Tiny Cooper!"

At the end of the song, my suspicions are confirmed when the lead singer says, to a reception of absolute silence, "Thank you! Thanks very much. NMH couldn't make it, but we're Ashland Avenue, and we're here to rock!" *No*, I think. *You're Ashland Avenue and you're here to suck.* Someone taps me on the shoulder then and I turn around and find myself staring at this unspeakably hot twenty-something girl with a labret piercing, flaming red hair, and boots up her calves. She says, askingly, "We thought Neutral Milk Hotel was playing?" and I look down and say, "Me—" I stammer for a second, and then say "too. I'm here for them, too."

The girl leans into my ear to shout above the atonal arrhythmic affront to decency that is Ashland Avenue. "Ashland Avenue is no Neutral Milk Hotel."

Something about the fullness of the room, or the strangeness of the stranger, has made me talkative, and I shout back, "Ashland Avenue is what they play to terrorists to make them talk." The girl smiles, and it's only now that I realize that she's conscious of the age difference. She asks me where I'm in school, and I say "Evanston," and she says, "*High* school?" And I say, "Yeah but don't tell the bartender," and she says, "I feel like a real pervert right now," and I say, "Why?" and she just laughs. I know the girl isn't really into me, but I still feel marginally pimping.

And then this huge hand settles on my shoulder, and I look down and see the middle school graduation ring he's worn on his pinkie ever since eighth grade and know immediately that it's Tiny. And to think, some idiots claim that the gays have fashion sense.

I turn around and Tiny Cooper is crying huge tears. One of Tiny Cooper's tears could drown a kitten. And I mouth

WHAT'S WRONG because Ashland Avenue is sucking too loudly for him to hear me, and Tiny Cooper just hands me his phone and walks away. It's showing me Tiny's Facebook feed, zoomed in on a status update.

Zach is like the more i think about it the more i think y ruin a gr8 frendship? i still think tiny's awesum tho.

I push my way through a couple people to Tiny, and I pull down his shoulder and scream into his ear, "THAT'S PRETTY FUCKING BAD," and Tiny shouts back, "I GOT DUMPED BY STATUS UPDATE," and I answer, "YEAH, I NOTICED. I MEAN, HE COULD HAVE AT LEAST TEXTED. OR E-MAILED. OR SENT A PASSENGER PIGEON."

"WHAT AM I GOING TO *DO*?" Tiny shouts in my ear, and I want to say, "Hopefully, go find a guy who knows there is no u in *awesome*," but I just shrug my shoulders and pat him firmly on the back, and guide him away from Ashland Avenue and toward the bar.

Which, as it turns out, is something of a mistake. Just before we get to the bar, I see Possibly Gay Jane hovering by a tall table. She tells me Gary has left in disgust. "It was a publicity ploy by Ashland Avenue, apparently," she says.

I say, "But no NMH fan would *ever* listen to this drivel."

Then Jane looks up at me all pouty and big-eyed and says, "My brother is the guitarist."

I feel like a total asshole and say, "Oh, sorry, dude."

And she says, "Christ, I'm kidding. If he were, I'd disown him." At some point during our four-second conversation I have managed to completely lose Tiny, which is no easy task, so I tell Jane about Tiny's great Facebook wall of dumpage, and she is still laughing when Tiny appears at our table with a round tray holding six shot glasses full of a greenish liquid. "I don't really drink," I remind Tiny, and he nods. He pushes a shot toward Jane, and Jane just shakes her head.

Tiny takes a shot, grimaces, and exhales. "Tastes like Satan's fire cock," Tiny says, and then pushes another shot in my direction. "Sounds delightful," I say, "but I'll pass."

"How can he just," Tiny yells, and then he takes a shot, "dump me," and another shot, "on his STATUS after I say I LOVE him," and another. "What is the goddamned world coming to?" Another. "I really do, Grayson. I know you think I'm full of shit, but I knew I loved him the moment we kissed. Goddamn it. What am I going to *do*?" And then he stifles a sob with the last shot.

Jane tugs on my shirtsleeve and leans in to me. I can feel her breath warm against my neck, and she says, "We're going to have a big frickin' problem when he starts feeling those shots," and I decide that Jane is right, and anyway, Ashland Avenue is terrible, so we need to leave the Hideout posthaste.

I turn to tell Tiny it's time to go, but he has disappeared. I glance back at Jane, who's looking toward the bar with a look of profound concern on her face. Shortly thereafter, Tiny Cooper returns. Only two shots this time, thank God.

"Drink with me," he says, and I shake my head, but then Jane pokes me in the back, and I realize that I have to take a bullet for Tiny. I dig into my pocket and hand Jane my car keys. The only sure way to prevent him from drinking the rest of the plutonium-green booze is to down one myself. So I grab the shot glass and Tiny says, "Aw, fuck him, anyway, Grayson. Fuck everybody," and I say, "I'll drink to that," and I do, and then it hits my tongue and it's like a burning Molotov cocktail—glass and all. I involuntarily spit the entire shot out onto Tiny Cooper's shirt.

"A monochrome Jackson Pollock," Jane says, and then tells Tiny, "We gotta bolt. This band is like a root canal *sans* painkiller."

Jane and I walk out together, figuring (correctly, as it turns out) that Tiny, wearing my shot of nuclear fallout, will follow us. Since I've failed at drinking both the alcoholic beverages Tiny bought me, Jane tosses the keys back to me in a high arc. I grab them and get behind the wheel after Jane climbs into the back. Tiny tumbles into the passenger seat. I start the car, and my date with massive aural disappointment comes to an end. But I hardly think about it on the way home because Tiny keeps going on about Zach. That's the thing about Tiny: his problems are so huge that yours can hide behind them.

"How can you just be so *wrong* about something?" Tiny is asking over the noisy screechiness of Jane's favorite (and my least favorite) NMH song. I'm cruising up Lake Shore and can hear Jane singing along in the back, a little off-key but closer than I'd be if I sang in front of people, which I don't, due to the Shutting Up Rule. And Tiny is saying, "If you can't trust your gut then what can you trust?" And I say, "You can trust that caring, as a rule, ends poorly," which is true. Caring doesn't sometimes lead to misery. It always does.

"My *heart* is broken," Tiny says, as if the thing has never happened before to him, as if it has never happened before to anyone. And maybe that's the problem: maybe each new breakup feels so radically new to Tiny that, in some way, it *hasn't* happened before. "And Yaw naht helping," he adds, which is when I notice he's slurring his words. Ten minutes from his house if we don't catch traffic, and then straight to bed.

But I can't drive as fast as Tiny can deteriorate. By the time I exit Lake Shore—six minutes to go—he's slurring his words *and* bawling, going on and on about Facebook and the death of polite society and whatever. Jane's got her hands, with fingernails painted black, kneading Tiny's elephantine shoulders, but he can't seem to stop crying, and I'm missing all the lights as Sheridan slowly unwinds before us, and the snot and tears mix until Tiny's T-shirt is just a wet mess. "How far?" Jane asks, and I say, "He lives off Central," and she says, "Jesus. Stay calm, Tiny. You just need to go to sleep, baby. Tomorrow makes everything a little better."

Finally, I turn into the alley and steer around the potholes until we get behind Tiny's coach house. I jump out of the car and push my seat forward so Jane can get out behind me. Then we walk around to the passenger seat. Jane opens the door, reaches across Tiny, manages through a miracle of dexterity to unfasten his seat belt, and then says, "All right, Tiny. Time for bed," and Tiny says, "I'm a fool," and then unleashes a sob that probably registers on the Richter scale in Kansas. But he gets up and weaves toward his back door. I follow, just to make sure he gets to bed all right, which turns out to be a good idea, because he doesn't get to bed all right.

Instead, about three steps into the living room, he stops dead in his tracks. He turns around and stares at me, his eyes squinting as if he's never seen me before and can't figure out why I'm in his house. Then he takes off his shirt. He's still looking at me quizzically when, sounding stone sober, he says, "Grayson, something needs to happen," and I say, "Huh?" And Tiny says, "Because otherwise what if we just end up like everybody at the Hideout?" And I'm about to say *huh* again, because those people were far cooler than our classmates and also far cooler than us, but then I know what he means. He means, What if we become grown-ups waiting for a band that's never coming back? I notice Tiny looking blankly at me, swaying back and forth like a skyscraper in the wind. And then he falls facefirst.

"Oh boy," Jane says behind me, and only then do I realize she's here. Tiny, his face buried in carpet, has taken to crying again. I look at Jane for a long time and a slow smile creeps over her face. Her whole face changes when she smiles—this eyebrow-lifting, perfect-teeth-showing, eye-crinkling smile I've either never seen or never noticed. She becomes pretty so suddenly that it's almost like a magic trick—but it's not like I want her or anything. Not to sound like a jerk, but Jane isn't really my type. Her hair's kinda disastrously curly and she mostly hangs out with guys. My type's a little girlier. And honestly, I don't even like my type of girl that much, let alone other types. Not that I'm asexual—I just find Romance Drama unbearable.

"Let's get him in bed," she says finally. "Can't have his parents find this in the morning."

I kneel down and tell Tiny to get up, but he just keeps crying and crying, so finally Jane and I get on his left side and roll him over onto his back. I step over him, and then reach down, getting a good grip under his armpit. Jane mimics me on his other side.

"One," says Jane, and I say, "Two," and she says, "Three," and grunts. But nothing happens. Jane is small—I can see her upper arm narrow as she flexes her muscles. And I can't lift my half of Tiny either, so we resolve to leave him there. By the time Jane places a blanket on top of Tiny and a pillow beneath his head, he's snoring.

We're about to leave when all of Tiny's snotting finally catches up with him, and he begins to make these hideous noises that sound like snoring, except more sinister, and also more wet. I lean down to his face and see that he's inhaling and exhaling these disgusting bubbly strands of snot from the last throes of his cryathon. There's so much of the stuff that I worry he'll choke.

"Tiny," I say. "You gotta get the snot outta your nose, man," but he doesn't stir. So I get down right by his eardrum and shout, "Tiny!" Nothing. Then Jane smacks him across the face, really rather hard. Nada. Just the awful, drowning-in-snot snoring.

And that is when I realize that Tiny Cooper cannot pick his nose, countering the second part of my dad's theorem. And shortly thereafter, with Jane looking on, I disprove the theorem entirely when I reach down and clear Tiny's airways of snot. In short: I cannot pick my friend; he cannot pick his nose; and I can—nay, I *must*—pick it for him.

chapter two

i am constantly torn between killing myself and killing everyone around me.

those seem to be the two choices. everything else is just killing time.

right now i'm walking through the kitchen to get to the back door.

mom: have some breakfast.

i do not eat breakfast. i never eat breakfast. i haven't eaten breakfast since i was able to walk out the back door without eating breakfast first.

mom: where are you going?

school, mom. you should try it some time.

mom: don't let your hair fall in your face like that — i can't see your eyes.

but you see, mom, that's *the whole fucking point*.

i feel bad for her — i do. a damn shame, really, that i had to have a mother. it can't be easy having me for a son. nothing can prepare someone for that kind of disappointment.

me: bye

i do not say 'good-bye.' i believe that's one of the bullshittiest words ever invented. it's not like you're given the choice to say 'bad-bye' or 'awful-bye' or 'couldn't-care-less-about-you-bye.' every time you leave, it's supposed to be a good one. well, i don't believe in that. i believe *against* that.

mom: have a good d—

the door kinda closes in the middle of her sentence, but it's not like i can't guess where it's going. she used to say 'see you!' until one morning i was so sick of it i told her, 'no, you don't.'
she tries, and that's what makes it so pathetic. i just want to say, 'i feel sorry for you, really i do.' but that might start a conversation, and a conversation might start a fight, and then i'd feel so guilty i might have to move away to portland or something.
i need coffee.

every morning i pray that the school bus will crash and we'll all die in a fiery wreck. then my mom will be able to sue the school bus company for never making school buses with seat belts, and she'll be able to get more money for my

tragic death than i would've ever made in my tragic life. unless the lawyers from the school bus company can prove to
the jury that i was guaranteed to be a fuckup. then they'd
get away with buying my mom a used ford fiesta and calling it even.

maura isn't exactly waiting for me before school, but
i know, and she knows i'll look for her where she is. we
usually fall back on that so we can smirk at each other or
something before we're marched off. it's like those people
who become friends in prison even though they would
never really talk to each other if they weren't in prison.
that's what maura and i are like, i think.

me: give me some coffee.
maura: get your own fucking coffee.

then she hands me her XXL dunkin donuts crappaccino
and i treat it like it's a big gulp. if i could afford my own
coffee i swear i'd get it, but the way i see it is: her bladder
isn't thinking i'm an asshole even if the rest of her organs
do. it's been like this with me and maura for as long as I
can remember, which is about a year. i guess i've known
her a little longer than that, but maybe not. at some point
last year, her gloom met my doom and she thought it was
a good match. i'm not so sure, but at least i get coffee out
of it.

derek and simon are coming over now, which is good
because it's going to save me some time at lunch.

me: give me your math homework.
simon: sure. here.

what a friend.

the first bell rings. like all the bells in our fine institution of lower learning, it's not a bell at all, it's a long beep, like you're about to leave a voicemail saying you're having the suckiest day ever. and nobody's ever going to listen to it.

i have no idea why anyone would want to become a teacher. i mean, you have to spend the day with a group of kids who either hate your guts or are kissing up to you to get a good grade. that has to get to you after a while, being surrounded by people who will never like you for any real reason. i'd feel bad for them if they weren't such sadists and losers. with the sadists, it's all about the power and the control. they teach so they can have an official reason to dominate other people. and the losers make up pretty much all the other teachers, from the ones who are too incompetent to do anything else to the ones who want to be their students' best friends because they never had friends when they were in high school. and there are the ones who honestly think we're going to remember a thing they say to us after final exams are over. right.

every now and then you get a teacher like mrs. grover, who's a sadistic loser. i mean, it can't be easy being a french teacher, because nobody really needs to know how to speak french anymore. and while she kisses the honors kids' *derrieres*, with standard kids she resents the fact that we're taking up her time. so she responds by giving us quizzes every day and giving us gay projects like 'design your own ride for euro disney' and then acting all surprised when i'm like 'yeah, my ride for euro disney is minnie using a baguette as a dildo to have some fun with mickey.' since i don't have any idea how to say 'dildo' in french (*dildot?*), i just say 'dildo' and she pretends to have no idea what i'm talking about and says that minnie and mickey eating baguettes isn't a ride. no doubt she gives me a check-minus for the day. i know i'm supposed to care, but really it's hard to imagine something i could care less about than my grade in french.

the only worthwhile thing i do all period — all morning, really — is write *isaac, isaac, isaac* in my notebook and then draw spider-man spelling it out in a web. which is completely lame, but whatever. it's not like i'm doing it to be cool.

i sit with derek and simon at lunch. the way it is with us, it's like we're sitting in a waiting room. every now and then we'll say something, but mostly we stick to our own chair-sized spaces. occasionally we'll read magazines. if someone comes over, we'll look up. but that doesn't happen often.

we ignore most of the people who walk by, even the ones we're supposed to lust after. it's not like derek and simon are into girls. basically, they like computers.

derek: do you think the X18 software will be released before summer?

simon: i read on trustmaster's blog that it might. that would be cool.

me: here's your homework back.

when i look at the guys and girls at the other tables, i wonder what they could possibly have to say to each other. they're all so boring and they're all trying to make up for it by talking louder. i'd rather just sit here and eat.

i have this ritual, that when it hits two o'clock i allow myself to get excited about leaving. it's like if i reach that point i can take the rest of the day off.

it happens in math, and maura is sitting next to me. she figured out in october what i was doing, so now every day at two she passes me a slip of paper with something on it. like 'congratulations' or 'can we go now?' or 'if this period doesn't end soon i am going to slit my own skull.' i know i should write her back, but mostly i nod. i think she wants us to go out on a date or something, and i don't know what to do about that.

everyone in our school has afterschool activities.
mine is going home.

sometimes i stop and board for a while in the park, but not in february, not in this witch-twat-frigid chicago suburb (known to locals as naperville). if i go out there now, i'll freeze my balls off. not that i'm putting them to any use whatsoever, but i still like to have them, just in case.

plus i've got better things to do than have the college dropouts tell me when i can ramp (usually about . . . never) and have the skatepunks from our school look down at me because i'm not cool enough to smoke and drink with them and i'm not cool enough to be straightedge. i'm no-edge as far as they're concerned. i stopped trying to be in their in-crowd-that-doesn't-admit-it's-an-in-crowd when i left ninth grade. it's not like boarding is my life or anything.

i like having the house to myself when i get home. i don't have to feel guilty about ignoring my mom if she's not around.

i head to the computer first and see if isaac's online. he's not, so i fix myself a cheese sandwich (i'm too lazy to grill it) and jerk off. it takes about ten minutes, but it's not like i'm timing it.

isaac's still not on when i get back. he's the only person on my 'buddy list,' which is the stupidest fucking name for a list. what are we, three years old?

me: hey, isaac, wanna be my buddy!?
isaac: sure, buddy! let's go *fishin'*!

isaac knows how stupid i find these things, and he finds them just as stupid as i do. like lol. now, if there's anything stupider than buddy lists, it's lol. if anyone ever uses lol with me, i rip my computer right out of the wall and smash it over the nearest head. i mean, it's not like anyone is laughing out loud about the things they lol. i think it should be spelled loll, like what a lobotomized person's tongue does. loll. loll. i can't think any more. loll. loll!

or ttyl. bitch, you're not actually *talking*. that would require actual *vocal contact*. or <3. you think that looks like a heart? if you do, that's only because you've never seen scrotum.

(rofl! what? are you really rolling on the floor laughing? well, please stay down there a sec while I KICK YOUR ASS.)

i had to tell maura that my mom made me get rid of my instant messenger in order for her to stop popping up whenever i was trying to do something.

gothblood4567: 'sup?
finalwill: i'm working.
gothblood4567: on what?
finalwill: my suicide note. i can't figure out how to end it.
gothblood4567: lol

so i killed my screenname and resurrected myself under another. isaac's the only person who knows it, and it's going to stay that way.

i check my email and it's mostly spam. what i want to know is this: is there really someone in the whole world who gets an email from <u>hlyywkrrs@hothotmail.com</u>, reads it, and says to himself, 'you know, what i really need to do is enlarge my penis 33%, and the way to do it would be to send $69.99 to that nice lady ilena at VIRILITY MAXI-MUS CORP via this handy internet link!' if people are actually falling for that, it's not their dicks they should be worried about.

i have a friend request from some stranger on facebook and i delete it without looking at the profile because that doesn't seem natural. 'cause friendship should not be as easy as that. it's like people believe all you need to do is like the same bands in order to be soulmates. or books. *omg . . . U like the outsiders 2 . . . it's like we're the same person!* no we're not. it's like we have the same english teacher. there's a difference.

it's almost four and isaac's usually on by now. i do that stupid reward thing with my homework — it's like *if i look up what date the mayans invented toothpicks, i can check to see if isaac's online yet.* then *if i read three more paragraphs about the importance of pottery in indigenous cultures, i can check my yahoo account.* and finally *if i finish answering all three of these questions and isaac isn't on yet, then i can jerk off again.*

i'm only halfway through answering the first question, some bullshit about why mayan pyramids are *so much cooler* than egyptian ones, when i cheat and look at my buddy list and see that isaac's name is there. i'm about to think *why hasn't he IM'ed me?* when the box appears on the screen. like he's read my mind.

boundbydad: u there?
grayscale: yes!
boundbydad: ☺
grayscale: ☺ x 100
boundbydad: i've been thinking about you all day
grayscale: ???
boundbydad: only good things
grayscale: that's too bad ☺
boundbydad: depends on what you think of as good
☺☺

it's been like this from the beginning. just being comfortable. i was a little freaked out at first by his screenname, but he quickly told me it was because his name was isaac, and ultimatelymydadchosetokillthegoatinsteadofme was too long to be a good screenname. he asked me about my old screenname, finalwill, and i told him my name was will, and that's how we started to get to know each other. we were in one of those lame chatrooms where it falls completely silent every ten seconds until someone goes 'anyone in here?' and other people are like 'yeah' 'yup' 'here!' without saying anything. we were supposed to be in a forum for this singer i used to like, but there wasn't much to say about him except which songs were better than the other songs. it was really boring, but it's how isaac and i met, so i guess we'll have to hire the singer to play at our wedding or something. (that is so not funny.)

soon we were swapping pictures and mp3s and telling each other about how everything pretty much sucked, but of course the ironic part was that while we were talking about it the world didn't suck as much. except, of course, for the part at the end when we had to return to the real world.

it is so unfair that he lives in ohio, because that should be close enough, but since neither of us drives and neither of us would ever in a million years say, 'hey, mom, do you want to drive me across indiana to see a boy?,' we're kind of stuck.

> grayscale: i'm reading about the mayans.
> boundbydad: angelou?
> grayscale: ???
> boundbydad: nevermind. we skipped the mayans. we
>   only read 'american' history now.
> grayscale: but aren't they in the americas?

boundbydad: not according to my school. **groans**

grayscale: so who did you almost kill today?

grayscale: and by 'kill,' i mean 'wish would disappear,'
just in case this conversation is being monitored by
administrators

boundbydad: potential body count of eleven. twelve if
you count the cat.

grayscale: . . . or homeland security

grayscale: goddamn cat!

boundbydad: goddamn cat!

i haven't told anyone about isaac because it's none of
their business. i love that he knows who everyone is but
nobody knows who he is. if i had actual friends that i felt i
could talk to, this might cause some conflict. but since right
now there'd only need to be one car to take people to my
funeral, i think it's okay.

eventually isaac has to go, because he isn't really supposed to be using the computer at the music store where he
works. lucky for me that it doesn't seem to be a busy music
store, and his boss is like a drug dealer or something and
is always leaving isaac in charge while he goes out to 'meet
some people.'

i step away from the computer and finish my homework
quickly. then i go in the den and turn on law & order, since
the only thing i can really count on in life is that whenever i
turn on the tv there will be a law & order episode. this time
it's the one with the guy who strangles blonde after blonde
after blonde, and even though i'm pretty sure i've seen it
like ten times already, i'm watching it like i don't know that

the pretty reporter he's talking to is about to have the curtain cord around her neck. i don't watch that part, because
it's really stupid, but once the police catch the guy and the
trial's going on, they're all

> lawyer: dude, the cord knocked this microscopic piece
> of skin off your hand while you were strangling her,
> and we ran it under the microscope and found out
> that you're totally fucked.

you gotta know he wishes he'd worn gloves, although
the gloves probably would've left fibers, and he would've
been totally fucked anyway. when that's all over, there's another episode i don't think i've seen before, until this celebrity runs over a baby in his hummer and i'm like, oh, it's the
one where the celebrity runs over the baby in his hummer. i
watch it anyway, because it's not like i have anything better
to do. then mom comes home and finds me there and it's
like we're a rerun, too.

> mom: how was your day?
> me: mom, i'm watching tv.
> mom: will you be ready for dinner in fifteen minutes?
> me: *mom*, i'm watching tv!
> mom: well, set the table during the commercials.
> me: FINE.

i totally don't get this — is there anything more boring
and pathetic than setting the table when there are only two
of you? i mean, with place mats and salad forks and ev-

erything. who is she kidding? i would give anything not to have to spend the next twenty minutes sitting across from her, because she doesn't believe in letting silence go. no, she has to fill it up with talk. i want to tell her that's what the voices in your head are for, to get you through all the silent parts. but she doesn't want to be with her thoughts unless she's saying them out loud.

    mom: if i get lucky tonight, maybe we'll have a few
        more dollars for the car fund.
    me: you really don't need to do that.
    mom: don't be silly. it gives me a reason to go to girls'
        poker night.

i really wish she would stop it. she feels worse about me not having a car than i do. i mean, i'm not one of those jerks who thinks that as soon as you turn seventeen it's your god-given american right to have a brand-new chevrolet in the driveway. i know what our situation is, and i know she doesn't like that i have to work weekends at cvs in order to afford the things we need to pick up at cvs. having her constantly sad about it doesn't make me feel better. and of course there's another reason for her to go play poker be-sides the money. she needs more friends.

she asks me if i took my pills before i ran off this morn-ing and i tell her, yeah, wouldn't i be drowning myself in the bathtub if i hadn't? she doesn't like that, so i'm all like 'joke, joke' and i make a mental note that moms aren't the best audience for medication humor. i decide not to get her that *world's greatest mom of a depressive fuckup* sweatshirt for mother's day like i'd been planning. (okay, there's not really a sweatshirt like that, but if there was, it would have kittens on it, putting their paws in sockets.)

truth is, thinking about depression depresses the shit out of me, so i go back into the den and watch some more law & order. isaac's never back at his computer until eight, so i wait until then. maura calls me but i don't have the energy to say anything to her except what's happening on law & order, and she hates it when i do that. so i let the voicemail pick up.

me: this is will. why the fuck are you calling me? leave
    a message and maybe i'll call you back. [BEEP]
maura: hey, loser. i'm so bored i'm calling you. i figured
    if you weren't doing anything i could bear your
    children. oh, well. i guess i'll just go call joseph and
    ask him to do me in the manger and begat another
    holy child.

by the time i care, it's almost eight. and even then, i don't care enough to call her back. we have this thing about calling each other back, in that we don't do it very much. instead i head to the computer and it's like i turn into a little girl who's just seen her first rainbow. i get all giddy and nervous and hopeful and despairing and i tell myself not to look obsessively at my buddy list, but it might as well be projected onto the insides of my eyelids. at 8:05 his name pops up, and i start to count. i only get to twelve before his IM pops up.

boundbydad: greetings!

grayscale: and salutations!

boundbydad: so glad u're here.

grayscale: so glad to be here

boundbydad: work today = lamest! day! ever! this girl tried to shoplift and wasn't even subtle about it. i used to have some sympathy for shoplifters

boundbydad: but now i just want to see them behind bars. i told her to put it back and she acted all 'put what back?' until i reached into her pocket and took the disc out. and what does she say to that? 'oh.'

grayscale: not even 'sorry'?

boundbydad: not even.

grayscale: girls suck.

boundbydad: and boys are angels? ☺

we go on like this for about an hour. i wish we could talk on the phone, but his parents won't let him have a cell and i know my mom sometimes checks my phone log when i'm in the shower. this is nice, though. it's the only part of my day when the time actually seems worth it.

we spend our usual ten minutes saying good-bye.

boundbydad: i really should go.

grayscale: me too.

boundbydad: but i don't want to.

grayscale: me neither.

boundbydad: tomorrow?

grayscale: tomorrow!

boundbydad: i wish you.

grayscale: i wish you, too.

this is dangerous because as a rule i don't let myself wish for things. too many times when i was a kid, i would put my hands together or squinch my eyes shut and i would devote myself fully to hoping for something. i even thought that there were some places in my room that were better for wishing than others — under the bed was okay, but on the bed wasn't; the bottom of the closet would do, as long as my shoebox of baseball cards was in my lap. never, ever at my desk, but always with the sock drawer open. nobody had told me these rules — i'd figured them out for myself. i could spend hours setting up a particular wish — and every single time, i'd be met with a resounding wall of complete indifference. whether it was for a pet hamster or for my mom to stop crying — the sock drawer would be open and i would be sitting behind my toy chest with three action figures in one hand and a matchbox car in the other. i never hoped for everything to get better — only for one thing to get better. and it never did. so eventually i gave up. i give up every single day.

but not with isaac. it scares me sometimes. wishing it to work.

later that night i get an email from him.

i feel like my life is so scattered right now. like it's all these small pieces of paper and someone's turned on the fan. but talking to you makes me feel like the fan's been turned off for a little bit. like things could actually make sense. you completely unscatter me, and i appreciate that so much.

GOD I AM SO IN LOVE.

chapter three

Nothing happens for a week. I don't mean this figuratively, like there is a shortage of significant events. I mean that no things occur. Total stasis. It's sort of heavenly, to tell you the truth.

There's the getting up, and the showering, and the school, and the miracle of Tiny Cooper and the desk, and the plaintive glancing at my Burger King Kids Meal Magic School Bus watch during each class, and the relief of the eighth period bell, and the bus home, and the homework, and the dinner, and the parents, and the locking the door, and the good music, and the Facebook, and the reading of people's status updates without writing my own because my policy on shutting up extends to textual communication, and then there's the bed and the waking and the shower and the school again. I don't mind it. As lives go, I'll take the quietly desperate over the radically bipolar.

And then on Thursday night, I go home and Tiny calls me, and some things start happening. I say hello, and then Tiny, by way of introduction, says, "You should come to the Gay-Straight Alliance meeting tomorrow."

And I say, "Nothing personal, Tiny, but I don't really go

in for alliances. Anyway, you know my policy on extracurricular activities."

"No, I don't," Tiny says.

"Well, I'm opposed to them," I say. "Just the curricular activities are plenty. Listen, Tiny. I gotta go. Mom's on the other line." I hang up. Mom's not on the other line, but I need to hang up, because I can't get talked into anything.

But then Tiny calls back. And he says, "Actually I *need* you to come because we have to get our membership numbers up. Our school funding is partly decided by meeting attendance."

"Why do you need money from the school? You've got your own *house*."

"We need money so that we can stage our production of *Tiny Dancer*."

"Oh. My. Sweet. Holy. God," I say, because *Tiny Dancer* is this musical, written by Tiny. It's basically Tiny's slightly fictionalized life story, except it is sung, and it is—I mean, I don't use this adjective lightly—the gayest single musical in all of human history. Which is really saying something. And by gay, I don't mean that it sucks. I just mean that it's gay. It is actually—as musicals go—quite good. The songs are catchy. I'm particularly fond of "The Nosetackle (Likes Tight Ends)," which includes the memorable couplet, "The locker room isn't porn for me / 'cause you're all too damned pimple-ey."

"*What?*" whines Tiny.

"I just worry it might be, uh—what did Gary say the other day—'bad for the team,'" I say.

"That's *exactly* the kind of thing that you can say

tomorrow!" Tiny answers, only a hint of disappointment in his voice.

"I'll go," I say, and hang up. He calls back, but I don't answer, because I'm on Facebook, looking at Tiny's profile, paging through his 1,532 friends, each cuter and trendier than the last. I'm trying to figure out who, precisely, is *in* the Gay-Straight Alliance, and whether they could develop into a suitably nonannoying Group of Friends. So far as I can tell, though, it's just Gary and Nick and Jane. I'm squinting at Jane's tiny profile pic in which she appears to have her arm around some kind of life-size mascot on ice skates.

And right then, I get a friend request from her. A couple seconds after I accept it, she IMs me.

Jane: Hey!
Me: Hey.
Jane: Sorry, that might have been inappropriate exclamation point use.
Me: Ha. All good.

I look at her profile. The list of favorite music and favorite books is obscenely long, and I can only get through the *A*'s of the music list before giving up. She looks cute in her pictures, but not quite like she looks in real life—her picture smile isn't her smile.

Jane: I hear Tiny's recruiting you to the GSA.
Me: Indeed.
Jane: You should come. We need members. It's kind of pathetic, actually.
Me: Yeah, I think I will.

Jane: Cool. I didn't know you had a Facebook. Your profile is funny. I like "ACTIVITIES: ought to involve sunglasses."

Me: You have more favorite bands than Tiny has ex-boyfriends.

Jane: Yeah, well. Some people have lives; some people have music.

Me: And some people have neither.

Jane: Cheer up, Will. You're about to be the hottest straight guy in the Gay-Straight Alliance.

I have the distinct feeling that flirting is occurring. Now, don't get me wrong. I enjoy flirting as much as the next guy, provided the next guy has repeatedly seen his best friend torn asunder by love. But nothing violates the rules of shutting up and not caring so much as flirting—except possibly for that enchantingly horrible moment when you act upon the flirting, that moment where you seal your heartbreak with a kiss. There should be a third rule, actually: 1. Shut up. 2. Don't care too much. And 3. Never kiss a girl you like.

Me, after a while: How many straight guys are there in the GSA?

Jane: You're it.

I lol, and feel like a fool for even thinking her a flirt. Jane's just a smart, snarky girl with too-curly hair.

And so it comes to this: At 3:30 the next afternoon, the eighth period bell rings, and for a nanosecond, I feel the endorphins sizzling through my body that usually indicate I have successfully survived another school day without anything happening, but then I remember: day ain't over yet.

I trudge upstairs while a flood of people race down, on their way to the weekend.

I get to Classroom 204A. I open the door. Jane is facing away from me with her butt on a desk and her feet on a chair. She's wearing a pale yellow T-shirt and the way she's leaned over, I can see a little of the small of her back.

Tiny Cooper is splayed out across the thin carpet, using his backpack as a pillow. He's wearing skinny jeans, which look very much like denim sausage casings. At this moment, the three of us constitute the Gay-Straight Alliance.

Tiny says, "Grayson!"

"This is the Homosexuality Is An Abomination Club, right?"

Tiny laughs. Jane just sits facing away from me, reading. My eyes return to Jane's back, because they have to go somewhere, and Tiny says, "Grayson, are you abandoning your asexuality?"

Jane turns around as I cut Tiny a look and mumble, "I'm not asexual. I'm arelationshipal."

And Tiny says to Jane, "I mean, it's such a tragedy, isn't it? The only thing Grayson has going for him is that he's adorable, and yet he refuses to date."

Tiny likes to hook me up. He does it for the pure-driven pleasure of pissing me off. And it works. "Shut up, Tiny."

"I mean, I don't see it," he says. "Nothing personal, Grayson, but you're not my type. A. You don't pay enough attention to *hygiene*, and B. All the crap you've got going for you is the crap I find totally uninteresting. I mean, Jane, I think we can agree that Grayson has nice arms."

Jane looks mildly panicked, and I jump in to save her from having to talk. "You have the oddest way of coming on to me, Tiny."

"I would never come on to you, because you're not gay. And, like, boys who like girls are *inherently* unhot. Why would you like someone who can't like you back?"

The question is rhetorical, but if I wasn't trying to shut up, I'd answer it: You like someone who can't like you back because unrequited love can be survived in a way that once-requited love cannot.

After a moment, Tiny says, "Straight girls think he's cute, that's all I'm saying." And then I realize the full extent of the insanity. Tiny Cooper has brought me to a Gay-Straight Alliance meeting to hook me up with a girl.

Which is of course idiotic in the kind of profound and multivalent way that only an English teacher could fully elucidate. At least Tiny finally shuts up, whereupon I begin staring at my watch and wondering whether this is what happens at a GSA meeting—maybe the three of us just sit here for an hour in silence with Tiny Cooper periodically rendering the room toxically uncomfortable with his un-subtle comments, and then at the end we go into a huddle and shout GO GAY! or something. But then Gary and Nick come in with some guys I vaguely recognize, a girl with a tomboy cut wearing a gigantic Rancid T-shirt that extends nearly to her knees, and this English teacher, Mr. Fortson, who has never taught me in English, which perhaps ac-counts for why he smiles at me.

"Mr. Grayson," says Mr. Fortson. "Nice to have you here. Enjoyed your letter to the editor a few weeks back."

"Biggest mistake of my life," I tell him.

"Why's that?"

Tiny Cooper jumps in then. "It's a long story involving shutting up and not caring." I just nod. "Oh my God, Grayson," Tiny stage-whispers. "Did I tell you what Nick said to me?" I'm thinking *nick nick nick, who the hell is nick?* And then I glance over at Nick, who is not sitting next to Gary, which is Clue A. He is also burying his head in his arms, which is Clue B. Tiny says, "He said he can see himself with me. Those words. I can see myself with you. Isn't that just the most fantastic thing you've ever heard?" From Tiny's inflection, I can't tell whether the thing is fantastically hilarious or fantastically wonderful, so I just shrug.

Nick sighs, his head against the desk, mumbles, "Tiny, not now." Gary runs his fingers through his hair and sighs. "Bad for the team, all your polyamory."

Mr. Fortson calls the meeting to order with a gavel. A real gavel. Poor bastard. I imagine that back in college or whatever, he did not imagine that gavel use would be part of his teaching career.

"Okay, so we've got eight people today. That's great, guys. I believe the first order of business is Tiny's musical, *Tiny Dancer*. We need to decide whether to ask the administration to fund this play, or if we'd like to focus on different things. Education, awareness, etc."

Tiny sits up and announces, "*Tiny Dancer* is all about education *and* awareness."

"Yeah," says Gary sarcastically. "Making sure everyone is aware of and educated about Tiny Cooper."

The two guys sitting with Gary snicker, and before I can think it through I say, "Hey, don't be a jerk, Gary," because I can't help but defend Tiny.

Jane says, "Look, are people going to make fun of it? Absuh-freakin'-lutely. But it's honest. It's funny, and it's accurate, and it's not full of crap. It shows gay people as whole and complicated—not just like 'oh my God I have to tell my daddy that I like boys and wah-wah it's so hard.'"

Gary rolls his eyes and exhales through pursed lips like he's smoking. "Right. You know how hard it is," he says to Jane, "since you're—oh, wait. Right. You're *not gay.*"

"That's irrelevant," Jane responds. I glance over at Jane, who's giving Gary a look as Mr. Fortson starts talking about how you can't have Alliances within the Alliance or else there's no overarching Alliance. I'm wondering how many times he can possibly use the word *alliance* in one sentence when Tiny Cooper cuts Mr. Fortson off by saying, "Hey, wait, Jane, you're straight?"

And she nods without really looking up and then mumbles, "I mean, I think so, anyway."

"You should date Grayson," Tiny says. "He thinks you're super cute."

If I were to stand on a scale fully dressed, sopping wet, holding ten-pound dumbbells in each hand and balancing a stack of hardcover books on my head, I'd weigh about 180 pounds, which is approximately equal to the weight of Tiny Cooper's left tricep. But in this moment, I could beat the holy living shit out of Tiny Cooper. And I would, I swear to God, except I'm too busy trying to disappear.

I'm sitting here thinking, *God, I swear I will take a vow of silence and move to a monastery and worship you for all my days if you just this once provide me with an invisibility cloak, come on come on, please please invisibility cloak now now now.* It's very possible that Jane is thinking the same thing, but I have no idea, because she's not talking either, and I can't look at her on account of how I'm blinded by embarrassment.

The meeting lasts thirty more minutes, during which time I do not speak or move or in any way respond to stimuli. I gather that Nick gets Gary and Tiny to sort of make up, and the alliance agrees to seek money for both *Tiny Dancer* and a series of flyers aimed at education. There's some more talking, but I don't hear Jane's voice again.

And then it's over, and out of my peripheral vision I see everyone leaving, but I stay put. In the past half hour, I've collected a mental list of approximately 412 ways I might kill Tiny Cooper, and I'm not going to leave until I've settled on just the right one. I finally decide I'm going to just stab him a thousand times with a ballpoint pen. Jailhouse-style. I stand up ramrod straight and walk outside. Tiny Cooper's leaning against a row of lockers, waiting for me.

"Listen, Grayson," he says, and I walk up to him, and grab a fistful of his Polo, and I'm up on my tiptoes, and my eyes are about at his Adam's apple, and I say, "Of all the miserable things you've ever done, you cocksucker."

Tiny laughs, which only makes me madder, and he says, "You can't call me a cocksucker, Grayson, because A. It's not an insult, and B. You know I'm not one. Yet. Tragically."

I let go of his shirt. There's no physically intimidating Tiny. "Well, whatever," I say. "Shitbag. Dumbass. Vagina lover."

"Now *that's* an insult," he says, "But listen, dude. She likes you. When she walked out just now she came up to me and she was like, 'Did you really mean that or were you just joking?' and I was like, 'Why do you ask?' and she was like, 'Well, he's nice is all,' and then I told her I wasn't kidding, and then she smiled all goofy."

"Seriously?"

"Seriously."

I take a long, deep breath. "That's *terrible*. I'm not into her, Tiny."

He rolls his eyes. "And you think *I'm* crazy? She's adorable. I just totally made your life!"

I realize this is not, like, boyish. I realize that properly speaking guys should only think about sex and the acquisition of it, and that they should run crotch-first toward every girl who likes them and etc. But: The part I enjoy most is not the doing, but the noticing. Noticing the way she smells like oversugared coffee, and the difference between her smile and her photographed smile, and the way she bites her lower lip, and the pale skin of her back. I just want the pleasure of noticing these things at a safe distance—I don't want to have to acknowledge that I am noticing. I don't want to *talk* about it or *do stuff* about it.

I did think about it while we were there with unconscious, snot-crying Tiny below us. I thought about stepping over the fallen giant and kissing her and my hand on her face and her improbably warm breath, and having a girlfriend who gets mad at me for being so quiet and then only getting quieter because the thing I liked was one smile with a sleeping leviathan between us, and then I feel like crap for a while until finally we break up, at which point I reaffirm my vow to live by the rules.

I could do that.

Or I could just live by the rules.

"Trust me," I tell him. "You are not improving my life. Just stop interfering, okay?"

He answers with a shrug that I take for a nod. "So, listen," Tiny says. "About Nick. The thing is that he and Gary were together for a really long time and, like, they only broke up yesterday, but there's a real spark."

"Supremely bad idea," I say.

"But they broke up," says Tiny.

"Right, but what would happen if someone broke up with you and then the next day was flirting with one of your friends?"

"I'll think about it," says Tiny, but I know he can't possibly restrain himself from having another brief and failed romance. "Oh, hey." Tiny perks up. "You should go with us to the Storage Room on Friday. Nick and I are going to see this band, the uh—the Maybe Dead Cats. Intellectual pop punk. Dead Milkmen-ey, but less funny ha-ha."

"Thanks for inviting me before," I say, elbowing Tiny in the side. He pushes me back playfully, and I almost fall down the stairs. It's like being best friends with a fairy-tale giant: Tiny Cooper can't help but hurt you.

"I just figured you wouldn't want to come, after the disaster last week."

"Oh, wait, I can't. The Storage Room is over-twenty-one."

Tiny Cooper, walking ahead of me, reaches the door. He throws his hips against the metal bar, and the door flings open. Outside. The weekend. The brisk bare light of Chicago. The cold air floods over me, and the light rushes in, and Tiny Cooper is backlit by the sinking sun, so I can

48

barely see him when he turns back around to me and pulls out his phone.

"Who are you calling?" I ask, but Tiny doesn't answer. He just holds the phone in his gigantic meaty hand and then he says, "Hey, Jane," and my eyes get wide, and I do the slit-the-throat motion, and Tiny smiles and says, "Listen, so Grayson wants to come with us to the Maybe Dead Cats on Friday. Maybe get some dinner first?"

"..."

"Well, the only problem is that he doesn't have an ID, and don't you know some guy?"

"..."

"You aren't home yet, are you? So just come back and pick his skinny ass up." Tiny hangs up and says to me, "She's on her way," and then I'm left standing in the doorway as Tiny races down the steps and starts skipping—yeah, skipping—toward the junior parking lot. "Tiny!" I shout, but he doesn't turn around; he just keeps skipping. I don't start to skip after his crazy ass or anything, but I do kinda smile. He may be a malevolent sorcerer, but Tiny Cooper is his own goddamned man, and if he wants to be a gigantic skipper, then that's his right as a huge American.

I figure I can't ditch Jane, so I'm sitting on the front steps when she shows up two minutes later behind the wheel of an ancient, hand-painted orange Volvo. I've seen the car before in the parking lot—you can't miss it—but I've never attached it to Jane. She seems quieter than the car implies. I walk down the steps, open the passenger door, and climb in, my feet landing in a pile of fast-food wrappers.

"Sorry. I realize it's disgusting."

"Don't worry," I say. This would be an excellent time to make a joke, but I'm thinking *shut up shut up shut up*. After a while the silence feels too weird, so I say, "Do you know this band, the uh, Maybe Dead Cats?"

"Yeah. They're not bad. They're sort of a poor man's early Mr. T Experience, but they've got one song I like—it's like fifty-five seconds long and it's called 'Annus Miribalis,' and it basically explains Einstein's theory of relativity."

"Cool," I say. She smiles, shifts into drive, and we jolt off toward the city.

Maybe a minute later, we come to a stop sign and Jane pulls over to the side of the road and looks at me. "I'm quite shy," she says.

"Huh?"

"I'm quite shy, so I understand. But don't hide behind Tiny."

"I'm not," I say.

And then she ducks beneath her seat belt and I'm wondering why she's doing that, and then she leans across the gearbox, and I realize what's happening, and she closes her eyes and tilts her head and I turn away, staring down at the fast-food bags on the floor of her car. She opens her eyes and jolts backward. Then I start talking to fill the silence. "I'm not really, uh, I think you're awesome and pretty but I'm not, like, I'm not, like, I guess I don't, um, really want a relationship right now."

After a second, very quietly, she says, "I think I might have gotten some unreliable information."

"Possible," I say.

"I'm really sorry."

"Me too. I mean, you really are—"

"No no no stop, that only makes it worse. Okay. Okay. Look at me." I look at her. "I can totally forget that ever happened if, and only if, you can totally forget it ever happened."

"Nothing happened," I say, and then correct myself. "Nothing didn't happen."

"Exactly," she says, and then our thirty-second stop at the stop sign ends, and my head is thrown back against the seat. Jane drives like Tiny dates.

We're exiting Lake Shore near downtown and talking about Neutral Milk Hotel and whether there might be some recordings out there that no one has heard, just demos, and how interesting it would be to hear what their songs sounded like before they were songs, how maybe we could break into their recording studio and copy every recorded moment of the band's existence. The Volvo's ancient heating system makes my lips feel dry and the leaning-in thing feels actually, literally forgotten—and it occurs to me that I am weirdly disappointed about how entirely un-upset Jane seems to feel, which in turn causes me to feel strangely rejected, which in turn causes me to think that perhaps a special wing at the Museum of Crazy should be erected in my honor.

We find a parking space on the street a couple blocks away from the place, and Jane leads me to a nondescript glass door next to a hot-dog restaurant. A sign on the door reads GOLD COAST COPY AND PRINT. We head up the stairs, the smell of delicious pork lips wafting through the air, and enter a tiny officelike shop. It is extremely sparsely decorated, which is to say that there are two folding chairs, a

HANG IN THERE kitten poster, a dead potted plant, a computer, and a fancy printer.

"Hey, Paulie," says Jane, to a heavily tattooed guy who appears to be the shop's sole employee. The hot-dog smell has dissipated, but only because Gold Coast Copy and Print stinks of pot. The guy comes around the counter and gives Jane a one-armed hug, and then she says, "This is my friend, Will," and the guy reaches out his hand, and as I shake his hand, I see that he has the letters, H-O-P-E tattooed on his knuckles. "Paulie and my brother are good friends. They went to Evanston together."

"Yeah, *went* together," Paulie says. "But we sure didn't graduate together, 'cause I still ain't graduated." Paulie laughs.

"Yeah, so, Paulie. Will lost his ID," explains Jane.

Paulie smiles at me. "That's a shame, kid." He hands me a blank sheet of computer paper and says, "I need your full name, your address, date of birth, social, height, weight, and eye color. And a hundred bucks."

"I, uh—" I say, because I don't happen to carry hundred dollar bills around with me. But before I can even form the words, Jane puts five twenties on the counter.

Jane and I sit down on the folding chairs, and together we invent my new identity: My name is Ishmael J. Biafra, my address is 1060 W. Addison Street, the location of Wrigley Field. I've got brown hair, blue eyes. I'm five ten, weigh 160 pounds, my social security number is nine randomly selected numbers, and I turned twenty-two last month. I hand the paper to Paulie, and then he points to a strip of duct tape and tells me to stand there. He holds a digital camera up to his eye and says, "Smile!" I didn't smile for my real driver's license picture, and I'm sure as hell not going to smile for this one.

"I'll just be a minute," Paulie says, and so I lean against the wall, and I feel nervous enough about the ID to forget being nervous about my proximity to Jane. Even though I know I'm about the three millionth person to get a fake ID, I'm still pretty sure it's a felony, and I'm generally opposed to committing felonies. "I don't even drink," I say out loud, half to myself and half to Jane.

"Mine's just for concerts," she says.

"Can I see it?" I ask. She grabs her backpack, which has been inked all over with band names and quotes, and fishes out her wallet.

"I keep it hidden back here," she says, unzipping a flap in the wallet, "because if I, like, die or something, I don't want the hospital trying to call Zora Thurston Moore's parents." Sure enough, that's her name, and the license looks completely real to me. Her picture is brilliant: Her mouth seems right on the edge of laughing, and this is exactly how she looked at Tiny's house, unlike all her Facebook pictures.

"This is a great picture of you. This is what you look like," I tell her. And it's true. That's the problem: so many things are true. It's true that I want to smother her with compliments and true that I want to keep my distance. True that I want her to like me and true that I don't. The stupid, endless truth speaking out of both sides of its big, stupid mouth. It's what keeps me, stupidly, talking. "Like, you can't know what you look like, right? Whenever you see yourself in the mirror, you know you're looking at you, so you can't help but pose a little. So you never *really* know. But this—that's what you look like."

Jane puts two fingers against the face on the license, which I'm holding against my leg, so her fingers are on my leg if you don't count the license, and I look at them for a moment and then look up to her and she says, "Paulie, for all his criminality, is actually kinda a good photographer."

Right then, Paulie comes out waving a driver's licenseish piece of plastic in the air. "Mr. Biafra, your identification."

He hands it to me. The knuckles on this hand read L-E-S-S.

It is perfect. All the holograms of a real Illinois license, all the same colors, the same thick, laminated plastic, the same organ donor info. I even look half okay in the picture. "Christ," I say. "It's magnificent. It's the *Mona Lisa* of IDs."

"No problem," says Paulie. "Ahright, kids, I gotta take care of some business." Paulie smiles and holds up a joint. I'm mystified as to how someone so pot-addled could be such a genius in the field of false identification. "See you later, Jane. Tell Phil to give me a call."

"Aye aye, cap'n," Jane says, and then we're walking down the stairs, and I can feel my fake ID in my front pocket, tight against my thigh, and it feels like I've got a ticket to the whole frakking world.

We get outside onto the street, the cold a permanent surprise. Jane takes off running ahead of me and I don't know whether I'm supposed to follow her or not, but then she turns around toward me and starts skipping backward. The wind in her face, I can barely hear her shout, "Come on, Will! Skip! After all, you're a *man* now."

And I'll be damned if I don't start skipping after her.

chapter four

i am shelving metamusil in aisle seven when maura stalks in. she knows my boss is an asshole about me standing around and talking while i'm working, so she pretends to look at vitamins while she's talking to me. she's telling me there's something really disturbing about the word 'chewable' and then all of a sudden the clock strikes 5:12 and she figures it's time to ask personal questions.

> maura: are you gay?
> me: what the fuck?
> maura: it would be okay with me if you were.
> me: oh, good, because the thing i'd be worried about
>   the most is whether you were okay with it.
> maura: i'm just saying.
> me: noted. now will you just shut up and let me work,
>   okay? or do you want me to use my employee
>   discount to get you something for your cramps?

i think there really needs to be a rule against calling a guy's sexuality into question while he's working. and anyway, i really don't want to talk about it with maura no matter where we are. because, here's the thing — we're not that

close. maura is the kind of friend i enjoy swapping doomsday scenarios with. she's not, however, someone who makes
me want to prevent doomsday from happening. for the year
or so we've hung out, this has always been a problem. i
know if i told her about liking guys, she'd probably stop
wanting to date me, which would be a huge plus. but i also
know i'd immediately become her gay pet, and that's the
last kind of leash i want. and it's not like i'm really *that* gay.
i fucking hate madonna.

> me: there should be a cereal for constipated people
>   called metamueslix.
> maura: i'm serious.
> me: and i'm seriously telling you to fuck off. you
>   shouldn't call me gay just because i don't want to
>   sleep with you. a lot of straight guys don't want to
>   sleep with you, either.
> maura: fuck you.
> me: ah, but the point is, you won't.

she comes over and messes up all the bottles that i've
been putting in rows. i almost pick one up and throw it at
the back of her head while she leaves, but the truth is if i
brained her here, my manager would make me clean it up,
and that would suck. the last thing i need is gray matter on
my new shoes. do you know how hard that shit is to get
out? anyway, i really need this job, which means i can't do
things like yell or pin my stupid name tag upside down or
wear jeans that have rips in them or sacrifice puppies in the
toy aisle. i don't really mind it, except when my manager is

around or when people i know come by and are all weird because i'm working and they don't have to.

i'm thinking maura will swing back into aisle seven, but she doesn't, and i know i'm going to have to act nice to her (or at least not act mean to her) for the next three days. i make a mental note to buy her coffee or something, but my mental noteboard is a joke, because as soon as i put something on there it disappears. and the truth is that the next time we talk, maura's going to pull her whole hurt routine, and that's only going to annoy me more. i mean, she's the one who opened her mouth. not my fault if she can't take the answer.

cvs closes at eight on saturdays, which means i'm out by nine. eric and mary and greta are all talking about parties they're going to, and even roger, our square-headed manager, is telling us that he and his wife are going to be 'having a night in' — wink wink, nudge nudge, hump hump, spew spew. i'd rather picture a festering wound with maggots crawling into it. roger is bald and fat and his wife is probably bald and fat, too, and the last thing i want to hear about is them having bald and fat sex. especially 'cause you know that he's making it sound all wink-nudge when the truth is he'll probably get home and the two of them will watch a tom hanks movie and then one of them will lie in bed listening to the other one pee and then they'll switch places and then when the second person is done in the bathroom, the lights will go off and they'll go to sleep.

greta asks me if i want to come along with her, but she's like twenty-three or something and her boyfriend vince acts like he'll disembowel me if i use any SAT words in his presence. so i just get a ride home, and mom is there, and isaac's not online, and i hate the way mom never has saturday night plans and isaac always has saturday night plans. i mean, i don't want him sitting at home waiting for me to get back and IM, because one of the cool things about him is that he has a life. there's an email from him saying he's going out to the movies for kara's birthday, and i tell him to wish her a happy birthday from me, but of course by the time he gets the message her birthday will be over and i don't know whether he's told kara about me, anyway.

mom is on our lime-green couch, watching the *pride & prejudice* miniseries for the seven-zillionth time, and i know i'll be totally girling out if i sit there and watch it with her. the weird thing is that she also really likes the *kill bill* movies, and i've never been able to sense a difference in her mood between when she's watching *pride & prejudice* and when she's watching *kill bill*. it's like she's the same person no matter what's happening. which can't be right.

i end up watching *pride & prejudice* because it's fifteen hours long, so i know that when it's over, isaac will probably be home. my phone keeps ringing and i keep not answering. that's one of the good things about knowing he can't call me — i never have to worry it's him.

the doorbell rings right when the guy's about to tell the girl all the shit he needs to tell her, and at first i ignore it the same way i'm ignoring my cellphone. the only problem is that people at the door don't go to voicemail, so there's another ring, and mom's about to get up, so i say i'll get it, figuring it must be the door equivalent of a wrong number.

only when i get there it's maura on the other side of the door, and she's heard my footsteps so she knows i'm here.

maura: i need to talk to you.
me: isn't it like midnight or something?
maura: just open the door.
me: are you going to huff and puff?
maura: c'mon, will. just open it.

it's always a little scary when she gets all direct with me. so while i'm opening the door i'm already trying to figure out how to dodge her. it's like some instinct kicks in.

mom: who is it?
me: it's only maura.

and, oh fuck, maura's taking the 'only' personally. I want her to just draw the teardrop under her eye and get it over with. she has enough black eyeliner on to outline a corpse, and her skin's so pale she looks like she's just broken dawn. only without the two dots of blood on her neck.

we're hovering there in the doorway because i don't really know where we should go. i don't think maura's ever really been inside my house before, except maybe the kitchen. she definitely hasn't been in my room, because that's where the computer is, and maura's the kind of girl who the moment you leave her alone will go right for the diary or the computer. plus, you know, asking someone to your room could be taken to mean something, and i definitely don't want maura to think i'm going to get all 'hey-why-don't-we-sit-on-my-bed-and-hey-since-we're-sitting-on-my-bed-how-'bout-i-put-my-dick-inside-you?' with her. but the kitchen and the living room are off-limits now because of mom, and mom's bedroom is off-limits because it's mom's bedroom. which is how i find myself asking maura if she wants to go into the garage.

> maura: the garage?
> me: look, it's not like i'm going to ask you to go down on a tailpipe, okay? if i wanted us to do a suicide pact, i'd opt for bathtub electrocution. you know, with a hair dryer. like poets do.
> maura: fine.

mom's maxiseries hasn't come yet to its austen shitty limits, so i know maura and i will be able to talk undisturbed. or, at least, we'll be the only disturbed ones in the garage. it seems really stupid to sit in the car, so i clear a space for us by the things of dad's that mom never got around to throwing out.

> me: so what's up?
> maura: you're a prick.
> me: this is a news flash?
> maura: shut up for a second.
> me: only if you shut up, too.
> maura: stop it.
> me: you started it.
> maura: just stop it.

i decide, okay, i'll shut up. and what do i get? fifteen fucking seconds of silence. then it's all

> maura: i always tell myself that you don't mean to hurt
> me, which makes it less hurtful, you know. but
> today — i'm just so fucking sick of it. of you. just
> so you know, i don't want to sleep with you, either.
> i would never sleep with someone i can't even be
> friends with.
> me: wait a second — now we're not friends?
> maura: i don't know what we are. you won't even tell
> me that you're gay.

this is a classic maura maneuver. if she doesn't get an answer she wants, she will create a corner to back you into. like the time she went through my bag when i was in the bathroom and found my pills — i hadn't taken them in the morning, so i brought them along with me to school. she waited a good ten minutes before asking me if i was on any medication. this seemed a little random to me, and i didn't really want to talk about it, so i told her no. and then what does she do? she reaches into my bag and pulls out the pill bottles and asks me what they're for. she got her answer, but it didn't exactly inspire trust. she kept telling me i didn't need to be ashamed of my 'mental condition,' and i kept telling her i wasn't ashamed — i just didn't want to talk about it with her. she couldn't understand the difference.

so now we're back in another corner, and this time it's the gay thing.

me: whoa, wait a second. even if i was gay, wouldn't
      that be my decision? to tell you?
maura: who's isaac?
me: fuck.
maura: you think i can't see what you draw in your
      notebook?
me: you're kidding me. this is about *isaac*?
maura: just tell me who he is.

i fundamentally don't want to tell her. he's mine, not
hers. if i give her just a piece of the story, she'll want the
whole thing. i know in some twisted way she's doing this
because she thinks it's what i want — to talk about everything, to have her know everything about me. but that's not
what i want. that's not what she can have.

me: maura maura maura . . . isaac's a character. he
      doesn't actually exist. fuck! it's just this thing i'm
      working on. this — i don't know — *idea*. i have all
      these stories in my head. starring this character,
      isaac.

i don't know where this shit comes from. it's like it's just
being given to me by some divine force of fabrication.
      maura looks like she wants to believe it, but doesn't really.

me: like pogo dog. only he's not a dog, and he's not on
      a pogo stick.
maura: god, i forgot all about pogo dog.
me: are you kidding? he was going to make us rich!

and she's buying it. she's leaning against me and, i swear to god, if she was a guy i'd be able to see the boner in her pants.

maura: i know it's awful, but i'm kind of relieved that you're not hiding something that big from me.

i figure this would be a bad time to point out that i've never actually said i wasn't gay. i just told her to fuck off.

i don't know if there's anything more horrifying than a goth girl getting all cuddly. maura's not only leaning, but now she's examining my hand like somebody stamped it with the meaning of life. in braille.

me: i should probably get back to my mom.
maura: tell her we're hanging out.
me: i promised her i would watch this thing with her.

the key here is to blow off maura without her realizing i'm blowing her off. because i really don't want to hurt her, not when i just managed to bring her back from the brink of the last hurt i allegedly inflicted. i know as soon as maura gets home, she's going to dive right into her notebook of skull-blood poetry, and i'm doing my best not to get a bad review. maura once showed me one of her poems.

hang me
like a dead rose
preserve me
and my petals won't fall
until you touch them
and i dissolve

and i wrote her a poem back

> *i am like*
> *a dead begonia*
> *hanging upside down*
> *because*
> *like a dead begonia*
> *i don't give a fuck*

to which she replied

> *not all flowers*
> *depend on light*
> *to grow*

so now maybe tonight i'll inspire

> *i thought his soil was gay*
> *but maybe there's a chance*
> *i can get myself some play*
> *and get into his pants*

hopefully i'll never have to read it or know about it or even think about it ever again.

i stand up and open the garage door so maura can leave that way. i tell her i'll see her monday in school and she says 'not if i see you first' and i go har har har until she's a safe distance away and i can shut the garage door again.

the sick thing is, i'm sure that someday this is going to

come back to haunt me. that someday she's going to say i
led her on, when the truth is i was only holding her off.
i have to set her up with somebody else. soon. it's not me
she wants — she just wants anybody who will make it all
about her. and i can't be that guy.

when i get back to the living room, *pride & prejudice* is
almost over, which means that everyone knows pretty much
where they stand with everyone else. usually my mom is a
crumpled-tissue mess at this point, but this time there's not
a wet eye in the house. she pretty much confirms it when
she turns the dvd off.

> mom: i really have to stop doing this. i need to get a
> life.

i think she's directing this at herself, or the universe, not
really at me. still, i can't help thinking that 'getting a life'
is something only a complete idiot could believe. like you
can just drive to a store and get a life. see it in its shiny box
and look inside the plastic window and catch a glimpse of
yourself in a new life and say, 'wow, i look much happier — i
think this is the life i need to get!' take it to the counter,
ring it up, put it on your credit card. if getting a life was
that easy, we'd be one blissed-out race. but we're not. so it's
like, mom, your life isn't out there waiting, so don't think all
you have to do is find it and get it. no, your life is right here.
and, yeah, it sucks. lives usually do. so if you want things
to change, you don't need to get a life. you need to get off
your ass.

of course i don't say any of these things to her. moms

don't need to hear that kind of shit from their kids, unless they're doing something really wrong, like smoking in bed, or doing heroin, or doing heroin while they're smoking in bed. if my mom were a jock guy in my school, all of her jock-guy friends would be saying, 'dude, you just need to get laid.' but sorry, geniuses, there's no such thing as a fuck cure. a fuck cure is like the adult version of santa claus.

it's kind of sick that my mind has gone from my mom to fucking, so i'm glad when she complains about herself a little more.

> mom: it's getting old, isn't it? mom at home on a
>   saturday night, waiting for darcy to show up.
> me: there's not an actual answer to that question, is
>   there?
> mom: no. probably not.
> me: have you actually asked this darcy guy out?
> mom: no. i haven't actually found him.
> me: well, he's not going to show up until you ask him
>   out.

me giving my mom romantic advice is kind of like a goldfish giving a snail advice on how to fly. i could remind her that not all guys are dickheads like my dad, but she perversely hates it when i say bad things about him. she's probably just worried about the day i'll wake up and realize half my genes are so geared toward being a bastard that i'll wish i *was* a bastard. well, mom, guess what — that day came a long time ago. and i wish i could say that's where the pills come in, but the pills only deal with the side effects.

god bless the mood equalizers. *and all moods shall be created equal.* i am the fucking civil rights movement of moods.

it's late enough for isaac to be home, so i tell my mom i'm heading off to bed and then, to be nice, tell her that if i see any cute guys wearing, like, knickers and riding a horse sexily on the way to the mall, i'll be sure to slip 'em her number. she thanks me for that, and says it's a better idea than any of her friends at girls poker night have had. i wonder if she'll be asking the mailman for his opinion soon.

there's a dangling IM waiting for me when i banish my screen saver and check what's up.

boundbydad: u there?
boundbydad: i'm wishin'
boundbydad: and hopin'
boundbydad: and prayin'

all sorts of yayness floods my brain. love is such a drug.

grayscale: please be the one voice of sanity left in the
    world
boundbydad: you're there!
grayscale: just.
boundbydad: if you're relying on me for sanity, it must
    be pretty bad.
grayscale: yeah, well, maura stopped by cvs for a hag
    audition, then when i told her that tryouts were
    canceled, she decided she'd go for some
grayscale: nookie instead. and then my mom started

saying she had no life. oh, and i have homework to
do. or not.

boundbydad: it's hard to be you, isn't it?

grayscale: clearly.

boundbydad: do you think maura knows the truth?

grayscale: i'm sure she thinks she does.

boundbydad: what a nosy bitch.

grayscale: not really. it's not her fault i don't really want
to get into it. i'd rather share it with you.

boundbydad: and so you are. meanwhile, no big
saturday night plans? more quality time with mom?

grayscale: you, my dear, are my saturday night plans.

boundbydad: i'm honored.

grayscale: you should be. how was the bday
celebration?

boundbydad: small. kara just wanted to see a movie
with me and janine. good time, lame movie. the
one with the guy who learns that the girl he
marries is a sucubus

boundbydad: sucubbus?

boundbydad: succubus?

grayscale: succubus

boundbydad: yeah, one of those. it was really stupid.
then it was really boring. then it got loud and
stupid. then there were about two minutes where
it was so stupid it was funny. then it went back to
being dumb, and finally ended lame.

boundbydad: good times, good times

grayscale: how's kara?

boundbydad: in recovery.

grayscale: meaning?

boundbydad: she talks a lot about her problems in the past tense as a way to convince us they're in the past. and maybe they are.

grayscale: did you say hi to her for me?

boundbydad: yeah. i think i phrased it as 'will says he wants you inside of him,' but the effect was the same. she said hi back.

grayscale: **sighs forlornly** i wish i could've been there.

boundbydad: i wish i was there with you right now.

grayscale: really? ☺

boundbydad: yessirreebob.

grayscale: and if you were here . . .

boundbydad: what would i do?

grayscale: ☺

boundbydad: let me tell you what i'd do.

this is a game we play. most of the time we're not serious. like, there are different ways it could go. the first is we basically make fun of people who have IM sex by inventing our own ridiculous scornographic dialogue.

grayscale: i want you to lick my clavicle.

boundbydad: i am licking your clavicle.

grayscale: ooh my clavicle feels so good.

boundbydad: naughty, naughty clavicle.

grayscale: mmmmmm

boundbydad: wwwwwww

grayscale: rrrrrrrrrrrrrrrrr

boundbydad: tttttttttttttttttttttt

other times we go for the romance novel approach. corn
porn.

boundbydad: thrust your fierce quavering manpole at
    me, stud
grayscale: your dastardly appendage engorges me with
    hellfire
boundbydad: my search party is creeping into your no
    man's land
grayscale: baste me like a thanksgiving turkey!!!

and then there are nights like tonight, when the truth
is what comes out, because it's what we need the most. or
maybe just one of us needs it the most, but the other knows
the right time to give it.
    like now, when what i want most in the universe is to
have him beside me. he knows this, and he says

boundbydad: if i was there, i would stand behind your
    chair and put my hands on your shoulders, lightly,
    and would rub them gently until you finished your
    last sentence
boundbydad: then i would lean forward and trace
    my hands down your arms and curve my neck into
    yours and let you turn into me and rest there for a
    while
boundbydad: rest
boundbydad: and when you were ready, i'd kiss you

once and lift myself away, sit back on your bed and
wait for you there, just so we could lie there, and
you could hold me, and i could hold you
boundbydad: and it would be so peaceful. completely
peaceful. like the feeling of sleep, but being awake
in it together.
grayscale: that would be so wonderful.
boundbydad: i know. i would love it, too.

i can't imagine us saying these things to each other out
loud. but even if i can't imagine hearing these words, i can
imagine living them. i don't even picture it. instead i'm in it.
how i would feel with him here. that peace. it would be so
happy, and it makes me sad because it only exists in words.

early on, isaac let me know that he always finds pauses
awkward – if too much time went by without me respond-
ing, he'd think i was typing something else in another window, or had left the computer, or was IMing twelve other
boys besides him. and i had to admit that i felt the same
fears. so now we do this thing whenever we're pausing. we
just type

grayscale: i'm here
boundbydad: i'm here
grayscale: i'm here
boundbydad: i'm here

until the next sentence comes.

grayscale: i'm here

boundbydad: i'm here

grayscale: i'm here

boundbydad: what are we doing?

grayscale: ???

boundbydad: i think it's time

boundbydad: time for us to meet

grayscale: !!!

grayscale: seriously?

boundbydad: deliriously

grayscale: you mean i would get a chance to see you

boundbydad: hold you for real

grayscale: for real

boundbydad: yes

grayscale: yes?

boundbydad: yes.

grayscale: yes!

boundbydad: am i crazy?

grayscale: yes! ☺

boundbydad: i'll go crazy if we don't.

grayscale: we should.

boundbydad: we should.

grayscale: ohmygodwow

boundbydad: it's going to happen, isn't it?

grayscale: we can't go back now.

boundbydad: i'm so excited . . .

grayscale: and terrified

boundbydad: . . . and terrified

grayscale: . . . but most of all excited?

boundbydad: but most of all excited.

it's going to happen. i know it's going to happen.

giddily, terrifyingly, we pick a date.

friday. six days away

only six days.

in six days, maybe my life will actually begin.

this is so insane.

and the most insane thing of all is that i'm so excited that i want to immediately tell isaac all about it, even though he's the one person who already knows it's happened. not maura, not simon, not derek, not my mom — nobody in this whole wide world but isaac. he is both the source of my happiness and the one i want to share it with.

i have to believe that's a sign.

chapter five

It's one of those weekends where I don't leave the house at all—literally—except briefly with Mom to go to the White Hen. Such weekends usually don't bother me, but I keep sort of hoping Tiny Cooper and/or Jane might call and give me an excuse to use the ID I've hidden in the pages of *Persuasion* on my bookshelf. But no one calls; neither Tiny nor Jane even shows up online; and it's colder than a witch's tit in a steel bra, so I just stay in the house and catch up on homework. I do my precalc homework, and then when I'm done I actually sit with the textbook for like three hours and try to understand what I just did. That's the kind of weekend it is—the kind where you have so much time you go past the answers and start looking into the ideas.

Then on Sunday night while I'm at the computer checking to see if anyone's online, my dad's head appears in my doorway. "Will," he says, "do you have a sec to talk in the living room?" I spin around in the desk chair and stand up. My stomach flips a bit because the living room is the room least likely to be lived in, the room where the nonexistence of Santa is revealed, where grandmothers die, where grades are frowned upon, and where one learns that a man's station wagon goes inside a woman's garage, and then exits the garage, and then enters again, and so on until an egg is fertilized, and etc.

My dad is very tall, and very thin, and very bald, and he has long thin fingers, which he taps against an arm of a floral-print couch. I sit across from him in an overstuffed, overgreen armchair. The finger tapping goes on for about thirty-four years, but he doesn't say anything, and then finally I say, "Hey, Dad."

He has a very formalized, intense way of talking, my dad. He always talks to you as if he's informing you that you have terminal cancer—which is actually a big part of his job, so it makes sense. He looks at me with those sad, intense you-have-cancer eyes, and he says, "Your mother and I are wondering about your plans."

And I say, "Uh, well. I thought I would, uh, go to bed pretty soon. And then, just go to school. I'm going to a concert on Friday. I already told Mom."

He nods. "Yes, but after that."

"Uh, after that? You mean, like, get into college and get a job and get married and give you grandchildren and stay off drugs and live happily ever after?"

He almost smiles. It is an exceedingly hard thing, to get my dad to smile. "There's one facet of that process in which your mother and I are particularly interested at this particular juncture in your life."

"College?"

"College," he says.

"Don't have to worry about it until next year," I point out.

"It's never too early to plan," he says. And then he starts talking about this program at Northwestern where you do both college and medical school in, like, six years so that you can be in residency by the time you're twenty-five, and you can stay close to home but of course live on campus and whatever whatever whatever, because after about eleven seconds, I realize he and Mom have decided I should go to this particular program, and that they are introducing me to the idea early, and that they will periodically bring this program up over the next year, pushing and pushing and pushing. And I realize, too, that if I can get in, I will probably go. There are worse ways to make a living.

You know how people are always saying your parents are always right? "Follow your parents' advice; they know what's good for you." And you know how no one ever listens to this advice, because even if it's true it's so annoying and condescending that it just makes you want to go, like, develop a meth addiction and have unprotected sex with eighty-seven thousand anonymous partners? Well, I listen to my parents. They know what's good for me. I'll listen to anyone, frankly. Almost everyone knows better than I do.

Andbutso little does my dad know, but all his explanation of this future is lost on me; I'm already fine with it. No, I'm thinking about how little I feel in this absurdly immense chair, and I'm thinking about the fake ID warming up Jane Austen's pages, and I'm thinking about whether I'm more mad at Tiny or in awe of him, and thinking about Friday, steering clear of Tiny in the mosh pit as he tries to dance like everyone else, and the heat turned on too high in the club and everyone sweating through their clothes and the music so uptempo and goose bumps that I don't even care what they're singing about.

And I say, "Yeah, it sounds really cool, Dad," and he's talking about how he knows people there, and I'm just nodding nodding nodding.

I'm at school Monday morning twenty minutes early because Mom has to get to the hospital by seven—I guess someone has an extralarge tumor or something. So I lean against the flagpole on the lawn in front of school waiting for Tiny Cooper, shivering in spite of the gloves and the hat and the coat and the hood. The wind tears across the lawn, and I can hear it whipping the flag above me, but I'll be damned if I'm going to enter that building a nanosecond before the first period bell rings.

The buses let off, and the lawn starts to fill up with freshmen, none of whom seems particularly impressed by me. And then I see Clint, a tenured member of my former Group of Friends, walking toward me from the junior parking lot, and I'm able to convince myself that he's not really walking toward *me* until his visible breath is blowing over me like a small, malodorous cloud. And I'm not going to lie: I kind of hope he's about to apologize for the small-mindedness of certain of his friends.

"Hey, fucker," he says. He calls everyone *fucker*. Is it a compliment? An insult? Or maybe it is both at once, which is precisely what makes it so useful.

I wince a little from the sourness of his breath, and then just say, "Hey." Equally noncommittal. Every conversation I ever had with Clint or any of the Group of Friends is identical: all the words we use are stripped bare, so that no one ever knows what anyone else is saying, so that all kindness is cruelty, all selfishness generous, all care callous.

And he says, "Got a call from Tiny this weekend about his musical. Wants student council to fund it." Clint is student council vice president. "He told me all the fuck about it. A musical about a big gay bastard and his best friend who uses tweezers to jack off 'cause his dick's so small." He's saying all this with a smile. He's not being mean. Not exactly.

And I want to say, *That's so incredibly original. Where do you come up with these zingers, Clint? Do you own some kind of joke factory in Indonesia where you've got eight-year-olds working ninety hours a week to deliver you that kind of top-quality witticism? There are boy bands with more original material.* But I say nothing.

"So yeah," Clint finally continues. "I think I might help Tiny out at the meeting tomorrow. Because that play sounds like a fantastic idea. I've only got one question: are you going to sing your own songs? Because I'd pay to see that."

I laugh a little, but not too much. "I'm not much for drama," I say, finally. Right then, I feel an enormous presence behind me. Clint raises his chin way the hell up to look at Tiny and then nods at him. He says, "'Sup, Tiny," and then walks away.

"He trying to steal you back?" Tiny asks.

I turn around, and *now* I can talk. "You go all weekend without logging on or calling me and yet you find time to call *him* in your continuing attempts to ruin my social life through the magic of song?"

"First off, *Tiny Dancer* isn't going to ruin your social life, because you don't have a social life. Second off, you didn't call me, either. Third off, I was so busy! Nick and I spent almost the entire weekend together."

"I thought I explained to you why you couldn't date Nick," I say, and Tiny's just starting to talk again when I see Jane, hunched forward, plowing through the wind. She's wearing a not-thick-enough hoodie and walking up to us.

I say hi, and she says hi, and she comes and stands next to me as if I'm a space heater or something, and she squints into the wind, and I say, "Hey, take my coat." I take it off and she buries herself in it. I'm still trying to think of a question to ask Jane when the bell goes off, and we all hustle inside.

I don't see Jane at all during the entire school day, which is a little frustrating, because it's even-the-hallways-are-freezing cold, and I keep worrying that after school I'm gonna freeze to death on the walk to Tiny's car. After my last class, I race downstairs and unlock my locker. My coat is stuffed inside it.

Now, it is possible to slip a note into a locked locker through the vents. Even, with some pushing, a pencil. Once, Tiny Cooper slipped a Happy Bunny book into my locker. But I find it extraordinarily difficult to imagine how Jane, who, after all, is not the world's strongest individual, managed to stuff an entire winter coat through the tiny slits in my locker.

But I'm not here to ask questions, so I put my coat on and walk out to the parking lot, where Tiny Cooper is sharing one of those hand-shake-followed-by-one-armed-hug things with none other than Clint. I open the passenger door and get into Tiny's Acura. He shows up soon afterward, and although I'm pissed at him, even I am able to appreciate the fascinating and complex geometry involved in Tiny Cooper inserting himself into a tiny car.

"I have a proposition," I tell him as he engages in another miracle of engineering—that of fastening his seat belt.

"I'm flattered, but I'm not gonna sleep with you," Tiny answers.

"Not funny. Listen, my proposition is that if you back off this *Tiny Dancer* business, I will—well, what do you want me to do? Because I'll do anything."

"Well, I want you to hook up with Jane. Or at least call her. After I so artfully arranged for you to be alone together, she seems to have gotten the impression that you don't want to date her."

"I don't," I say. Which is entirely true and entirely not. The stupid, all-encompassing truth.

"What do you think this is, eighteen thirty-two? When you like someone and they like you, you fucking put your lips against their lips and then you open your mouth a little, and then just a little hint of tongue to spice things up. I mean, *God*, Grayson. Everybody's always got their panties in a twist about how the youth of America are debaucherous, sex-crazed maniacs passing out handjobs like they were lollipops, and you can't even kiss a girl who *definitely likes you*?"

"I don't like her, Tiny. Not like that."

"She's *adorable*."

"How would you know?"

"I'm gay, not blind. Her hair's all poofy and she's got a great nose. I mean, a *great* nose. And, what? What do you people like? Boobs? She seems to have boobs. They seem to be of approximately normal boob size. What else do you want?"

"I don't want to talk about this."

He starts the car and then begins banging his tetherball of a head against the car's horn rhythmically. *Ahnnnk. Ahhhnk. Ahhhnk.*

"You're embarrassing us," I shout over the horn.

"I'm going to keep doing this until I get a concussion or you say you'll call her."

I jam my fingers into my ears, but Tiny keeps headbutting the horn. People are looking at us. Finally I just say, "Fine. Fine! FINE!" And the honking ceases.

"I'll call Jane. I'll be nice to her. But I still don't want to date her."

"That is your choice. Your stupid choice."

"So then," I say hopefully, "no production of *Tiny Dancer*?"

Tiny starts the car. "Sorry, Grayson, but I can't do it. *Tiny Dancer* is bigger than you or me, or any of us."

"Tiny, you have a really warped understanding of compromise."

He laughs. "Compromise is when you do what I tell you and I do what I want. Which reminds me: I'm gonna need you to be in the play."

I stifle a laugh, because this shit won't be funny anymore if it's staged in our goddamned auditorium. "Absolutely not. No. NO. Also, I insist that you write me out of it."

Tiny sighs. "You just don't get it, do you? Gil Wrayson isn't *you*; he's a fictional character. I can't just change my art because you're uncomfortable with it."

I try a different tack. "You're gonna humiliate yourself up there, Tiny."

"It's going to happen, Grayson. I've got the support on the student council for the money. So shut up and deal with it."

I shut up and deal with it, but I don't call Jane that night. I'm not Tiny's errand boy.

The next afternoon I take the bus home, because Tiny is busy at the student council meeting. He calls me as soon as it's over.

"Great news, Grayson!" he shouts.

"Great news for someone is always bad news for someone else," I answer.

And sure enough, the student council has approved a thousand dollars for the staging and production of the musical *Tiny Dancer*.

That night I'm waiting for my parents to come home so we can eat, and I'm trying to work on this essay about Emily Dickinson, but mostly I'm just downloading everything the Maybe Dead Cats have ever recorded. I kind of absolutely love them. And as I keep listening to them, I keep wanting to tell someone how good they are, and so I call Tiny, but he doesn't pick up, and so I do exactly what Tiny wants— just like always. I call Jane.

"Hey, Will," she says.

"I kind of absolutely love the Maybe Dead Cats," I say.

"They're not bad, yeah. A bit pseudointellectual but, hey, aren't we all?"

"I think their band name is a reference to, like, this physicist guy," I say. In fact, I *know* it. I've just looked the band up on Wikipedia.

"Yeah," she says. "Schrödinger. Except the band name is a total fail, because Schrödinger is famous for pointing out this paradox in quantum physics where, like, under certain circumstances, an unseen cat can be *both* alive *and* dead. Not *maybe* dead."

"Oh," I say, because I can't even pretend to have known that. I feel like a total dumbass, so I change the subject. "So I hear Tiny Cooper worked his Tiny Magic and the musical's on."

"Yeah. What's your problem with *Tiny Dancer*, anyway?"

"Have you ever *read* it?"

"Yeah. It's amazing, if he can pull it off."

"Well, I'm, like, the costar. Gil Wrayson. That's me, obviously. And it's just, it's embarrassing."

"Don't you think it's kind of awesome to be, like, the costar of Tiny's life?"

"I don't really want to be the costar of *anyone*'s life," I say. She doesn't say anything in response. "So how are you?" I ask after a second.

"I'm okay."

"Just okay?"

"Did you get the note in your coat pocket?"

"The what—no. There was a note?"

"Yeah."

"Oh. Hold on." I put the phone down on the desk and ransack my pockets. The thing about my coat pockets is that if I have a small amount of trash—like, say, a Snickers wrapper—but I don't see a garbage can, my pockets end up becoming the garbage can. And I'm not great when it comes to taking out the pocket trash. So it takes me a few minutes before I find a folded piece of notebook paper. On the outside it says:

To: Will Grayson
From: The Locker Houdini

I grab the phone and say, "Hey, I found it." I feel a little sick to my stomach, in a way that is both nice and not.

"Well, did you read it?"

"No," I say, and I wonder if maybe the note is not better left unread. I shouldn't have called her in the first place. "Hold on." I unfold the paper:

Mr. Grayson,
You should always make sure no one's watching when you unlock your locker. You never know (18) when someone (26) will memorize (4) your combination. Thanks for the coat. I guess chivalry isn't dead.

yours,
Jane

p.s. I like how you treat your pockets the way I treat my car.

Upon finishing the note, I read it again. It makes both truths more true. I want her. I don't. Maybe I am a robot after all. I have no idea what to say, so I go ahead and say the worst possible thing. "Very cute." This is why I should adhere to Rule 2.

In the ensuing silence, I have time to contemplate the word cute—how dismissive it is, how it's the equivalent of calling someone little, how it makes a person into a baby, how the word is a neon sign burning through the dark reading, "Feel Bad About Yourself."

And then finally she says, "Not my favorite adjective."

"Sorry. I mean, it's—"

"I know what you mean, Will," she says. "I'm sorry. I, uh, I don't know. I just got out of a relationship, and I think I'm, like, kind of just looking to fill that hole, and you're the most obvious candidate to fill the hole, and oh my God that sounds dirty. Oh, God. I'm just gonna hang up."

"I'm sorry about cute. It wasn't cute. It was—"

"Forget it. Forget the note, really. I don't even . . . Just don't worry about it, Grayson."

After an awkward hanging up, I realize the intended ending of the "I don't even . . ." sentence. "I don't even . . . like you, Grayson, because you're kind of how can I say this politely not that smart. Like, you had to look up that physicist on Wikipedia. I just miss my boyfriend, and you wouldn't kiss me, so I kind of want to just because you wouldn't, and it's really actually not a big deal but I can't find a way to tell you that without hurting your feelings, and since I'm far more compassionate and thoughtful than you with your *cutes*, I'm just going to stop the sentence at *I don't even*."

I call Tiny again, this time not about the Maybe Dead Cats, and he picks up on the first half-ring and says, "Good evening, Grayson."

I ask him if he agrees with me about what the end of

her sentence probably was, and then I ask him what short-circuited in my brain to call the note cute, and how is it even possible to be both attracted and not attracted to someone at the very same moment, and whether maybe I am a robot incapable of real feelings, and do you think that actually, like, trying to follow the rules about shutting up and not caring has made me into some kind of hideous monster whom no one will ever love or marry. I say it all, and Tiny says nothing, which is a basically unprecedented turn of events, and then when I finally stop, Tiny says *hrmm* in the little way that he has and then he says—and I am quoting him directly here—"Grayson, sometimes you are *such. a. girl.*" And then he hangs up on me.

The unfinished sentence stays with me all night. And then my robot heart decides to do something—the kind of something that would be enjoyed by a hypothetical girl-I-would-like.

At school on Friday, I eat lunch superfast, which is easy enough to do because Tiny and I are sitting with a table full of Drama People, and they are discussing *Tiny Dancer*, all of them speaking more words per minute than I speak in a day. The conversational curve follows a distinct pattern—the voices get louder and faster, crescendoing until Tiny, talking over everyone, makes a joke, and the table explodes in laughter and then things calm briefly, and then the voices start again, building and building into the coming Tiny eruption. Once I notice this pattern, it becomes difficult not to pay attention to it, but I try to focus on wolfing down my enchiladas. I chug a Coke and then stand up.

Tiny holds up his hand to quiet the chorus. "Where ya going, Grayson?"

"I gotta go check on something," I say.

I know the *approximate* location of her locker. It is approximately across from the hallway mural in which a poorly painted version of our school mascot, Willie the Wildkit, says in a speech bubble, "Wildkits Respect EVERYONE," which is hilarious on at least fourteen different levels, the fourteenth being that *there is no such thing as a wildkit.* Willie the Wildkit looks approximately like a mountain lion, though, and while I am admittedly not an expert in zoology, I'm reasonably sure that mountain lions do not, in fact, respect everyone.

So I'm leaning against the Willie the Wildkit mural in such a way that it appears that I'm the one saying that Wildkits Respect EVERYONE, and I have to wait like that for about ten minutes, just trying to look like I'm doing something and wishing I'd brought a book or whatever so I wouldn't look so aggressively stalkerish, and then finally the period bell rings and the hallway floods with people.

Jane gets to her locker, and I step into the middle of the hallway, and people make way for me, and I take a step to the left to get the angle just right, and I can see her hand reach up to the lock, and I squint, and 25-2-11. I turn into the flow of people and walk to history.

Seventh period, I take this video game–design class. It turns out that designing video games is incredibly hard and not nearly as fun as playing them, but the one advantage of the class is that I have Internet access and my monitor faces away from the teacher most of the time.

So I e-mail the Maybe Dead Cats.

From: williamgrayson@eths.il.us
To: thiscatmaybedead@gmail.com
Subject: Make My Life
Dear Maybe Dead Cats,
If you happen to play "Annus Miribalis" tonight,
could you possibly dedicate it to 25-2-11 (a certain
girl's locker combination)? That would be amazing.
Sorry about the short notice,
                    Will Grayson

The reply comes before the period is even over.

Will,
Anything for love.
MDC

So after school on Friday, Jane and Tiny and I go to Frank's Franks, a hot-dog restaurant a few blocks away from the club. I sit in a small booth next to Jane, her hip against my hip. Our coats are all bunched up across from us along with Tiny. Her hair is falling in all these big curls on her shoulders, and she's wearing this non weather–appropriate top with thin straps and quite a lot of eye makeup.

Because this is a classy hot-dog joint, a waiter takes our order. Jane and I each want one hot dog and a soda. Tiny orders four hot dogs with buns, three hot dogs without buns, a bowl of chili, and a Diet Coke.

"A *Diet* Coke?" asks the waiter. "You want four hot dogs

with buns, three hot dogs without buns, a bowl of chili, and a *Diet* Coke?"

"That's correct," says Tiny, and then explains, "simple sugars don't really help me put on muscle mass." And the waiter just shakes his head and says, "Uh-huh."

"Your poor digestive system," I say. "One day your intestinal tract is going to revolt. It's going to reach up and strangle you."

"You know Coach says ideally I should put on thirty pounds for the start of next season. If I want to get scholarships from Division I schools? You gotta be *big*. And it's just so hard for me to put on weight. I try and I try, but it's a constant battle."

"You've got a real hard life, Tiny," says Jane. I laugh, and we exchange glances, and then Tiny says, "Oh my God, just *do* it already," which leads to an uncomfortable silence that lasts until Jane asks, "So where are Gary and Nick?"

"Probably getting back together," Tiny says. "I broke up with Nick last night."

"That was the right thing to do. It was doomed from the start."

"I know, right? I really think I want to be single for a while."

I turn to Jane and say, "I bet you five bucks he'll be in love within four hours."

She laughs. "Make it three and you're on."

"Deal."

We shake.

After dinner, we walk around the neighborhood for a little

while to kill time and then get in line outside the Storage Room. It's cold out, but up against the building, we're out of the wind at least. In line, I pull out my wallet, move the fake ID to the front picture window, and hide my real driver's license between a health insurance card and my dad's business card.

"Let me see it," says Tiny, and I hand him my wallet, and he says, "Damn, Grayson, for once in your life you don't look like a bitchsquealer in a picture."

Just before we get to the front of the line, Tiny pushes me in front of him—I guess so he can have the pleasure of watching me use the ID for the first time. The bouncer wears a T-shirt that doesn't quite extend over his belly.

"ID," he tells me. I pull my wallet from my back pocket, slide the ID out, and hand it to him. He shines a flashlight on it, then turns the flashlight onto my face, and then back to the ID, and then he says, "What, you think I can't add?"

And I say, "Huh?"

And the bouncer says, "Kid, you're twenty."

And I say, "No, I'm twenty-two." And he hands me my ID and says, "Well, your goddamned driver's license says you're twenty." I stare at it, and do the math. It says I turn twenty-one next January.

"Uh," I say. "Um, yeah. Sorry."

That stupid h-o-p-e-l-e-s-s stoner put the wrong fucking year on my ID. I step away from the club's entrance, and Tiny walks up to me, laughing his ass off. Jane is giggling, too. Tiny claps me too hard on the shoulder and says, "Only Grayson could get a fake ID that says he's twenty. It's totally worthless!"

And I say to Jane, "Your friend made it with the wrong year," and she says, "I'm sorry, Will," but she can't be *that* sorry, or else she'd stop laughing.

"We can try to get you in," Jane suggests, but I just shake my head.

"You guys just go," I say. "Just call me when it's over. I'll just hang out at Frank's Franks or something. And, like, call me if they play 'Annus Miribalis.'"

And here's the thing: they go. They just get back into line and then I watch them walk into the club, and neither of them even tries to say *no, no, we don't want to see the show without you.*

Don't get me wrong. The band is great. But being passed over for the band still sucks. Standing in line I hadn't felt cold, but now it's freezing. It's miserable out, the kind of cold where breathing through your nose gives you brain freeze. And I'm out here alone with my worthless fucking hundred-dollar ID.

I walk back to Frank's Franks, order a hot dog, and eat it slowly. But I know I can't possibly eat this one hot dog for the two or three hours they'll be gone—you can't savor a hot dog. My phone's on the table, and I just watch it, stupidly hoping Jane or Tiny might call. And sitting here, I only get more and more pissed. This is a hell of a way to leave someone—sitting alone in a restaurant—just staring straight ahead, not even a book to keep me company. It's not even just Tiny and Jane; I'm pissed at myself, for giving them an out, for not checking the date on the stupid ID, for sitting here waiting for the phone to ring even though I could be driving home.

And thinking about it, I realize the problem with going where you're pushed: sometimes you're pushed here.

I'm tired of going where I'm pushed. It's one thing to get pushed around by my parents. But Tiny Cooper pushing me toward Jane, and then pushing me toward a fake ID, and then laughing at the fuckup that resulted, and then leaving me here alone with a goddamned second-rate hot dog when I don't even particularly like first-rate hot dogs—that's bullshit.

I can see him in my mind, his fat head laughing. *It's totally worthless. It's totally worthless.* Not so! I can buy cigarettes, although I don't smoke. I can possibly illegally register to vote. I can—oh, hey. Huh. Now there's an idea.

See, across from the Storage Room, there's this place. A neon-sign-and-no-windows kind of place. Now, I don't particularly like or care about porn—or the "Adult Books" promised by the sign outside the door—but I'll be damned if I'm going to spend my entire night at Frank's Franks *not* using my fake ID. No. I'm going to the porn store. Tiny Cooper doesn't have the nuts to walk into a place like that. No way. I'm thinking about the story I'll have when Tiny and Jane get out of the concert. I put a five on the table—a 50 percent tip—and walk four blocks. As I get near the door, I start to feel anxious—but I tell myself that being outside in the dead of winter in downtown Chicago is much more dangerous than any business establishment could possibly be.

I pull the door open, and step into a room bright with fluorescent light. To my left, a guy with more piercings than a pincushion stands behind a counter, staring at me.

"You browsing or you want tokens?" he asks me. I don't have the first idea what tokens are, so I say, "Browsing?"

"Okay. Go on in," he tells me.

"What?"

"Go ahead."

"You're not going to ID me?"

The guy laughs. "What, are you sixteen or something?"

He nailed it exactly, but I say, "No, I'm twenty."

"Well, yeah. So that's what I figured. Go ahead."

And I'm thinking, *Oh, my God. How hard can it fucking be to successfully use a fake ID in this town?* This is ridiculous! I won't stand for it. "No," I say, forcefully. "ID me."

"All right, man. If that's what gets your maracas shakin'." And then, real dramatically, he asks, "Can I see some ID, please?"

"You may," I answer, and hand it to him. He glances at it, hands it back, and says, "Thanks, Ishmael."

"You're welcome," I say, exasperated. And then I'm in a porn store.

It's kinda boring, actually. It looks like a regular store—shelves of DVDs and old VHS tapes and a rack of magazines, all under this harsh fluorescent glow. I mean, there *are* some differences from a regular video store, I guess, like A. At the regular video store, very few of the DVDs have the words *guzzling* or *slut* in them, whereas here the opposite seems to be the case, and also B. I'm pretty sure the regular video store doesn't have any devices used for spanking, whereas this place has several. Also, C. There are very few items for sale at the regular video store that make you think, "I have no earthly idea what that is supposed to do or where it is supposed to do it."

Other than Señor Muy Pierced, the place is empty, and I very much want to leave because this is possibly the most uncomfortable and unpleasant portion of what has heretofore been a pretty uncomfortable and unpleasant day. But the whole trip is completely worthless if I don't get a memento to prove I was here. My goal is to find the item that will make for the funniest show-and-tell, the item that will make Tiny and Jane feel like I had a night of hilarity they can only glimpse, which is how I finally come to settle upon a Spanish-language magazine called *Mano a Mano*.

chapter six

at this moment, i want to jump ahead in time. or, if that doesn't work, i'll settle for traveling back in time.

i want to jump ahead in time because in twenty hours i will be with isaac in chicago, and i am willing to skip everything in between in order to get to him faster. i don't care if in ten hours i'm going to win the lottery, or if in twelve hours i'm going to get the chance to graduate early from high school. i don't care if in fourteen hours i am going to be jerking off and have the most life-altering orgasm in all of unrecorded history. i would fast-forward past it all to be with isaac instead of having to settle for thinking about him.

as for traveling back in time, it's really simple — i want to go back in time and kill the guy who invented math. why? because right now i'm at the lunch table and derek is saying

derek: aren't you psyched for mathletes tomorrow?

with that simple word — *mathletes* — it's like every ounce of anesthesia i've ever collected in my body wears off at once.

me: holy sweet f-ing a

there are four mathletes in our school. i am number four. derek and simon are numbers one and two, and in order to enter competitions they need at least four members. (number three is a freshman whose name i deliberately forget. his pencil has more personality than he does.)

simon: you do remember, right?

they've both put their meatburgers down (that's what the cafeteria menu calls them — meatburgers), and they're staring at me with looks so blank i swear i can see the computer screens reflected in their glasses.

me: i dunno. i'm not feeling very mathletic. maybe you
    should find a subset-stitute?
derek: that's not funny.
me: ha ha! wasn't meant to be!
simon: i've told you — you don't have to do anything.
    in a mathletic competition, you enter as a team,
    but are judged as individuals.
me: you guys know i'm your biggest mathletic
    supporter. but, um, i kind-of made other plans
    for tomorrow.
derek: you can't do that.
simon: you said you'd come.
derek: i promise it'll be fun.
simon: nobody else will do it.
derek: *we'll have a good time.*

i can tell derek's upset because it looks like he's considering having a slight emotional response to the informational stimuli being presented to him. maybe it's too much, because he puts down his meatburger, picks up his tray, murmurs something about library fines, and leaves the table.

there's no doubt in my mind that i'm going to bail on these guys. the only question is whether i can do it without feeling like shit. i guess it's a sign of desperation, but i decide to tell simon something remotely resembling the truth.

> me: look, you know that ordinarily i'd be all over
> mathletes. but this is like an emergency. i made
> like a — i guess you could call it a date. and i
> really, really have to see this person, who's coming
> a long way to see me. and if there was any way to
> do it and go to the mathletic competition with you,
> i would. but i can't. it's like . . . if a train is traveling
> at ninety miles an hour and it needs to get from
> the mathletics competition to the middle of chicago
> in, like, two minutes for a date, it's never going to
> make it in time. so i have to jump on the express,
> because ultimately the tracks that lead to the date
> are only being laid down this one time, and if i get
> on the wrong train, i'm going to be more miserable
> than any equation could ever account for.

it feels so strange to be telling someone this, especially simon.

simon: i don't care. you said you'd be there and you
      have to be there. this is an instance where four
      minus one equals zero.
me: but simon . . .
simon: stop whining and find another warm body to
      get in mr. nadler's car with us. or even a cold body
      if it can stay propped up for an hour. it would be a
      change of pace to have someone who can actually
      add, but i swear i won't be choosy, *you fart*.

it's amazing how i usually make it through the day
without realizing i don't have that many friends. i mean,
once you get out of the top five you'll find a lot more of
the custodial staff than members of the student body. and
while janitor jim doesn't mind if i swipe a roll of toilet
paper every now and then for 'art projects,' i have a feeling
he wouldn't be willing to forfeit his friday night for a trip
with the calcsuckers and their faculty groupies.

i know i only have one shot, and it ain't an easy one.
maura's been in a good mood all day — well, a maura version of a good mood, which means the forecast calls for
drizzle instead of thunderstorms. she hasn't brought up the
gay thing, and lord knows i haven't either.

i wait until last period, knowing that if the pressure's
on, she's more likely to say yes. even though we're sitting
next to each other, i take my phone out under the desk and
text her.

me: whatre u doing tmrw night?
maura: nothing. wanna do something?

me: i wish. i have to go to chicago with my mom.
maura: fun?
me: i need you to sub for me in mathletes. otherwise
   s&d are screwed.
maura: ure kidding, right?
me: no, theyll really be screwed.
maura: and y would i?
me: because ill o u 1. and ill give you 20 bucks.
maura: o me 3 and make it 50.
me: deal.
maura: im saving these texts.

truth? i probably just rescued maura from an afternoon of shopping with her mom or doing homework or poking a pen into her veins to get some material for her poetry. after class, i tell her that she'll no doubt meet some other deadbeat fourth-string mathlete from some town we've never heard of, and the two of them will sneak out for clove cigarettes and talk about how lame everyone else is while derek and simon and that stupid freshman get smashed on theorems and rhombazoids. really, i'm doing wonders for her social life.

maura: don't push it.
me: i swear, it'll be hot.
maura: i want twenty bucks up front.

i'm just glad i didn't have to lie and say that i had to go visit my sick grandma or something. those kind of lies are dangerous, because you know the minute you say your grandma's sick the phone's going to ring and your mom's going to come into the room with really bad news about grandma's pancreas, and even though you'll know that little white lies do not cause cancer, you'll still feel guilty for the rest of your life. maura asks me more about my trip to chicago with my mom, so i make it sound like it's necessary bonding time, and since maura has two happy parents and i have one bummed-out one, i win the sympathy vote. i'm thinking about isaac so much that i'm completely scared i'm just going to blurt him out, but luckily maura's interest keeps me on my guard.

when it's time for her to go her way and me to go mine, she makes one more stab for the truth.

maura: is there anything you want to tell me?
me: yeah. i want to tell you that my third nipple is
    lactating and my butt cheeks are threatening to
    unionize. what do you think i should do about it?
maura: i feel you're not telling me something.

here's the thing about maura: it's always about her. always. now, normally i don't mind this, because if everything's about her, then nothing has to be about me. but sometimes her spotlight clinging drags me in, and that's what i hate.

she's pouting at me now, and, to give her credit, it's a genuine pout. it's not like she's trying to manipulate me by pretending to be annoyed. maura doesn't do that kind of crap, and that's why i put up with her. i can take everything on her face at face value, and that's valuable in a friend.

me: i'll tell you when i have something to tell you,
    okay? now go home and practice your math. here . . .
    i made you flash cards.

i reach into my bag and take out these cards i made
seventh period, kinda knowing maura was going to say yes.
they're not actually cards, since it's not like i carry a set of
index cards around in my bag for indexing emergencies. but
i made all these dotted lines on the piece of paper so she'll
know where to cut. each card has its own equation.

$2 + 2 = 4$
$50 \times 40 = 2000$
$834620 \times 375002 =$ *who really gives a fuck?*
$x + y = z$
cock + *pussy* = *a happy rooster-kitten couple*
red + *blue* = *purple*
me − *mathletes* = *me* + *gratitude to you*

maura looks at them for a second, then folds the piece of
paper along the dotted lines, squaring it together like a map. she
doesn't smile or anything, but she looks unpissed for a second.

me: don't let derek and simon get too frisky, okay?
    always wear pocket protection.
maura: i think i'll be able to keep my maidenhead at a
    mathletes competition.
me: you say that now, but we'll see in nine months. if
    it's a girl, you should name her *logorrhea*. if it's a
    boy, go for *trig*.

it does occur to me that because of the way life works, maura probably *will* get some hot math-reject guy to put his plus in her minus, while i bomb out with isaac and come home to the comfort of my own hand.

i decide not to tell maura this, 'cause why jinx us both?

maura gives me an actual 'good-bye' before she goes, and she looks like she has something else to say, but has decided not to say it. another reason for me to be grateful.

i thank her again. and again. and again.

when that's done, i head home and email with isaac once he gets home from school — no work for him today. we go over our plan about two thousand times. he says a friend of his suggested we meet at a place called frenchy's, and since i don't really know chicago that much outside of places where you'd go on a class trip, i tell him that's fine by me, and print out the directions he sends me.

when we're through, i go on facebook and look at his profile for the millionth thousandth time. he doesn't really change it that often, but it's a good enough reminder to me that he's real. i mean, we've exchanged photos and have talked enough for me to know that he's real — it's not like he's some forty-six-year-old who's already prepared a nice spot in the back of his unmarked van for me. i'm not that stupid. we're meeting in a public place, and i have my phone. even if isaac has a psychotic break, i'll be prepared.

before i go to sleep, i look at all the pictures i have of him, as if i haven't already memorized them. i'm sure i'll recognize him the moment i see him. and i'm sure it'll be one of the best moments of my life.

friday after school is brutal. i want to commit murder about a thousand different ways, and it's my closet i want to kill. i have no fucking idea what to wear — and i am *not* a what-do-i-wear kind of guy at all, so it's like i can't even begin to comprehend the task at hand. every single goddamn piece of clothing i own seems to have chosen now to reveal its faults. i put on this one shirt which i've always thought made me look good, and sure enough it makes my chest look like it actually has some definition. but then i realize it's so small that if i raise my arms even an inch, my belly pubes are on full display. so then i try this black shirt which makes me look like i'm trying too hard, and then this white shirt which is cool until i find this stain near the bottom which i'm hoping is orange juice, but is probably from when i tucked before i tapped. band t-shirts are too obvious — if i wear a shirt from one of his favorites, it's like i'm being a kiss-ass, and if i wear one for a band he might not like, he might think my taste is lame. my gray hoodie is too blech and this blue shirt i have is practically the same color as my jeans, and looking all-blue is something only cookie monster can pull off.

for the first time in my life i realize why hangers are called hangers, because after fifteen minutes of trying things on and throwing them aside, all i want to do is hook one to the top of my closet door, lean my neck into the loop, and let my weight fall. my mother will come in and think it's some autoerotic asphyxiation where i didn't even have the time to get my dick out, and i won't be alive enough to tell her that i think autoerotic asphyxiation is one of the dumbest things in the whole universe, right up there with gay republicans.

but, yeah, i'll be dead. and it'll be like an episode of *CSI: FU*, where the investigators will come in and spend forty-three minutes plus commercials scouring over my life, and at the end they'll bring my mother to the station house and they'll sit her down and give her the truth.

cop: ma'am, your son wasn't murdered. he was just getting ready for a first date.

i'm kind-of smiling, picturing how the scene would be shot, then i remember that i'm standing shirtless in the middle of my room, and i have a train to catch. finally i just pick this shirt that has a little picture of this robot made out of duct tape or something, with the word *robotboy* in small lowercase underneath it. i don't know why i like it, but i do. and i don't know why i think isaac will like it, but i do.

i know i must be nervous, because i'm actually thinking about *how my hair looks*, but when i get to the bathroom mirror, i decide my hair's going to do what it wants to do, and since it usually looks better when it's windy, i'll just stick my head out of the train window or something on my way there. i could use my mother's hair stuff, but i have no desire to smell like butterflies in a field. so i'm done.

i've told mom that the mathletes competition is in chicago — i figured if i was going to lie, she might as well think we made the state finals. i claimed the school had chartered a bus, but instead i head to the train station, no problem. my nerves are completely jangling by now. i try to read *to kill a mockingbird* for english class, but it's like the letters are this nice design on the page and don't mean anything more to me than the patterns on the train seats. it could be an action movie called *die, mockingbird, die!* and i still wouldn't be into it. so i close my eyes and listen to my ipod, but it's like it's been preprogrammed by a mean-ass cupid, because every single song makes me think of isaac. he's become the one the songs are about. and while part of me knows he's probably worth that, another part is yelling at me to *slow the fuck down*. while it's going to be exciting to see isaac, it's also going to be awkward. the key will be to not let that awkwardness get to us.

i take about five minutes to think about my dating history — five minutes is really all i can fill — and i'm sent back to the traumatic experience of drunkenly groping carissa nye at sloan mitchell's party a couple months ago. the kissing part was actually hot, but then when it got more serious, carissa got this stupidly earnest look on her face and i almost cracked up. we had some serious problems with her bra cutting off the circulation to her brain, and when i finally had her boobs in my hands (not that i'd asked for them), i didn't know what to do with them except pet them, like they were puppies. the puppies liked that, and carissa decided to give me a rub or two also, and i liked that, because when it all comes down to it, hands are hands, and touch is touch, and your body's going to react the way your body's going to react. it doesn't give a damn about all the conversations you're going to have afterward — not just with carissa, who wanted to be my girlfriend and who i tried to let down easy, but ended up hurting anyway. no, there was also maura to deal with, because the moment she heard (not from me) she was pissed (all at me). she said she thought carissa was using me, and she acted like she thought i was using carissa, when really the whole thing was useless, and no matter how many times i told maura this, she refused to let me off the hook. for weeks i had her shouting 'well, why don't you give carissa a call, then?' whenever we disagreed. for that alone, the groping wasn't worth it.

isaac, of course, is completely different. not just in the groping sense. although there is certainly that. i'm not heading into the city just to mess around with him. it might not be the last thing on my mind, but it isn't near the first, either.

i thought i was going to be early, but of course by the time i get near where we're supposed to meet, i'm later than a pregnant girl's period. i walk along michigan avenue with the right-before-curfew tourist girls and tourist boys, who all look like they've just come from basketball practice or watching basketball on tv. i definitely eye a few specimens, but it's purely scientific research. for the next, oh, ten minutes, i can save myself for isaac.

i wonder if he's already there. i wonder if he's as nervous as i am. i wonder if he has spent as much time this morning as i did picking a shirt out. i wonder if by some freak of nature we'll be wearing the same thing. like this is so meant to be that god's decided to make it *really* obvious.

sweaty palms. *check*. shaky bones. *check*. the feeling that all oxygen in the air has been replaced by helium. *yup*. i look at the map fifteen times a second. five blocks to go. four blocks to go. three blocks to go. two blocks to go. state street. the corner. looking for frenchy's. thinking it's going to be a hip diner. or a coffee shop. or an indie record store. or even just a rundown restaurant.

then: getting there and finding out . . . it's a porn shop.

thinking maybe the porn shop was named after something else nearby. maybe this is the frenchy's district, and everything is named frenchy's, like the way you can go downtown and find downtown bagels and the downtown cleaners and the downtown yoga studio. but no. i loop the block. i try the other side. i check the address over and over and over.

and there i am. back at the door.

i remember that isaac's friend suggested the place. or at least that's what he said. if that's true, maybe it's a joke, and poor isaac got here first and was mortified and is waiting for me inside. or maybe this is some kind of cosmic test. i have to cross the river of extreme awkwardness in order to get to the paradise on the other side.

what the fuck, i figure.

cold wind blowing all around me, i head inside.

chapter seven

I hear the electronic *bing* and turn around to see a kid walking in. Naturally, he doesn't get carded, and while he is on the hairy side of puberty, there's no way he's eighteen. Small and big-eyed and towheaded and absolutely terrified—as scared as I would probably be had I not already been driven to the brink by the anti-Will Grayson conspiracy encompassing A. Jane, and B. Tiny, and C. The well-pierced specimen behind the counter, and D. Stonedy McKopyShoppy.

But, anyway, the kid is staring at me with a level of intensity that I find very troubling, particularly given that I am holding a copy of *Mano a Mano*. I'm sure there are a number of fantastic ways to indicate to the underage stranger standing next to a Great Wall of Dildos that you are not, in fact, a fan of *Mano a Mano*, but the particular strategy I choose is to mumble, "It's, uh, for a friend." Which is true, but A. It's not a terribly convincing excuse, and B. It implies that I'm the kind of guy who is friends with the kind of guy who likes *Mano a Mano*, and further implies that C. I'm the kind of guy who buys porn magazines for his friends. Immediately after saying "It's for a friend," I realize that I should have said, "I'm trying to learn Spanish."

The kid just continues to stare at me, and then after a while he narrows his eyes, squinting. I hold his stare for a few seconds but then glance away. Finally, he walks past me and into the video aisles. It seems to me that he is looking for something specific, and that the something specific is not related to sex, in which case I rather suspect he will not find it here. He meanders toward the back of the store, which contains an open door that I believe may in some way be related to "Tokens." All I want to do is get the hell out of here with my copy of *Mano a Mano*, so I walk up to the pierced guy and say, "Just this, please."

He rings it up on the cash register. "Nine eighty-three," he says.

"Nine DOLLARS?" I ask, incredulous.

"And eighty-three cents," he adds.

I shake my head. This is turning into an extraordinarily expensive joke, but I'm not very well going to return to the creepy magazine rack and look for a bargain. I reach into my pockets and come out with somewhere in the neighborhood of four dollars. I sigh, and then reach for my back pocket, handing the guy my debit card. My parents look at the statement, but they won't know *Frenchy's* from *Denny's*.

The guy looks at the card. He looks at me. He looks at the card. He looks at me. And just before he talks, I realize: my card says William Grayson. My ID says Ishmael J. Biafra.

Quite loud, the guy says, "William. Grayson. William. Grayson. Where *have* I seen that name before? Oh, right. NOT on your driver's license."

I consider my options for a moment and then say, real quietly, "It's my card. I know my pin. Just—ring it up."

He swipes it through the card machine and says, "I don't give a shit, kid. It all spends the same." And just then I can feel the guy right behind me, looking at me again, and so I wheel around, and he says, "What did you say?" Only he's not talking to me, he's talking to Piercings.

"I said I don't give a shit about his ID."

"You didn't call me?"

"What the fuck are you talking about, kid?"

"William Grayson. Did you say William Grayson? Did someone call here for me?"

"Huh? No, kid. William Grayson is this guy," he says, nodding toward me. "Well, two schools of thought on that, I guess, but that's what *this* card says."

And the kid looks at me confused for a minute and finally says, "What's your name?"

This is freaking me out. Frenchy's isn't a place for *conversation*. So I just say to Piercings, "Can I have the magazine?" and Piercings hands it to me in an unmarked and thoroughly opaque black plastic bag for which I am very grateful, and he gives me my card and my receipt. I walk out the door, jog a half block down Clark, and then sit down on the curb and wait for my pulse to slow down.

Which it is just starting to do when my fellow underage Frenchy's pilgrim runs up to me and says, "Who *are* you?"

I stand up then and say, "Um, I'm Will Grayson."

"W-I-L-L G-R-A-Y-S-O-N?" he says, spelling impossibly fast.

"Uh, yeah," I say. "Why do you ask?"

The kid looks at me for a second, his head turned like he thinks I might be putting him on, and then finally he says, "Because I am also Will Grayson."

"No shit?" I ask.

"Shit," the guy says. I can't decide if he's paranoid or schizophrenic or both, but then he pulls a duct-taped wallet out of his back pocket and shows me an Illinois driver's license. Our middle names are different, at least, but—yeah.

"Well," I say, "good to meet you." And then I start to turn away, because nothing against the guy but I don't care to strike up a conversation with a guy who hangs out at porn stores, even if, technically speaking, I am myself a guy who hangs out at porn stores. But he touches my arm, and he seems too small to be *dangerous*, so I turn back around, and he says, "Do you know Isaac?"

"Who?"

"Isaac?"

"I don't know anyone named Isaac, man," I say.

"I was supposed to meet him at that place, but he's not there. You don't really look like him but I thought—I don't know what I thought. How the—what the hell is going on?" The kid spins a quick circle, like he's looking for a cameraman or something. "Did Isaac put you up to this?"

"I just told you, man, I don't know any Isaac."

He turns around again, but there's no one behind him. He throws his arms in the air, and says, "I don't even know *what* to freak out *about* right now."

"It's been a bit of a crazy day for Will Graysons everywhere," I say.

He shakes his head and sits down on the curb then and I follow him, because there is nothing else to do. He looks over at me, then away, then at me again. And then he actually, physically pinches himself on the forearm. "Of course not. My dreams can't make up shit this weird."

"Yeah," I say. I can't figure out if he wants me to talk to him, and I also can't figure out if I want to talk to him, but after a minute, I say, "So, uh, how do you know meet-me-at-the-porn-store Isaac?"

"He's just—a friend of mine. We've known each other online for a long time."

"Online?"

If possible, Will Grayson manages to shrink into himself even more. His shoulders hunched, he stares intently into the gutter of the street. I know, of course, that there are other Will Graysons. I've Googled myself enough to know that. But I never thought I would see one. Finally he says, "Yeah."

"You've never physically seen this guy," I say.

"No," he says, "but I've seen him in like a thousand pictures."

"He's a fifty-year-old man," I say, matter-of-factly. "He's a pervert. One Will to another: No way that Isaac is who you think he is."

"He's probably just—I don't know, maybe he met another freaking Isaac on the bus and he's stuck in Bizarro World."

"Why the hell would he ask you to go to Frenchy's?"

"Good question. Why *would* someone go to a porn store?" He kind of smirks at me.

"Fair point," I say. "Yeah, that's true. There's a story to it, though."

I wait for a second for Will Grayson to ask me about my story, but he doesn't. Then I start telling him anyway. I tell him about Jane and Tiny Cooper and the Maybe Dead

Cats and "Annus Miribalis" and Jane's locker combination and the copy shop clerk who couldn't count, and I weasel a couple of laughs out of him along the way, but mostly he just keeps glancing back toward Frenchy's, waiting for Isaac. His face seems to alternate between hope and anger. He pays very little attention to me actually, which is fine, really, because I'm just telling my story to tell it, talking to a stranger because it's the only safe kind of talking you can do, and the whole time my hand is in my pocket holding my phone, because I want to make sure I feel it vibrate if someone calls.

And then he tells me about Isaac, about how they've been friends for a year and that he always wanted to meet him because there's just no one like Isaac out in the suburb where he lives, and it dawns on me pretty quickly that Will Grayson likes Isaac in a not-altogether-platonic way. "So, I mean what perverted fifty-year-old would do that?" Will says. "What pervert spends a year of his life talking to me, telling me everything about his fake self, while I tell him everything about my real self? And if a perverted fifty-year-old *did* do that, why wouldn't he show up at Frenchy's to rape and murder me? Even on a totally impossible night, that is *totally impossible*."

I mull it over for a second. "I don't know," I say finally. "People are pretty fucking weird, if you haven't noticed."

"Yeah." He's not looking back to Frenchy's anymore, just forward. I can see him out of the corner of my eye, and I'm sure he can see me out of the corner of his, but mostly we are looking not at each other, but at the same spot on the street as cars rumble past, my brain trying to make sense of all the impossibilities, all the coincidences that brought me here, all the true-and-false things. And we're quiet for a while, so long that I take my phone out of my pocket and look at it and confirm that no one has called and then put it back, and then finally I feel Will turning his head away from the spot on the street and toward me and he says, "What do you think it means?"

"What?" I ask.

"There aren't that many Will Graysons," he says. "It's gotta mean something, one Will Grayson meeting another Will Grayson in a random porn store where neither Will Grayson belongs."

"Are you suggesting that God brought two of Chicagoland's underage Will Graysons into Frenchy's at the same time?"

"No, asshole," he says, "but I mean, it must mean *something*."

"Yeah," I say. "It's hard to believe in coincidence, but it's even harder to believe in anything else." And just then, the phone jumps to life in my hand, and as I am pulling it out of my pocket, Will Grayson's phone starts ringing.

And even for me, that's a lot of coincidences. He mutters, "God, it's Maura," as if I'm going to know who Maura is, and he just stares at the phone, seeming unsure of whether to answer. My call is from Tiny. Before I flip open the phone, I say to Will, "It's my friend Tiny," and I'm looking at Will—at cute, confuzzled Will.

I flip open the phone.

"Grayson!" Tiny shouts over the din of the music. "I'm in love with this band! We're gonna stay for like two more songs and then I'm gonna come get you. Where are you, baby! Where's my pretty little baby Grayson!"

"I'm across the street," I shout back. "And you better get down on your knees and thank the sweet Lord, because man, Tiny, have I got a guy for you."

chapter eight

i am so freaked out, you could pull a clown out of my ass and i wouldn't be at all surprised.

it would make maybe a little sense if this OTHER WILL GRAYSON standing right next to me wasn't a will grayson at all but was instead the gold medal champion of the mind-fuck olympics. it's not like when i first saw him i thought to myself, *hey, that kid must be named will grayson, too.* no, the only thing i thought was, *hey, that's not isaac.* i mean, right age, but entirely wrong face pic. so i ignored him. i turned back to the dvd case i was pretending to study, which was for this porno called *the sound and the furry.* it was all about 'moo sex,' with these people pictured on the cover wearing cow suits (one udder). i was glad that no real cows were harmed (or pleasured) in the making of the film. but still. not my thing. next to it was a dvd called *as i get laid dying,* which had a hospital scene on the front. it was like *grey's anatomy,* only with less grey and more anatomy. i totally thought for a moment, *i can't wait to tell isaac about this,* forgetting, of course, that he was supposed to be with me.

it's not like i wouldn't have noticed him come in; the place was empty except for me, o.w.g., and the clerk, who looked like the pillsbury doughboy if the dough had been left out for a week. i guess everyone else was using the internet to get their porn. and frenchy's wasn't exactly inviting — it was lit like a 7-eleven, which made all the plastic seem much more plastic, and the metal seem much more metal, and the naked people on the covers of the dvd cases look even less hot and more like cheap porn. passing up *go down on moses* and *afternoon delight in august*, i found myself in this bizarre penis produce section. because my mind is, at heart, full of fucked up shit, i immediately started to picture this sequel to *toy story* called *sex toy story*, where all these dildos and vibrators and rabbit ears suddenly came to life and have to do things like cross the street in order to get back home.

again, as i was having all these thoughts, i was also thinking about sharing them with isaac. that was my default.

i was only distracted when i heard my name being said by the guy behind the counter. which is how i found o.w.g.

so, yeah, i go into a porn shop looking for isaac and i get another will grayson instead.

god, you're one nasty fucker.

of course, right now isaac is ranking up there in nasty fuckerdom, too. i'm hoping that he's actually a nervous fucker instead — like, maybe he showed up and discovered that the place his friend recommended was a porn shop and was so mortified that he ran away crying. i mean, it's possible. or maybe he's just late. i have to give him at least an hour. his train could've gotten stuck in a tunnel or something. it's not unheard of. he's coming from ohio, after all. people in ohio are late all the time.

my phone rings at practically the same time as o.w.g.'s. even though it's pathetically unlikely that it's going to be isaac, my hopes still do the up thing.

then i see it's maura.

me: god, it's maura.

at first i'm not going to answer, but then o.w.g. answers his.

o.w.g.: it's my friend tiny.

if o.w.g. is going to answer his, i figure i'd better answer mine, too. i also remember maura's doing me a favor today. if later on i learn that the mathletic competition was attacked by an uzi-wielding squad of frustrated humanties nerds, i'll feel guilty that i didn't answer the phone and let maura say good-bye.

me: quick — what's the square root of my underwear?
maura: hey will.
me: that answer earns you zero points.
maura: how's chicago?
me: there's no wind at all!
maura: what are you doing?
me: oh, hanging out with will grayson.
maura: that's what i thought.
me: what do you mean?
maura: where's your mom?

uh-oh. smells like a trap. has maura called my house? has she talked to my mom? pedal motion, backward!

me: am i my mother's keeper? (ha ha ha)
maura: stop lying, will.
me: okay, okay. i kinda needed to sneak in on my own.
    to go to a concert later.
maura: what concert?

fuck! i can't remember which concert o.w.g. said he was going to. and he's still on the phone, so i can't ask.

me: some band you've never heard of.
maura: try me.
me: um, that's their name. 'some band you've never
    heard of.'
maura: oh, i've heard of them.
me: yeah.
maura: i was just reading a review of their album in
    spin.
me: cool.
maura: yeah, the album's called 'isaac's not coming,
    you fucking liar.'

this is not good.

me: that's a pretty stupid name for an album.

what? what what what?

maura: give up, will.

me: my password.

maura: what?

me: you totally hacked my password. you've been reading my emails, haven't you?

maura: what are you talking about?

me: isaac. how do you know about me meeting up with isaac?

she must have looked over my shoulder when i checked my email at school. she must have seen the keys i typed. she stole my dumbass password.

maura: i *am* isaac, will.

me: don't be stupid. he's a guy.

maura: no he's not. he's a profile. i made him up.

me: yeah, right.

maura: i did.

no. no no no no no no no no no no no no no no no.

me: what?

no please no what no no please no fuck no NO.

maura: isaac doesn't exist. he's never existed.

me: you can't —

maura: you're so caught.

I'M so caught*?!?*

what the FUCK.

me: tell me you're joking.
maura: . . .
me: this can't be happening.

other will grayson's finished his conversation and is
looking at me now.

o.w.g.: are you okay?

it's hitting. that moment of 'did an anvil really just fall
on my head?' has passed and i am feeling that anvil. oh lord
am i feeling that anvil.

me: you. despicable. cunt.

yes, the synapses are conveying the information now.
newsflash: isaac never existed. it was only your friend pos-
ing. it was all a lie.
all a lie.

me: you. horrendous. bitch.
maura: why is it that girls are never called assholes?
me: i am not going to insult assholes that way. they at
    least serve a purpose.
maura: look, i knew you'd be mad . . .
me: you KNEW i would be MAD!?!
maura: i was going to tell you.
me: gee, thanks.

maura: but you never told me.

o.w.g.'s looking very concerned now. so i put my hand over the phone for a second and speak to him.

me: i'm actually not okay. in fact, i am probably having the worst minute of my life. don't go anywhere.

o.w.g. nods.

maura: will? look, i'm sorry.
me: . . .
maura: you didn't actually think he was meeting you at a porn store, did you?
me: . . .
maura: it was a joke.
me: . . .
maura: will?
me: it is only my respect for your parents that will prevent me from murdering you outright. but please understand this: i am never, ever speaking to you or passing notes to you or texting you or doing fucking sign language with you ever again. i would rather eat dog shit full of razor blades than have anything to do with you.

i hang up before she can say anything else. i switch off the phone. i sit down on the curb. i close my eyes. and i scream. if my whole world is going to crash down around me, then i am going to make the sound of the crashing. i want to scream until all my bones break.

once. twice. again.

then i stop. i feel the tears, and hope that if i keep my eyes closed i can keep them inside. i am so beyond pathetic because i want to open my eyes and see isaac there, have him tell me that maura's out of her mind. or have the other will grayson tell me that this, too, can be dismissed as coincidence. *he's* really the will grayson that maura's been emailing with. she's gotten her will graysons mixed up.

but reality. well, reality is the anvil.

i take a deep breath and it sounds clogged.

the whole time.

the whole time it was maura.

not isaac.

no isaac.

never.

there's hurt. there's pain. and there's hurt-and-pain-at-once.

i am experiencing hurt-and-pain-at-once.

o.w.g.: um . . . will?

he looks like he can see the hurt-and-pain-at-once very clearly on my face.

me: you know that guy i was supposed to meet?
o.w.g.: isaac.
me: yeah, isaac. well, it ends up he wasn't a fifty-year-old
    after all. he was my friend maura, playing a joke.
o.w.g.: that's one helluva mean joke.
me: yeah. i'm feeling that.

i have no idea whether i'm talking to him because he's also named will grayson or because he told me a little about what's going on with him or because he's the only person in the world who's willing to listen to me right now. all of my instincts are telling me to curl into a tiny ball and roll into the nearest sewer — but i don't want to do that to o.w.g. i feel he deserves more than being an eyewitness to my self-destruction.

me: anything like this ever happen to you before?

o.w.g. shakes his head.

o.w.g.: i'm afraid we're in new territory here. my best friend tiny was once going to enter me into *seventeen* magazine's boy of the month contest without telling me, but i don't think that's really the same thing.
me: how did you find out?
o.w.g.: he decided he needed someone to proofread his entry, so he asked me to do it.
me: did you win?
o.w.g.: i told him i'd mail it for him and then filed it away. he was really upset that i didn't win . . . but i think it would've been worse if i had.
me: you might have gotten to meet miley cyrus. jane would've died of jealousy.
o.w.g.: i think jane would've died of laughter first.

i can't help it — i imagine isaac laughing, too.
and then i have to kill that image.

because isaac doesn't exist.
i feel like i'm going to lose it again.

me: why?
o.w.g.: why would jane die laughing?
me: no, why would maura do this?
o.w.g: i can't honestly say.

maura. isaac.
isaac. maura.
anvil.
anvil.
anvil.

me: you know what sucks about love?
o.w.g.: what?
me: that it's so tied to truth.

the tears are starting to come back. because that pain
— i know i'm giving it all up. isaac. hope. the future. those
feelings. that word. i'm giving it all up, and that hurts.

o.w.g.: will?
me: i think i need to close my eyes for a minute and
      feel what i need to feel.

i shut my eyes, shut my body, try to shut out everything
else. i feel o.w.g. stand up. i wish he were isaac, even though
i know he's not. i wish maura weren't isaac, even though i
know she is. i wish i were someone else, even though i know

i'll never, ever be able to get away from what i've done and what's been done to me.

lord, send me amnesia. make me forget every moment i ever didn't really have with isaac. make me forget that maura exists. this must be what my mother felt when my dad said it was over. i get it now. i get it. the things you hope for the most are the things that destroy you in the end.

i hear o.w.g. talking to someone. a murmured recap of everything that's just happened.

i hear footsteps coming closer. i try to calm myself a little, then open my eyes . . . and see this *ginormous* guy standing in front of me. when he notices me noticing him, he gives me this broad smile. i swear, he has dimples the size of a baby's head.

ginormous guy: hello there. i'm tiny.

he offers his hand. i'm not entirely in a shaking mood, but it's awkward if i just leave him there, so i hold out my hand, too. instead of shaking it, though, he yanks me up to my feet.

tiny: did someone die?
me: yeah, i did.

he smiles again at that.

tiny: well, then . . . welcome to the afterlife.

chapter nine

You can say a lot of bad things about Tiny Cooper. I know,
because I have said them. But for a guy who knows absolutely
nothing about how to conduct his own relationships, Tiny
Cooper is kind of brilliant when it comes to dealing with
other people's heartbreak. Tiny is like some gigantic sponge
soaking up the pain of lost love everywhere he goes. And so
it is with Will Grayson. The other Will Grayson, I mean.

Jane's a storefront down standing in a doorway, talking
on the phone. I look over at her, but she's not looking at
me, and I'm wondering if they played the song. Something
Will—the other Will—said right before Tiny and Jane
walked up keeps looping around my head: love is tied to
truth. I think of them as unhappily conjoined twins.

"Obviously," Tiny is saying, "she's just a hot smoldering
pile of suck, but even so, I give her full credit for the name.
Isaac. Isaac. I mean, I could almost fall in love with a girl, if
she were named *Isaac.*"

The other Will Grayson doesn't laugh, but Tiny is un-
deterred. "You must have been so totally freaked out when
you realized it was a porn store, right? Like, who wants to
meet *there.*"

"And then also when his namesake was buying a magazine," I say, holding up the black bag, thinking that Tiny will snatch it and check out my purchase. But he doesn't. He just says, "This is even worse than what happened to me and Tommy."

"What happened with you and Tommy?" Will asks.

"He said he was a natural blonde, but his dye job was so bad it looked like a weave from Mattel—like Barbie. Also, Tommy wasn't short for *Tomas*, like he told me. It was short for regular old Thomas."

Will says, "Yes, this is worse. Much worse."

I clearly don't have much to contribute to the conversation, and anyway, Tiny is acting like I don't exist, so I smile and say, "I'm gonna leave you two boys alone now." And then I look at the other Will Grayson, and he's sort of swaying like he might fall over if the wind kicks up. I want to say something, because I feel really bad for him, but I never know what to say. So I just say what I'm thinking. "I know it sucks, but in a way, it's good." He looks at me like I've just said something absolutely idiotic, which of course I have. "Love and truth being tied together, I mean. They make each other possible, you know?"

The kid gives me about an eighth of a smile and then turns back to Tiny, who—to be fair—is clearly the better therapist. The black bag with *Mano a Mano* doesn't seem funny anymore, so I just drop it on the ground next to Tiny and Will. They don't even notice.

Jane's standing on the curb on her tiptoes now, almost leaning out into a street choked thick with cabs. A group of college guys walk past and look at her, one raising his eyebrows to another. I'm still thinking about the tying of love and truth—and it makes me want to tell her the truth—the whole, contradictory truth—because otherwise, on some level, am I not that girl? Am I not that girl pretending to be Isaac?

I walk over to her and try to touch the back of her elbow, but my touch is too soft and I only get her coat. She turns to me and I see that she's still on her cell. I make a gesture that is intended to convey, "Hey, no hurry, talk as long as you'd like," and probably actually conveys, "Hey, look at me! I have spastic hands." Jane holds up a finger. I nod. She speaks softly, cutely into the phone, saying, "Yeah, I know. Me too."

I step backward across the sidewalk and lean against the brick wall between Frenchy's and a closed sushi restaurant. To my right, Will and Tiny talk. To my left, Jane talks. I pull out my cell as though I'm going to send a text, but I just scroll through my contact list. Clint. Dad. Jane. Mom. People I used to be friends with. People I sorta know. Tiny. Nothing after the T's. Not much for a phone I've had three years.

"Hey," Jane says. I look up, flip the phone shut, and smile at her. "Sorry about the concert," she says.

"Yeah, it's okay," I answer, because it is.

"Who's the guy?" she asks, gesturing toward him.

"Will Grayson," I say. She squints at me, confused. "I met a guy named Will Grayson in that porn store," I say. "I was there to use my fake ID, and he was there to meet his fake boyfriend."

"Jesus, if I'd known that was gonna happen, I would've skipped the concert."

"Yeah," I say, trying not to sound annoyed. "Let's take a walk."

She nods. We walk over toward Michigan Avenue, the Magnificent Mile, home to all of Chicago's biggest, chainiest stores. Everything's closed now, and the tourists who flood the wide sidewalks during the day have gone back to their hotels, towering fifty stories above us. The homeless people who beg off the tourists are gone, too, and it is mostly just Jane and me. You can't tell the truth without talking, so I'm telling her the whole story, trying to make it funny, trying to make it grander than any MDC concert could ever be. And when I finish there's a lull and she says, "Can I ask you something random?"

"Yeah, of course." We're walking past Tiffany, and I stop for a second. The pale yellow streetlights illuminate the storefront just enough that through triple-paned glass and a security grate, I can see an empty display—a gray velvet outline of a neck wearing no jewelry.

"Do you believe in epiphanies?" she asks. We start walking again.

"Um, can you unpack the question?"

"Like, do you believe that people's attitudes can change? One day you wake up and you realize something, you see something in a way that you never saw it before, and boom, epiphany. Something is different forever. Do you believe in that?"

"No," I say. "I don't think anything happens all at once. Like, Tiny? You think Tiny falls in love every day? No way. He *thinks* he does, but he doesn't really. I mean, anything that happens all at once is just as likely to *un*happen all at once, you know?"

She doesn't say anything for a while. She just walks. My hand is down next to her hand, and they brush but nothing happens between us. "Yeah. Maybe you're right," she says finally.

"Why do you ask?" I say.

"I don't know. No reason, really." The English language has a long and storied history. And in all that time, no one has ever asked a "random question" about "epiphanies" for "no reason." "Random questions" are the least random of all questions.

"Who had the epiphany?" I ask.

"Um, I think you're actually, like, the worst possible person to talk to about this," she says.

"How's that?"

"I know it was pretty lame of me to go to the concert," she says randomly. We come to a plastic bench and she sits down.

"It's okay," I say, sitting down next to her.

"It's actually not okay on, like, the grandest possible scale. I guess the thing is that I'm a little confused." Confused. The phone. The sweet, girly voice. Epiphanies. I finally realize the truth.

"The ex-boyfriend," I say. I feel my gut sinking down like it's swimming in the ocean deep, and I learn the truth: I like her. She's cute and she's really smart in precisely the right slightly pretentious way, and there's a softness to her face that sharpens everything she says, and I like her, and it's not just that I *should* be honest with her; I want to. Such is the way these things are tied together, I guess. "I have an idea," I say.

I can feel her looking at me, and I cinch the hood of my coat. My ears feel cold like burning.

And she says, "What's the idea?"

"The idea is that for ten minutes, we forget that we have feelings. And we forget about protecting ourselves or other people and we just say the truth. For ten minutes. And then we can go back to being lame."

"I like the idea," she says. "But you have to start."

I push my coat sleeve back and look at my watch. 10:42. "Ready?" I ask. She nods. I look at my watch again. "Okay, and . . . go. I like you. And I didn't know whether I liked you until I thought of you at that concert with some other guy, but now I do know, and I realize that makes me a bitchsquealer, but yeah, I like you. I think you're great, and very cute—and by cute I mean beautiful but don't want to say beautiful because it's cliché but you are—and I don't even mind that you're a music snob."

"It's not snobbery; it's good taste. So I used to date this boy and I knew he was going to be at the concert and I wanted to go with you partly because I knew Randall would be there but then I wanted to go even without you because I knew he would be there and then he saw me while MDC was playing 'A Brief Overview of Time Travel Paradoxes,' and he was screaming in my ear about how he had an epiphany and he now knows that we're supposed to be together and I was, like, I don't think so and he quoted this e. e. cummings poem about how kisses are a better fate than wisdom and then it turns out that he had MDC dedicate a song to me which was the kind of thing that he would never have done before and I feel like I deserve someone who consistently likes me which you kind of don't and I don't know."

"What song?"

"'Annus Miribalis.' Uh, he's the only person who knows my locker combination, and he had them dedicate it to my locker combination, which is just, I mean, I don't know. That's just. Yeah."

Even though these are the minutes of truth, I don't tell her about the song. I can't. It's too embarrassing. The thing is, coming from your ex-boyfriend, it's sweet. And coming from the guy who wouldn't kiss you in your orange Volvo, it's just weird and maybe even mean. She's right that she deserves someone consistent, and maybe I can't be that. Nonetheless, I shred the guy. "I fucking hate guys who quote poetry to girls. Since we are being honest. Also, wisdom is a better fate than the vast majority of kisses. Wisdom is certainly a better fate than kissing douches who only read poetry so they can use it to get in girls' pants."

"Oh, my," she says. "Honest Will and Regular Will are so fascinatingly different!"

"To tell you the truth, I prefer just your average, run-of-the-mill, everyday jackass with his glass-eyed, slack-jawed obliviousness to the guys who try to hijack my cool by reading poetry and listening to halfway-good music. I worked hard for my cool. I got my ass kicked in middle school for my cool. I came by this shit honestly."

"Well, you don't even know him," she says.

"And I don't need to," I answer. "Look, you're right. Maybe I don't like you the way someone should like you. I don't like you in the call-you-and-read-you-a-poem-every-night-before-you-go-to-bed way. I'm crazy, okay? Sometimes I think, like, God, she's superhot and smart and kind of pretentious but the pretentiousness just makes me kind of *want* her, and then other times I think it's an amazingly bad idea, that dating you would be like a series of unnecessary root canals interspersed with occasional makeout sessions."

"Jesus, that's a burn."

"But not really, because I think both! And it doesn't matter, because I'm your Plan B. Maybe I'm your Plan B because I feel that way, and maybe I feel that way because I'm your Plan B, but regardless, it means you're supposed to be with Randall and I'm supposed to be in my natural state of self-imposed hookup exile."

"So different!" she says again. "Can you be like this permanently?"

"Probably not," I say.

"How many minutes do we have?"

"Four," I say.

And then we're kissing.

I lean in this time, and she doesn't turn away. It's cold, and our lips are dry, noses a little wet, foreheads sweaty beneath wool hats. I can't touch her face, even though I want to, because I'm wearing gloves. But God, when her lips come apart, everything turns warm and her sugar sweet breath is in my mouth, and I probably taste like hot dogs but I don't care. She kisses like a sweet devouring, and I don't know where to touch her because I want all of her. I want to touch her knees and her hips and her stomach and her back and her everything, but we're encased in all these clothes, so we're just two marshmallows bumping against each other, and she smiles at me while still kissing because she knows how ridiculous it is, too.

"Better than wisdom?" she asks, her nose touching my cheek.

"Tight race," I say, and I smile back as I pull her tighter to me.

I've never known before what it feels like to *want* someone—not to want to hook up with them or whatever, but to *want* them, to want *them*. And now I do. So maybe I do believe in epiphanies.

She pulls away from me just enough to say, "What's my last name?"

"I have no idea," I answer immediately.

"Turner. It's Turner." I slip in one last peck, and then she sits up properly, although her gloved hand still rests against my jacketed waist. "See, we don't even *know* each other. I have to find out if I believe in epiphanies, Will."

"I can't believe his name is Randall. He doesn't go to Evanston, does he?"

"No, he goes to Latin. We met at a poetry slam."

"Of course you did. My God, I can picture the slimy bastard: He's tall and shaggy-haired, and he plays a sport—soccer, probably—but he pretends like he doesn't even like it because all he likes is poetry and music and you, and he thinks you're a poem and tells you so, and he's slathered in confidence and probably body spray." She laughs, shaking her head. "What?" I ask.

"Water polo," she says. "Not soccer."

"Oh, Jesus. *Of course.* Water polo. Yeah, nothing says punk rock like water polo."

She grabs my arm and looks at my watch. "One minute," she says.

"You look better when your hair is pulled back," I tell her in a rush.

"Really?"

"Yeah, otherwise you look kinda like a puppy."

"You look better when you stand up straight," she says.

"Time!" I say.

"Okay," she says. "It's a shame we can't do that more often."

"Which part?" I ask smiling. She stands up.

"I should get home. Stupid midnight weekend curfew."

"Yeah," I say. I pull out my phone. "I'll call Tiny and tell him we're headed out."

"I'll just take a cab."

"I'll just call—"

But she's already standing on the edge of the sidewalk, the toes of her Chucks off the curb, her hand raised. A cab pulls over. She hugs me quickly—the hug all fingertips and shoulder blades—and is gone without another word.

I've never been alone in the city this late, and it's deserted. I call Tiny. He doesn't answer. I get the voice mail. "You've reached the voice mail of Tiny Cooper, writer, producer, and star of the new musical *Tiny Dancer: The Tiny Cooper Story*. I'm sorry, but it appears something more fabulous than your phone call is happening right now. When fabulous levels fall a bit, I'll get back to you. BEEP."

"Tiny, the next time that you try to set me up with a girl with a secret boyfriend can you at least *inform* me that she has a secret boyfriend? Also, if you don't call me back within five minutes, I'm going to assume you found a way back to Evanston. Furthermore, you are an asshat. That is all."

There are cabs on Michigan Avenue and a steady flow of

traffic, but once I get onto a side street, Huron, it's quiet. I walk past a church and then up State Street toward Frenchy's. I can tell from three blocks away that Tiny and Will aren't there anymore, but I still walk all the way to the storefront. I look up and down the street but see no one, and anyway, Tiny never shuts up, so I would hear him if he were nearby.

I fish through my coat pocket's detritus for my keys, then pull them out. The keys are wrapped in the note that Jane wrote me, the note from the Locker Houdini.

I'm walking down the street toward the car when I see a black plastic bag on the sidewalk, fluttering in the wind. *Mano a Mano.* I leave it, thinking I've probably just made someone's tomorrow.

For the first time in a long time, I drive with no music. I'm not happy—not happy about Jane and Mr. Randall Water Polo Doucheface IV, not happy about Tiny abandoning me without so much as a phone call, not happy about my insufficiently fake fake ID—but in the dark on Lake Shore with the car eating up all the sound, there's something about the numbness in my lips after having kissed her that I want to keep and hold onto, something in it that seems *pure*, that seems like the singular truth.

I get home four minutes before curfew, and my parents are on the couch, Mom's feet in Dad's lap. Dad mutes the TV and says, "How was it?"

"Pretty good," I say.

"Did they play 'Annus Miribalis'?" Mom asks, because I liked it so much I played it for her. I figure she's asking partly to seem hip and partly to make sure I went to the concert. She'll probably check the set list later. I *didn't* go to the concert, of course, but I know they played the song.

"Yeah," I say. "Yeah. It was good." I stare at them for a second, and then say, "Okay, I'm gonna go to bed."

"Why don't you watch some TV with us?" Dad asks.

"I'm tired," I say flatly, and turn to go.

But I don't go to bed. I go to my room and get online and start reading about e. e. cummings.

The next morning I get a ride to school early with Mom. In the hallways, I pass poster after poster for *Tiny Dancer*.

AUDITIONS TODAY NINTH PERIOD IN THE THEATER. PREPARE TO SING. PREPARE TO DANCE. PREPARE TO BE FABULOUS.

IN CASE YOU FAILED TO SEE THE PREVIOUS POSTER, AUDITIONS ARE TODAY.

.

SING & DANCE & CELEBRATE TOLERANCE IN THE MOST IMPORTANT MUSICAL OF OUR TIME.

I jog through the halls and then go upstairs to Jane's locker and carefully slip the note I wrote last night through the vent:

To: The Locker Houdini
From: Will Grayson
Re: An Expert in the Field of Good Boyfriends?

Dear Jane,

Just so you know: e. e. cummings cheated on both of his wives. With prostitutes.

Yours,
Will Grayson

chapter ten

tiny cooper.

tiny cooper.

tiny cooper.

i am saying his name over and over in my head.

tiny cooper.

tiny cooper.

it's a ridiculous name, and the whole thing is ridiculous, and i couldn't stop it if i tried.

tiny cooper.

if i say it enough times, maybe it will be okay that isaac doesn't exist.

it starts that night. in front of frenchy's. i am still in shock. i can't tell whether it's post-traumatic stress or post-stress trauma. whatever it is, a good part of my life has just been erased, and i have no desire to fill in the new blank. leave it empty, i say. just let me die.

tiny, though, won't let me. he's playing the i've-had-it-worse game, which never works, because either the person says something that's not worse at all ('he wasn't a natural blond') or they say something that's so much worse that you feel like all your feelings are being completely negated. ('well, i once had a guy stand me up for a date . . . and it ended up that he'd been eaten by a lion! his last word was my name!')

still, he's trying to help. and i guess i should take some when i need some.

for his part, o.w.g. is also trying to help. there's a girl hovering in the background, and i have no doubt it's the (in)famous jane. at first, o.w.g.'s attempt at help is even lamer than tiny's.

o.w.g.: i know it sucks, but in a way, it's good.

this is about as inspirational as a movie of hitler making out with his girlfriend and having a good time. it runs afoul of what i call the birdshit rule. you know, how people say it's good luck if a bird shits on you? and people believe it! i just want to grab them and say, 'dude, don't you realize this whole superstition was made up because no one could think of anything else good to say to a person who'd just been shit upon?' and people do that all the time – and not with something as temporary as birdshit, either. you lost your job? great opportunity! failed at life? there's only one way to go – up! dumped by a boyfriend who never existed? i know it sucks, but in a way, it's good!

i'm about to strip o.w.g. of his right to be a will grayson, but then he goes on.

o.w.g.: love and truth being tied together, i mean. they
        make each other possible, you know?

i don't know what hits me more — the fact that some stranger would listen to me, or the fact that he is, technically, absolutely correct.

the other will grayson heads off, leaving me with my new refrigerator-size companion, who's looking at me with such sincerity that i want to slap him.

me: you don't have to stay. really.
tiny: what, and leave you here to mope?
me: this is so far beyond moping. this is out-and-out despair.
tiny: *awwww.*

and then he hugs me. imagine being hugged by a sofa. that's what it feels like.

me (choking): i'm choking.
tiny (patting my hair): there, there.
me: dude, you're not helping.

i push him away. he looks hurt.

tiny: you just duded me!
me: i'm sorry. it's just, i —
tiny: i'm only trying to help!

this is why i should carry around extra pills. i think we could both use a double dose right now.

me (again): i'm sorry.

he looks at me then. and it's weird, because i mean, he's *really* looking at me. it makes me completely uncomfortable.

me: what?

tiny: do you want to hear a song from *tiny dancer: the tiny cooper story?*

me: excuse me?

tiny: it's a musical i'm working on. it's based on my life. i think one of the songs might help right now.

we are on a street corner in front of a porn shop. there are people passing by. *chicagoans* — you can't be less musical than chicagoans. i am in a completely demolished state. my mind is having a heart attack. the last thing i need is for the fat lady to sing. but do i protest? do i decide to live the rest of my life within the subway system, feeding off the rats? no. i just nod dumbly, because he wants to sing this song so badly that i'd feel like a jerk to say no.

with a dip of his head, tiny starts to hum a little to himself. once he's gotten the tune, he closes his eyes, opens his arms, and sings:

i thought you'd make my dreams come true
but it wasn't you, it wasn't you

i thought this time it would all be new
but it wasn't you, it wasn't you

i pictured all the things we'd do
but it wasn't you, it wasn't you

and now i feel my heart is through
but it isn't true, it isn't true

i may be big-boned and afraid
but my faith in love won't be mislaid!

though i've been completely knocked off course
i'm not getting off my faithful horse!

it wasn't you, it's true
but there's more to life than you

i thought you were a boy with a view,
you stuck-up, selfish, addled shrew

you may have kicked me till i was blue
but from that experience i grew

it's true, fuck you
there are better guys to woo

it won't be you, comprende vous?
it will never be you.

tiny doesn't just sing these words — he belts them. it's like a parade coming out of his mouth. i have no doubt the words travel over lake michigan to most of canada and on to the north pole. the farmers of saskatchewan are crying. santa is turning to mrs. claus and saying 'what the fuck is *that?*' i am completely mortified, but then tiny opens his eyes and looks at me with such obvious caring that i have no idea what to do. no one's tried to give me something like this in ages. except for isaac, and he doesn't exist. whatever you might say about tiny, he definitely exists.

he asks me if i want to walk. once again, i nod dumbly. it's not like i have anything better to do.

me: who *are* you?
tiny: tiny cooper!
me: you can't really be named tiny.
tiny: no. that's irony.
me: oh.
tiny (tsking): no need to 'oh' me. i'm fine with it. i'm
    big-boned.
me: dude, it isn't just your bones.
tiny: just means there's more of me to love!
me: but that requires so much more effort.
tiny: darling, i'm worth it.

the sick thing is, i have to admit there's something a little bit attractive about him. i don't get it. it's like, you know how sometimes you see a really sexy baby? wait, that sounds fucked up. that's not what i mean. but it's like, even though he's as big as a house (and i'm not talking about a poor person's house, either), he's got super-smooth skin and really green eyes and everything is in, like, proportion. so i'm not feeling the repulsion i would expect to feel toward someone three times my size. i want to tell him i should be out killing some people now, not taking a stroll with him. but he takes a little of the murder off my mind. it's not like it won't be there later.

as we walk over to millennium park, tiny tells me all

about *tiny dancer* and how hard he's struggled to write, act, direct, produce, choreograph, costume-design, lighting-design, set-design, and attain funding for it. basically, he's out of his mind, and since i'm trying really hard to get out of my mind, too, i attempt to follow. like with maura (fucking witch ass bitch mussolini al-qaeda darth vader non-entity), i don't have to say a word myself, which is fine.

when we get to the park, tiny makes a great-big beeline to the bean. somehow i'm not surprised.

the bean is this really stupid sculpture that they did for millennium park — i guess at the millennium — which originally had another name, but everyone started calling it the bean and the name stuck. it's basically this big reflective metal bean that you can walk under and see yourself all distorted. i mean, i've been here before on school trips, but i've never been here with someone as huge as tiny before. usually it's hard at first to locate yourself in the reflection, but this time i know i'm the wavy twig standing next to the big blob of humanity. tiny giggles when he sees himself like that. a genuine, tee-hee-hee giggle. i hate it when girls do that shit, because it's always so fake. but with tiny it isn't fake at all. it's like he's being tickled by life.

after tiny has tried ballerina pose, swing-batter-batter pose, pump-up-the-jam pose, and top-of-the-mountain-*sound-of-music* pose in the reflection of the bean, he walks us to a bench overlooking lake shore drive. i think he'll be all sweaty because, let's face it, most fat people get sweaty just from lifting the twinkie to their mouth. but tiny is just too fabulous to sweat.

tiny: so tell tiny your problems.

i can't answer, because the way he says it, it's like you could substitute the word 'mama' for the word 'tiny' and the sentence would still sound the same.

me: can tiny talk normal?
tiny (in his best anderson cooper voice): yes, he can.
    but it's not nearly as fun when he does it.
me: you just sound so gay.
tiny: um . . . there's a reason for that?
me: yeah, but. i dunno. i don't like gay people.
tiny: but surely you must like yourself?

holy shit, i want to be from this boy's planet. is he serious? i look at him and see that, yes, he is.

me: why should i like myself? nobody else does.
tiny: i do.
me: you don't know me at all.
tiny: but i want to.

it's so stupid, because all of a sudden i'm screaming

me: shut up! just shut up!

and he looks so hurt, so i have to say

me: no, ha, it's not you. okay? you're nice. i'm not. i'm
    not nice, okay? stop it!

because now he doesn't look hurt; he looks sad. sad for me. he sees me. christ.

me: this is so stupid.

it's like he knows that if he touches me, i will probably lose it on him and start hitting him and start crying and never want to see him again. so instead he just sits there as i put my head in my hands, as if i'm literally trying to hold my head together. and the thing is, he doesn't need to touch me, because with someone like tiny cooper, if he's next to you, you know it. all he has to do is stay, and you know he's there.

me: shit shit shit shit shit shit shit

here's the sick, twisted thing: part of me thinks i *deserve* this. that maybe if i wasn't such an asshole, isaac would have been real. if i wasn't such a lame excuse for a person, something right might happen to me. it's not fair, because i didn't ask for dad to leave, and i didn't ask to be depressed, and i didn't ask for us to have no money, and i didn't ask to want to fuck boys, and i didn't ask to be so stupid, and i didn't ask to have no real friends, and i didn't ask to have half the shit that comes out of my mouth come out of my mouth. all i wanted was one fucking break, one idiotic good thing, and that was clearly too much to ask for, too much to want.

i don't understand why this boy who writes musicals about himself is sitting with me. am i that pathetic? does he get a merit badge for picking up the pieces of a wrecked human being?

i let go of my head. it's not helping. when i surface, i look at tiny, and it's strange all over again. he's not just watching me — he's still *seeing* me. his eyes are practically gleaming.

tiny: i never kiss on the first date.

i look at him with total incomprehension, and then he adds

tiny: . . . but sometimes i make exceptions.

so now my shock from before is turning into a different kind of shock, and it's a charged shock, because at that moment, even though he's enormous, and even though he doesn't know me at all, and even though he's taking up roughly three times more of the bench than i am, tiny cooper is surprisingly, undeniably attractive. yeah, his skin is smooth, his smile is gentle, and most of all his eyes — his eyes have this crazy hope and crazy longing and ridiculous giddiness in them, and even though i think it's completely stupid and even though i am never going to feel the things that he feels, at the very least i don't mind the idea of kissing him and seeing what happens. he is starting to blush from what he's said, and he's actually too shy to lean down to me, so i find myself lifting to kiss him, keeping my eyes open because i want to see his surprise and see his happiness because there's no way for me to see or even feel my own.

it's not like kissing a sofa. it's like kissing a boy. finally, a boy.

he closes his eyes. he smiles when we stop.

tiny: this is not where i thought the night was going.
me: tell me about it.

i want to run away. not with him. i just don't want to go back to school or to life. if my mom wasn't waiting on the other end for me, i would probably do it. i want to run away because i've lost everything. i'm sure if i said this to tiny cooper, he'd point out that i've lost the bad things as well as the good things. he'd tell me the sun will come out tomorrow, or some shit like that. but then i wouldn't believe him. i don't believe any of it.

tiny: hey — i don't even know your name.
me: will grayson.

with that, tiny jumps off the bench, nearly knocking me to the grass.

tiny: no!
me: um . . . yes?
tiny: well, doesn't that just take the cake?

with that, he starts laughing, and calling out

tiny: i kissed will grayson! i kissed will grayson!

when he sees that this freaks me out more than sharks do, he sits back down and says

tiny: i'm glad it was you.

i think about the other will grayson. i wonder how he's doing with jane.

me: it's not like i'm *seventeen* magazine material, right?

tiny's eyes light up.

tiny: he told you about that?
me: yeah.
tiny: he was totally robbed. i was so mad, i wrote a
    letter to the editor. but they never printed it.

i have this deep pang of jealousy, that o.w.g. has a friend like tiny. i can't imagine anyone ever writing a letter to the editor for me. i can't even imagine them giving a quote for my obituary.

i think of everything that's happened, and how when i go home i won't really have anyone to tell it to. then i look at tiny and, surprising myself, kiss him again. because what the fuck. completely, what the fuck.

this goes on for some time. i am getting totally big-boned from kissing someone big-boned. and in between the making out, he's asking me where i live, what happened tonight, what i want to do with my life, what my favorite ice-cream flavor is. i answer the questions i can (basically, where i live and the ice-cream flavor) and tell him i have no idea about the rest of it.

nobody's really watching us, but i'm beginning to feel that they are. so we stop and i can't help but think about isaac, and how even though this whole tiny thing is an interesting development, all-in-all things still suck in a tornado-destroyed-my-home kind of way. tiny's like the one room left standing. i feel i owe him something for that, so i say

> me: i'm glad that you exist.
> tiny: i'm glad to be existing right now.
> me: you have no idea how wrong you are about me.
> tiny: you have no idea how wrong you are about
>   yourself.
> me: stop that.
> tiny: only if you stop it.
> me: i'm warning you.

i have no idea what truth has to do with love, and vice versa. i'm not even thinking in terms of love here. it's way, way, way early for that. but i guess i am thinking in terms of truth. i want this to be truthful. and even as i protest to tiny and i protest to myself, the truth is becoming increasingly clear.

it's time for us to figure out how the hell this is ever going to work.

chapter eleven

I'm sitting against my locker ten minutes before the first pe-riod bell when Tiny comes running down the hallway, his arms a jumble of *Tiny Dancer* audition posters.

"Grayson!" he shouts.

"Hey," I answer. I get up, grab a poster from him, and hold it against the wall. He lets the others fall to the ground and then starts taping, ripping off the masking tape with his teeth. He tapes the poster up, then we gather up the ones he dropped, walk a few paces, and repeat. And all the while, he talks. His heart beats and his eyelids blink and he breathes and his kidneys process toxins and he talks, and all of it utterly involuntary.

"So I'm sorry I didn't go back to Frenchy's to meet you, but I figured you'd guess I just took a cab, which I did, and anyway, Will and I had walked all the way down to the Bean and, like, Grayson, I know I've said this before but I *really like him*. I mean, you have to *really* like someone to go all the way to the Bean with them and listen to them talk about their boyfriend who was neither boy nor friend and also I sang for him. And Grayson, I mean really: can you believe I kissed Will Grayson? I. Freaking. Kissed. Will.

Grayson. And like nothing personal because like I've told you a gajillion times, I think you're a top-shelf person, but I would have bet my left nut that I would never make out with Will Grayson, you know?"

"Uh-hu—" I say, but he doesn't even wait for me to get through the *huh* before he starts up again.

"And I get texts from him like every forty-two seconds and he's a brilliant texter, which is nice because it's just a little pleasant leg vibration, just a reminder-in-the-thigh that he's—see, there's one." I keep holding up the poster while he pulls his phone out of his jeans. "Aww."

"What's it say?" I ask.

"Confidential. I think he kinda trusts me not to blab his texts, you know?"

I might point out the ridiculousness of anyone trusting Tiny not to blab anything, but I don't. He tapes up the poster and starts walking down the hallway. I follow.

"Well, I'm glad your night was so awesome. Meanwhile I was being blindsided about Jane's water polo–playing ex-boyf—"

"Well, first off," he says, cutting me off, "what do you care? You're *not into* Jane. And second off, I wouldn't call him a boy. He is a *man*. He is a sculpted, immaculately conceived, rippling hunk of ex-*man*friend."

"You're not helping."

"I'm just saying—not my type, but he is truly a wonder to behold. And his eyes! Like sapphires burning into the darkened corners of your heart. But anyway, I didn't know they ever dated. I'd never even heard of the guy. I just thought he was a hot guy hitting on her. Jane never

154

talks to me about guys. I don't know why; I'm totally trust-worthy about that sort of thing." There's enough sarcasm in his voice—just enough—that I laugh. Tiny talks over the laugh. "It's amazing what you don't know about people, you know? Like, I was thinking about that all weekend talking to Will. He fell for Isaac, who turned out to be made up. That *seems* like something that only happens on the Inter-net, but really it happens all the time i-r-l, too."

"Well, Isaac wasn't made up. He was just a girl. I mean, that girl Maura is Isaac."

"No, she's not," he says simply. I'm holding up the last of the posters as he tapes it to a boys' bathroom door. It says ARE YOU FABULOUS? IF SO, SEE YOU NINTH PERIOD TODAY AT THE AUDITORIUM. He finishes it up and then we walk toward precalc, the halls beginning to fill up.

The Isaac/Maura namescrewing reminds me of some-thing. "Tiny," I say.

"Grayson," he answers.

"Will you please rename that character in your play, the sidekick guy?"

"Gil Wrayson?" I nod. Tiny throws his hands up in the air and announces, "I can't change Gil Wrayson's name! It's thematically *vital* to the whole production."

"I'm really not in the mood for your bullshit," I say.

"I'm not bullshitting you. His name has to be Wrayson. Say it slow. Ray-sin. Rays-in. It's a double meaning—Gil Wrayson is undergoing a transformation. And he has to let the *rays* of sunlight *in*—those rays of sunlight coming in the form of Tiny's songs—in order to become his true self—no longer a plum, but a sun-soaked raisin. Don't you see?"

"Oh, come on, Tiny. If that's true, why the hell is his name *Gil*?"

That stops him for a moment. "Hmm," he says, squinting down the still-quiet hallway. "It just always sounded right to me. But I suppose I *could* change it. I'll think about it, okay?"

"Thank you," I say.

"You're welcome. Now please stop being a pussy."

"What?"

We get to our lockers, and even though other people can hear him, he talks as loud as ever. "Wah-wah, Jane doesn't like me even though I don't like her. Wah-wah, Tiny named a character after me in his play. Like, there are people in the world with real problems, you know? You gotta keep it in perspective."

"Dude, YOU'RE telling ME to keep it in perspective? Jesus Christ, Tiny. I just wanted to know she had a boyfriend."

Tiny closes his eyes and takes a deep breath like I'm the annoying one. "As I said, I didn't even know he *existed*, okay? But then I saw him talking to her, and I could tell he was into her just from his posture. And when he left, I just had to go up and ask who he was, and she was, like, 'My ex-boyfriend,' and I was, like, '*Ex*?! You need to scoop that beautiful man back up immediately!'"

I'm staring into the broad side of Tiny Cooper's face. He's looking away from me, into his locker. He looks sort of bored, but then his eyebrows dart up, and I think for a second he realizes how pissed I am about what he just said, but then he reaches into his jeans and pulls out the phone. "You didn't," I say.

"Sorry, I know I shouldn't read texts while we're talking, but I'm a little twitterpated at the moment."

"I'm not talking about *texts*, Tiny. You didn't tell Jane to get back together with that guy."

"Well, of course I did, Grayson," he answers, still looking at the phone. Now he's writing Will back while talking. "He was *gorgeous*, and you told me you didn't like her. So you like her now? Typical *boy*—you're interested as long as she isn't."

I want to slug him in the kidney, for being wrong and for being right. But it would only hurt me. I'm nothing but a bit character in the Tiny Cooper story, and there isn't a damn thing I can do about it except get jerked around until high school is over and I can finally escape his orbit, can finally stop being a moon of his fat planet.

And then I realize what I can do. The weapon I have. Rule 2: Shut up. I step past him and walk toward class.

"Grayson," he says.

I don't answer.

I say nothing in precalculus, when he miraculously inserts himself into his desk. And then I say nothing when he tells me that right now I am not even his favorite Will Grayson. I say nothing when he tells me how he has texted the other Will Grayson forty-five times in the last twenty-four hours, and do I think that's too much. I say nothing when he holds his phone under my nose, showing me some text from Will Grayson that I am supposed to find adorable. I say nothing when he asks me why the hell I'm not saying anything. I say nothing when he says, "Grayson, you were just getting on my nerves, and I only said all that stuff to

157

shut you up. But I didn't mean to shut you up *this much.*" I say nothing when he says, "No seriously, talk to me," and nothing when he says under his breath but still plenty loud enough for people to hear, "Honestly, Grayson, I'm sorry, okay? I'm sorry."

And then, blessedly, class starts.

Fifty minutes later, the bell rings, and Tiny follows me out into the hallway like a swollen shadow, saying, "Seriously, come on, this is ridiculous." It's not even that I want to torture him anymore. I'm just reveling in the glory of not having to hear the neediness and impotence of my own voice.

At lunch, I sit down by myself at the end of a long table featuring several members of my former Group of Friends. This guy Alton says, "How's it going, faggot?" and I say, "Pretty good," and then this other guy Cole says, "You coming to the party at Clint's? It's gonna be sick," which makes me think these guys don't in fact dislike me even though one of them just called me a faggot. Apparently, having Tiny Cooper as your best-and-only friend does not leave you well-prepared for the intricacies of male socialization.

I say, "Yeah, I'll try to stop by," even though I don't know when the party will be occurring. Then this shave-headed guy Ethan says, "Hey, are you trying out for Tiny's gay-ass play?"

"Hell, no," I say.

"I think I am," he says, and it takes me a second to tell if he's kidding. Everyone starts laughing and talking all at once, trying to get in the first insult, but he just laughs them off and says, "Girls love a sensitive man." He turns around in his chair and shouts at the table behind him, where his girlfriend, Anita, is sitting. "Baby, ain't my singing sexy?"

"Hell, yeah," she says. Then he just looks, satisfied, at all of us. Still, the guys rag on him. I mostly stay quiet, but by the end of my ham and cheese, I'm laughing at their jokes at the appropriate times, which I guess means I'm having lunch with them.

Tiny finds me when I'm putting my tray onto the conveyor belt, and he's got Jane with him, and they walk with me. Nobody talks at first. Jane is wearing an army green hoodie, the hood pulled up. She looks almost unfairly adorable, like she picked it out for the express purpose of taunting. Jane says, "Hilarious note, Grayson. So Tiny tells me you've taken a vow of silence."

I nod.

"Why?" she asks.

"I'm only talking to cute girls today," I answer, and smile. Tiny's right—the existence of the water-polo guy makes it easy to flirt.

Jane smiles. "I think Tiny's a fairly cute girl."

"But *why*?" Tiny begs as I turn down a hallway. The maze of identical hallways differentiated only by different Wildkit murals that used to scare the hell out of me. God, to go back to when my biggest fear was a hallway. "Grayson, please. You're KILLING me."

I am aware that for the first time in my memory, Tiny and Jane are following me.

Tiny decides to ignore me, and he tells Jane that he hopes one day to have enough texts from Will Grayson to turn them into a book, because his texts are like poetry.

Before I can stop myself, I say, "'Shall I compare thee to a summer's day' becomes 'u r hawt like august.'"

"He speaks!" Tiny shouts, and puts his arm around me. "I knew you'd come around! I'm so happy I'm renaming Gil Wrayson! He shall now be known as Phil Wrayson! Phil Wrayson, who must *fill* up on the rays of Tiny's sun in order to become his true self. It's perfect." I nod. People will still assume it's me, but he's—well, he's pretending to try. "Oh, text!" Tiny pulls out his phone, reads the text, sighs loudly, and begins trying to type a response with his meaty hands. While he's thumbing, I say, "I get to pick who plays him."

Tiny nods distractedly.

"Tiny," I repeat, "I get to pick who plays him."

He looks up. "What? No no no. I'm the director. I'm the writer, producer, director, assistant-costume designer, and casting director."

And Jane says, "I saw you nod, Tiny. You already agreed to it." He just scoffs, and then we're at my locker, and Jane kind of pulls me by the elbow away from Tiny and says quietly, "You know, you can't say that stuff."

"Damned if I talk, damned if I don't," I say, smiling.

"I just. Grayson, I just—you can't say those things."

"What things?"

"Cute girl things."

"Why not?" I ask.

"Because I am still doing research on the relationship between water polo and epiphanies." She tries a small, tight-lipped smile.

"You wanna go to the *Tiny Dancer* tryouts with me?" I ask. Tiny is still thumbing away.

"Grayson, I can't—I mean, I am kind of taken, you know?"

"I'm not asking you on a *date*. I'm asking you to an extracurricular activity. We will sit in the back of an auditorium and laugh at the kids auditioning to play me."

I haven't read Tiny's play since last summer, but as I recall, there are about nine meaty parts: Tiny, his mom (who has a duet with Tiny), Phil Wrayson, Tiny's love interests Kaleb and Barry, and then this fictional straight couple who make the character Tiny believe in himself or whatever. And there's a chorus. Altogether, Tiny needs thirty cast members. I figure there will be maybe twelve people at the auditions.

But when I arrive in the auditorium after chem, there are already at least fifty people lounging around the stage and the first few rows of seats waiting for the auditions to start. Gary is running around handing everyone safety pins and pieces of paper with handwritten numbers on them, which the auditioners are pinning to themselves. And, since they are theater people, they are all talking. All of them. Simultaneously. They do not need to be heard; they only need to be speaking.

I take a seat in the back row, one in from the aisle so that Jane can have the aisle. She shows up just after I do and sits down next to me, appraises the situation for a second, and then says, "Somewhere down there, Grayson, there's someone who will have to look into your soul in order to properly embody you."

I'm about to respond when Tiny's shadow passes over us. He kneels next to us, handing us each a clipboard. "Please write a brief note about each person who you'd consider for the role of Phil. Also I'm thinking of writing in a small role for a character named Janey."

Then he marches confidently down the aisle. "People!"

he shouts. "People, please take a seat." People scurry into the first few rows as Tiny hurtles onto the stage. "We haven't much time," he says, his voice weirdly affected. He's talking like he thinks theater people talk, I guess. "First, I need to know if you can sing. One minute of a song from each of you; if you're called back, you'll read for a part then. You may choose your song, but know this: Tiny. Cooper. Hates. Over. The. Rainbow."

He jumps off the stage dramatically, and then shouts, "Number One, make me love you."

Number 1, a mousy blonde who identifies herself as Marie F, climbs the stairs beside the stage and slouches to a microphone. She looks up through her bangs toward the back of the auditorium, where it says in large purple block letters WILDKITS ROCK. She proceeds to prove otherwise with a stunningly bad rendition of a Kelly Clarkson ballad.

"Oh, my God," Jane says under her breath. "Oh, God. Make it end."

"I don't know what you're talking about," I mumble. "This chick's a lock for the role of Janey. She sings off-key, loves corporate pop, and dates bitchsquealers." She elbows me.

Number 2 is a boy, a husky lad with hair too long to be considered normal but too short to be considered long. He sings a song by a band apparently called Damn Yankees— Jane knows them, natch. I don't know how the original sounds, but this guy's howler-monkey a cappella rendition of it leaves a lot to be desired. "He sounds like someone just kicked him in the nuts," Jane says; to which I respond, "If he doesn't stop soon, someone will." By Number 5, I'm *wishing* for a mediocre rendition of something inoffensive like "Over the Rainbow," and I suspect Tiny is, too, from the way his peppy, "That was great! We'll get back to you." has devolved into a, "Thanks. Next?"

The songs vary from jazz standards to boy band covers, but all the performers have one thing in common: they sort of suck. I mean, certainly, not everyone sucks in the same way, and not everyone sucks equally, but everyone sucks at least a little. I'm stunned when my lunch companion Ethan, Number 19, proves to be the best singer so far, singing a song from some musical called *Spring Awakening*. The dude can belt.

"He could play you," Jane says. "If he grew his hair out and developed a bad attitude."

"I don't have a bad attitude—"

"—is the kind of thing that people with bad attitudes say." Jane smiles.

I see a couple potential Janes over the next hour. Number 24 sings a weirdly good sticky-sweet version of a song from *Guys and Dolls*. The other girl, Number 43, has straight bleached hair streaked with blue and sings "Mary Had a Little Lamb." Something about the distance between children's songs and blue hair seems pretty Janeish to me.

"I vote for her," Jane says as soon as the girl gets to the second *Mary*.

The last auditionee is a diminutive, large-eyed creature named Hazel who sings a song from *Rent*. After she's finished, Tiny runs up onto the stage to thank everyone, and to say how brilliant they all were, and how impossibly hard this will be, and how callbacks will be posted the day after tomorrow. Everyone files out past us, and then finally Tiny slouches up the aisle.

"You've got your work cut out for you," I tell him.

He makes a dramatic gesture of futility. "We did not see a lot of future Broadway stars," he acknowledges.

Gary comes up and says, "I liked numbers six, nineteen, thirty-one, and forty-two. The others, well," and then Gary puts his hand to his chest and begins to sing, "Somewhere over the rainbow, way up high / The sound of singing Wild-kits, makes me want to die."

"Jesus," I say. "You're like a *real singer*. You sound like Pavarotti."

"Well, except he's a baritone," Jane says, her music pretension apparently extending even to the world of opera.

Tiny snaps the fingers of one hand excitedly while pointing at Gary. "You! You! You! For the part of Kaleb. Congratulations."

"You want me to play a fictionalized version of my own ex-boyfriend?" Gary asks. "I think not."

"Then Phil Wrayson! I don't care. Pick your part. My God, you sing better than all of them."

"Yes!" I say. "I cast you."

"But I'd have to kiss a girl," he says. "Ew." I don't remember my character kissing any girls, and I start to ask Tiny about it, but he cuts me off, saying, "I've been in rewrites." Tiny flatters Gary some more and then he agrees to play the part of me, and honestly, I'll take it. As we walk up the aisle on the way out of the cafeteria, Gary turns to me, cocking his head and squinting. "What's it like to *be* Will Grayson? I need to know what it's like from the inside."

He's laughing, but then he also seems to be waiting for an answer. I always thought that being Will Grayson meant being me, but apparently not. The other Will Grayson is also Will Grayson, and now Gary will be, too.

"I just try to shut up and not care," I say.

"Such stirring words." Gary smiles. "I will base your character upon the attributes of the boulders on the lakeshore: silent, apathetic, and—considering how little they exercise—surprisingly chiseled." Everybody laughs, except Tiny, who's texting. As we exit the hallway, I see Ethan standing against the Wildkit trophy stand, his backpack on. I walk up to him and say, "Not bad today," and he smiles and says, "I just hope I'm not too hot to play you." He smiles. I smile back, even though he seems a little serious. "See you on Friday at Clint's?" he asks.

"Yeah, maybe," I say. He adjusts the backpack over one shoulder and takes off with a nod. Behind me, I hear Tiny dramatically plead, "Someone tell me it will be okay!"

"It'll be okay," Jane says. "Mediocre actors rise to great material."

Tiny takes a deep breath, shakes some thought out of his mind, and says, "You're right. Together they will be greater than the sum of their parts. Fifty-five people tried out for my play! My hair looks amazing today! I got a B on an English paper!" His phone chirps. "And I just got a text from my new favorite Will Grayson. You're totally right, Jane: everything's coming up Tiny."

chapter twelve

it starts when i get home from chicago. i already have twenty-seven texts from tiny on my phone. and he has twenty-seven texts from me. that took up most of the train ride. the rest of the time, i figured out what i needed to do the moment i walked through the door. because if isaac's nonexistence is going to weigh me down, i have to let go of some other things in order not to crash right into the ground. i no longer give a fuck. i mean, i didn't think i gave a fuck before. but that was amateur not-giving-a-fuck. this is stop-at-nothing, don't-give-a-fuck freedom.

mom's waiting for me in the kitchen, sipping some tea, flipping through one of those stupid rich-celebrities-show-off-their-houses magazines. she looks up when i come in.

mom: how was chicago?
me: look, mom, i'm totally gay, and i'd appreciate it if you could get the whole freakout over with now, because, yeah, we have the rest of our lives to deal with it, but the sooner we get through the agony part, the better.
mom: the agony part?

me: you know, you praying for my soul and cursing me
    for not giving you grandbabies with a wifey and
    saying how incredibly disappointed you are.
mom: you really think i'd do that?
me: it's your right, i guess. but if you want to skip that
    step, it's fine with me.
mom: i think i want to skip that step.
me: really?
mom: really.
me: wow. i mean, that's cool.
mom: can i at least have a moment or two for surprise?
me: sure. i mean, it can't be the answer you were
    expecting when you asked me how chicago was.
mom: i think it's safe to say that wasn't the answer i
    was expecting.

i'm looking at her face to see if she's holding things back,
but it seems like it is what it is. which is pretty spectacular,
all things considered.

me: are you going to tell me you knew all along?
mom: no. but i was wondering who isaac was.

oh, shit.

me: isaac? were you spying on me, too?
mom: no. it's just —
me: what?
mom: you would say his name in your sleep. i wasn't
    spying. but i could hear it.

me: wow.

mom: don't be mad.

me: how could i be mad?

i know that's a silly question. i've proven that i can be mad about pretty much anything. there was this one time i woke up in the middle of the night and swore that my mother had installed a smoke alarm on the ceiling while i was asleep. so i burst into her room and started yelling about how could she just go and put something in my room without telling me, and she woke up and calmly told me the smoke alarm was in the hallway, and i actually dragged her out of bed to show her, and of course there wasn't anything on the ceiling – i'd just dreamed it. and she didn't yell at me or anything like that. she just told me to go back to sleep. and the next day was total crap for her, but not once did she say it was tied to me waking her up in the middle of the night.

mom: did you see isaac when you were in chicago?

how can i explain this to her? i mean, if i tell her i just traveled into the city to go to a porn store to meet some guy who didn't end up existing, the next few weeks' poker night earnings are going to be spent on a visit to dr. keebler. but she can tell when i'm lying if she's looking for it. i don't want to lie right now. so i bend the truth.

me: yeah, i saw him. his nickname's tiny. that's what i call him, even if he's huge. he's actually, you know, really nice.

we are in completely uncharted mother-son territory here. not just in this house — maybe in all of america.

> me: don't get all worried. we just went to millennium park and talked a while. some of his friends were there, too. i'm not going to get pregnant.

mom actually laughs.

> mom: well, *that's* a relief.

she gets up from the kitchen table and, before i know it, she's giving me a hug. and it's like for a moment i don't know what to do with my hands, and then i'm like, *you dumbfuck, hug her back.* so i do, and i expect her to start crying, because one of us should be crying. but she's dry-eyed when she pulls away — a little misty, maybe, but i've seen her when things aren't all right, when things have totally gone to shit, and so i know enough to recognize that this isn't one of those times. we're okay.

> mom: maura called a few times. she sounded upset.
> me: well, she can go to hell.
> mom: will!
> me: sorry. i didn't mean to say that out loud.
> mom: what happened?
> me: i don't want to get into it. i'm just going to tell you that she really, really hurt me, and i need for that to be enough. if she calls here, i want you to tell her that i never want to speak to her again. don't

tell her i'm not here. don't lie when i'm in the other
room. tell her the truth — that it's over and it's
never going to be un-over. please.

whether it's because she agrees or whether it's because
she knows there's no point in disagreeing when i'm like this,
mom nods. i have a very smart mom, all things considered.
it's time for her to leave the room — i thought that's
what was going to happen after the hug — but since she's
still hovering, i make the move.

me: i'm going to head off to bed. i'll see you in the
    morning.
mom: will . . .
me: really, it's been a long day. thank you for being so,
    you know, understanding. i owe you one. a big one.
mom: it's not about owing —
me: i know. but you know what i mean.

i don't want to leave until it's clear it's okay for me to
leave. i mean, that's the least i can do.
she leans in and kisses me on the forehead.

mom: good night.
me: good night.

then i go back to my room, turn on my computer, and
create a new screenname.

willupleasebequiet: tiny?
bluejeanbaby: here!

willupleasebequiet: are you ready?
bluejeanbaby: for what?
willupleasebequiet: the future
willupleasebequiet: because i think it just started

*

tiny sends me a file of one of the songs from *tiny dancer*. he says he hopes it will give me inspiration. i put it on my ipod and listen to it as i'm heading to school the next morning.

There was a time
When I thought I liked vagina
But then came a summer
When i realized something finer

I knew from the moment he took top bunk
How desperately i wanted into his trunk
Joseph Templeton Oglethorpe the Third
Left my heart singing like a little bird

Summer of gay!
So lovely! So queer!
Summer of gay!
Set the tone for my year!

Mama and Papa didn't know they were lighting the lamp
The moment they sent me to Starstruck Drama Camp

So many Hamlets to choose from
Some tortured, some cute

I was all ready to swordfight
Or take the Ophelia route

There were boys who called me sister
And sistahs who taught me about boys
Joseph whispered me sweet nothings
And i fed him Almond Joys

Summer of gay!
So fruity! So whole!
Summer of gay!
I realized Angel would be my role!

Mama and Papa didn't know how well their money was spent
When I learned about love from our production of Rent

Such kissing on the catwalks
Such competition for the leads
We fell in love so often and fully
Across all races and sexualities and creeds . . .

Summer of gay!
Ended soon! Lasted long!
Summer of gay!
My heart still carries its song!

Joseph and I didn't make it to September
But you can't unlight a gay-colored ember
I will never go back
To the heterosexual way

'Cause now every day
(Yes, every day)
Is the sum-mer
of gay!

since i've never really listened to musicals, i don't know if they all sound this gay, or if it's just tiny's. i suspect that i would find all of them this gay. i'm not entirely sure how this is supposed to inspire me to do anything except join drama club, which right now is about as likely as me asking maura on a date. still, tiny told me i was the first person to hear the song besides his mom, so that counts for something. even if it's lame, it's a sweet kind of lame.

it even manages to take my mind off of school and maura for a few minutes. but once i get there, she's right in front of me, and the mountain reminds me it's a volcano, and i can't help but want to spray lava everywhere. i walk right past the place we usually meet up, but that doesn't stop her. she launches right behind me, saying all the things that would be in a hallmark card if hallmark made cards for people who invented internet boyfriends for other people and then were suddenly caught in the lie.

> maura: i'm sorry, will. i didn't mean to hurt you or
> anything. i was just playing around. i didn't realize
> how serious you were taking it. and i'm a total
> bitch for that, i know. but i was only doing it
> because it was the only way to get through to you.
> don't ignore me, will. talk to me!

i am just going to pretend that she doesn't exist. because all the other options would get me expelled and/or arrested.

maura: please, will. i'm really, really sorry.

she's crying now, and i don't care. the tears are for her own benefit, not mine. let her feel the pain her poetry desires. it has nothing to do with me. not anymore.

she tries to pass me notes during class. i knock them off my desk and leave them on the ground. she sends me texts, and i delete them unread. she tries to come up to me at the beginning of lunch, and i build a wall of silence that no goth sorrow can climb.

maura: fine. i understand that you're mad. but i'm still going to be here when you aren't so angry.

when things break, it's not the actual breaking that prevents them from getting back together again. it's because a little piece gets lost — the two remaining ends couldn't fit together even if they wanted to. the whole shape has changed.

i am never, ever going to be friends with maura again. and the sooner she realizes it, the less annoying it's going to be.

when i talk to simon and derek, i find out that they vanquished the trigonometric challengers yesterday, so at least i know they're not still mad at me for ditching. my seat at the lunch table remains secure. we sit there and eat in silence for at least five minutes until simon speaks.

simon: so how was your big date in chicago?

me: do you really want to know?

simon: yeah — if it was big enough for you to bow out
of our competition, i want to know how it went.

me: well, at first he didn't exist, but then he existed
and it went pretty well. before, when i told you
about it, i was really careful not to use any
pronouns, but i don't give a fuck anymore.

simon: wait a sec — you're gay?

me: yup. i suppose that's the correct conclusion for you
to draw.

simon: that's disgusting!

this is not exactly the reaction i was expecting from simon.
i was betting on something a little closer to indifference.

me: what's disgusting?

simon: you know. that you put your thing in the place
where he, um, defecates.

me: first of all, i haven't put my thing anywhere. and
you do realize, don't you, that when a guy and
a girl get together, he puts his thing where she
urinates and gets her period?

simon: oh. i hadn't thought about that.

me: exactly.

simon: still, it's weird.

me: it's no weirder than jerking off to video game
characters.

simon: who told you that?

he whacks derek on the head with his plastic fork.

simon: did you tell him that?
derek: i didn't tell him anything!
me: i figured it out myself. honestly.
simon: it's only the girl characters.
derek: and some warlocks!
simon: SHUT UP!

this is not, i have to admit, how i thought being gay was going to be.

luckily, tiny texts me every five minutes or so. i don't know how he does it without getting caught in class. maybe he hides the phone in the folds of his stomach or something. whatever the case, i'm grateful. because it's hard to hate life too much when you have someone interrupting your day with things like

I'M THINKING HAPPY GAY THOUGHTS ABOUT U
and
I WANT TO KNIT U A SWEATER. WHAT COLOR?
and
I THINK I JUST FAILED A MATH TEST BECAUSE I WAS THINKING OF U 2 MUCH
and
WHAT RHYMES WITH SODOMY TRIAL?
then
LOBOTOMY VILE?
then
BOTTOM ME, KYLE?

then
BOTTOMY NILE
then
BOTTOMY GUILE!
then
BTW—ITS 4 THE SCENE WHEN OSCAR WILD'S
GHOST COMES TO ME IN A DREAM

i only know about half of what he's talking about, and usually that annoys the shit out of me. but with tiny, it doesn't matter as much. maybe someday i'll figure it out. and if not, being oblivious could be fun, too. the fatty's turning me into a softie. it's sick, really.

he also texts me all the questions about how it's going, what i'm doing, how i'm feeling, and when is he going to see me again. i can't help it — i think it's kind of like it was with isaac. only without the distance. this time, i feel i know who i'm talking to. because i get a sense that with tiny, what you see is how he is. he doesn't hold anything back. i want to be like that. only without having to gain, like, three hundred pounds to do it.

after school, maura catches me at my locker.

maura: simon told me you're officially gay now. that
        you 'met somebody' in chicago.

i don't owe you anything, maura. especially not an explanation.

maura: what are you doing, will? why did you tell him that?

because i did meet someone, maura.

maura: talk to me.

never. i am going to let the close of my locker speak for me. i am going to let the sound of my footsteps speak for me. i am going to let the way i don't look back speak for me.
  you see, maura, i don't give a fuck.

that night, tiny and i exchange IMs for four hours. mom leaves me alone and even lets me stay up late.
  someone with a fake profile leaves a comment on my myspace page calling me a fag. i don't think it's maura; someone else from school must've heard.
  when i look in my mailbox at all the messages i've gathered there, i see isaac's face has been replaced with a gray box with a red X through it.
  'profile no longer exists,' it says.
  so the mail from him remains, but he's gone.

i see a few people looking at me weird in school the next day, and i wonder if it would be possible to reconstruct the path the gossip took from derek or simon to the towering snot-nosed jock glaring at me. of course, it's possible that the towering snot-nosed jock always glared at me, and i'm just noticing it now. i try not to give a fuck.

maura's laying low, but i assume it's because she's planning her next assault. i want to tell her it's not worth it. maybe our friendship wasn't meant to last longer than a year. maybe the things that drew us together — doom, gloom, sarcasm — weren't meant to hold us together. the fucked-up thing is, i miss isaac and i don't miss her. even though i know she was isaac. none of those conversations count anymore. i am genuinely sorry that she went to such insane lengths to get me to tell her the truth — we would have been better off if we'd never been friends in the first place. i'm not going to try to punish her — i'm not going to tell everyone what she did, or bomb her locker, or yell at her in front of everyone else. i just want her to go away. that's all. the end.

right before lunch, this kid gideon catches me by my locker. we haven't really talked since seventh grade, when we were lab partners in earth science. then he went on the honors track and i didn't. i've always liked him and we've always been on hi-in-the-halls terms. he dj's a lot, mostly at parties i don't go to.

gideon: hey, will.
me: hey.

i'm pretty sure he's not here to bash me. the lcd sound-system shirt kinda gives that away.

gideon: so, yeah. i heard that you might be, you
    know . . .
me: ambidextrous? a philatelist? homosexual?

he smiles.

gideon: yeah. and, i don't know, when i realized i was
      gay, it really sucked that nobody was, like, 'way to
      go.' so i just wanted to come over and say . . .
me: way to go?

he blushes.

gideon: well, it sounds stupid like that. but that's the
      gist of it. welcome to the club. it's a very small club
      at this school.
me: i hope there aren't dues?

he stares at his shoes.

gideon: um, no. it's not *really* a club.

if tiny was at our school, i imagine it would be a club.
and he would be the president.
      i smile. gideon looks up and sees it.

gideon: maybe if you'd want to, i don't know, get some
      coffee or something after school . . . ?

it takes me a second.

me: are you asking me out?
gideon: um, maybe?

right here in the halls. there are all these people around us.
amazing.

me: here's the thing. i'd love to hang out. but . . . i have
    a boyfriend.

these words are actually leaving my lips.
uh–mazing.

gideon: oh.

i take out my phone and show him the inbox full of
texts from tiny.

me: i swear, i'm not making it up just to get out of
    going on a date with you. his name's tiny. he goes to
    school in evanston.
gideon: you're so lucky.

this is not a word that's usually thrown my way.

me: why don't you sit with me and simon and derek at
    lunch?
gideon: are they gay, too?
me: only if you're a warlock.

i text tiny a minute later.

MADE NEW GAY FRIEND.

and he texts back

PROGRESS!!!

then

YOU SHOULD FORM A GSA!

to which i reply

ONE STEP AT A TIME, BIG BOY

and he replies

BIG BOY – I LUV THAT!

the texting goes on for the rest of the day and into the night. it's pretty incredible, really, how frequently you can write someone when you're keeping the character count low. it's so stupid, because it feels like tiny's sharing the day with me. like he's there when i'm ignoring maura or talking to gideon or finding out that nobody's going to axe-murder me in gym class because i'm sending out a homosexual vibe.

still, it's not enough. because i felt that way sometimes with isaac. and i won't let this relationship be all in my head.

so that night i call tiny on the phone and talk to him. i tell him i want him to come visit. and he doesn't make excuses. he doesn't say it's not possible. instead, he says

tiny: how soon?

i will admit there's a certain degree of giving a fuck that goes into not giving a fuck. by saying you don't care if the world falls apart, in some small way you're saying you want it to stay together, on your terms.

when i hang up with tiny, mom comes into my room.

mom: how's it going?
me: fine.

and it's true, for once.

chapter thirteen

I awake to the sound of my alarm clock, blaring rhythmically, and it seems as loud as an air siren, shouting at me with such ferocity that it sort of hurts my feelings. I roll over in bed, and squint through the darkness: It's 5:43 in the morning. My alarm doesn't go off until 6:37.

And only then do I realize: That sound is not my alarm clock. It is a car horn, honking, sounding some kind of terrible siren song through the streets of Evanston, a howling warning of doom. Horns don't honk this early, not with such insistence. It must be an emergency.

I race out of bed, pull on a pair of jeans, and bolt toward the front door. I'm relieved to see both Mom and Dad alive, racing to the entryway. I say, "Jesus, what's going on?" and my mom just shrugs and my dad says, "Is it a car horn?" I make it to the door first and peer out the glass sidelight.

Tiny Cooper is parked outside my house, honking methodically.

I run outside and only when he sees me does he stop honking. The passenger window rolls down. "Christ, Tiny. You're going to wake the whole neighborhood."

I see a can of Red Bull dancing in his huge, shaky hand.

The other hand remains perched on the horn, ready to honk at any moment.

"We gotta go," he says, his voice rushed. "Gotta go go go go go go go go."

"What's wrong with you?"

"Gotta go to school. I'll explain later. Get in the car." He sounds so frantically serious, and I am so tired, that I don't think to question him. I just race back into the house, pull on some socks and shoes, brush my teeth, tell my parents I'm going to school early, and hurry into Tiny's car.

"Five things, Grayson," he says as he puts the car into drive and speeds off, without ever relinquishing his shaky hold on the can of Red Bull.

"What? Tiny, what's wrong?"

"Nothing's wrong. Everything's right. Things couldn't be righter. Things could be less tired. They could be less busy. They could be less caffeinated. But they couldn't be righter."

"Dude, are you on meth?"

"No, I'm on Red Bull." He hands me the Red Bull, and I sniff at it, trying to figure out whether it's laced with something. "Also coffee," he adds. "So but listen, Grayson. Five things."

"I can't believe you woke up my entire neighborhood at five forty-three for no reason."

"Actually," he says, his voice louder than seems entirely necessary at such a tender hour, "I woke you up for *five* reasons, which is what I've been trying to tell you, except that you keep interrupting me, which is just a very, like, Tiny Cooper thing of you to do."

I've known Tiny Cooper since he was a very large and very gay fifth grader. I've seen him drunk and sober, hungry and sated, loud and louder, in love and in longing. I have seen him in good times and bad, in sickness and in health. And in lo those many years, he has never before made a self-deprecating joke. And I can't help but think: maybe Tiny Cooper should fry his brain with caffeine more often.

"Okay, what are the five things?" I ask.

"One, I finished casting the show last night around eleven while I was skyping with Will Grayson. He helped me. I imitated all the potential auditioners, and then he helped me decide who was least horrible."

"The other Will Grayson," I correct him.

"Two," he says, as if he hasn't heard me. "Shortly there-after, Will went to bed. And I was thinking to myself, you know, it's been eight days since I met him, and I haven't technically liked someone who liked me back for eight days in my entire life, unless you count my relationship with Bethany Keene in third grade, which obviously you can't, since she's a girl.

"Three, and then I was thinking about that and lying in the bed staring up at the ceiling, and I could see the stars that we stuck up there in like sixth grade or whatever. Do you remember that? The glow-in-the-dark stars and the comet and everything?"

I nod, but he doesn't look over, even though we're stopped at a light. "Well," he goes on, "I was looking at those stars and they were fading away because it had been a few minutes since I'd turned out the light, and then I had a blinding light spiritual awakening. What is *Tiny Dancer* about? I mean, what is its subject, Grayson? You've read it."

I assume that, as usual, he is asking this question rhetorically, so I say nothing so he'll go on ranting, because as painful as it is for me to admit, there is something kind of wonderful about Tiny's ranting, particularly on a quiet street when I am still half asleep. There is something about the mere act of him speaking that is vaguely pleasurable even though I wish it weren't. It is something about his voice, not his pitch or his rapid-fire, caffeinated diction, but the voice itself—the familiarity of it, I guess, but also its inexhaustibility.

But he doesn't say anything for a while and then I realize he actually *does* want me to answer. I don't know what he wants to hear, so in the end I just tell him the truth. "*Tiny Dancer* is about Tiny Cooper," I say.

"*Exactly!*" he shouts, pounding the steering wheel. "And no great musical is ever about a person, not really. And that's the problem. That's the whole problem with the play. It's not about tolerance or understanding or love or anything. It's about *me*. And, like, nothing against me. I mean, I am pretty fabulous. Am I not?"

"You're a pillar of fabulosity in the community," I tell him.

"Yes, exactly," he says. He's smiling, but it's tough to tell how much he's kidding. We're pulling into school now, the place entirely dead, not even a car in the faculty lot. He turns into his usual spot, reaches into the back for his backpack, gets out, and starts walking across the desolate lot. I follow.

"Four," he says. "So I realized, in spite of my great and

terrible fabulousness, the play can't be about me. It must be about something even more fabulous: love. The polychromic many-splendored dreamcoat of love in all its myriad glories. And so it had to be revised. Also retitled. And so I had to stay up all night. And I've been writing like crazy, writing a musical called *Hold Me Closer*. We'll need more sets than I thought. Also! Also! More voices in the chorus. The chorus must be like a fucking *wall* of song, you know?"

"Sure, okay. What's the fifth thing?"

"Oh, right." He wiggles a shoulder out of his backpack and slings it around to his chest. He unzips the front pocket, digs around for a moment, and then pulls out a rose made entirely of green duct tape. He hands it to me. "When I get stressed," Tiny explains, "I get crafty. Okay. Okay. I'm gonna go to the auditorium and start blocking out some scenes, see how the new stuff looks onstage."

I stop walking. "Um, do you need me to help or something?"

He shakes his head no. "No offense, Grayson, but what exactly are your theater credentials?"

He's walking away from me, and I try to stand my ground, but then finally chase after him up the steps to school, because I've got a burning question. "Then why the hell did you wake me up at five forty-three in the morning?"

He turns to me now. It becomes impossible not to feel Tiny's immensity as he stands over me, shoulders back, his width almost entirely blocking the school behind him, his body a bundle of tiny tremors. His eyes are open unnaturally wide, like a zombie's. "Well, I needed to tell *someone*," he says.

I think about that a minute, and then follow him into the auditorium. For the next hour, I watch Tiny as he runs around the theater like a rampaging lunatic, mumbling to himself. He puts masking tape down on the floor to mark the spots of his imaginary sets; he pirouettes across the stage as he hums song lyrics in fast motion; and every so often he shouts, "It's not about Tiny! It's about love!" Then people start to file in for their first period drama class, so Tiny and I go to precalc, and Tiny performs the Big-Man-in-Small-Desk miracle, and I experience the traditional amazement, and school is boring, and then at lunch I'm sitting with Gary and Nick and Tiny, and Tiny is talking about his blinding light spiritual awakening in a manner that—nothing against Tiny—kind of implies that maybe Tiny has not fully internalized the idea that the earth does not spin around the axis of Tiny Cooper, and then I say to Gary, "Hey, where is Jane?"

And Gary says, "Sick."

To which Nick adds, "Sick in the I'm-spending-the-day-with-my-boyfriend-at-the-botanical-gardens kind of way." Gary shoots Nick a disapproving look.

Tiny quickly changes the subject, and I try to laugh at all the appropriate moments for the rest of lunch, but I'm not listening.

I know that she is dating Douchepants McWater Polo, and I know that sometimes when you date people you engage in idiotic activities like going to the botanical gardens, but in spite of all the knowledge that ought to protect me, I still feel like shit for the rest of the day. *One of these days*, I keep telling myself, *you'll learn to truly shut up and not care.*

And until then . . . well, until then I'll keep taking deep breaths because it feels like the wind got knocked out of me. For all my not crying, I sure feel a hell of a lot worse than I did at the end of *All Dogs Go to Heaven*.

I call Tiny after school, but I get his voice mail, so I send him a text: "The Original Will Grayson requests the pleasure of a phone call whenever possible." He doesn't call until 9:30. I'm sitting on the couch watching a dumb romantic comedy with my parents. The plates from our take-out-Chinese-put-on-real-plates-so-you-feel-like-it's-a-homemade dinner fill the coffee table. Dad is falling asleep, as he always does when he's not working. Mom sits closer to me than seems necessary.

Watching the movie, I can't stop thinking about wanting to be at the ridiculous botanical gardens with Jane. Just walking around, her in that hoodie, and me making jokes about the Latin names of the plants, and her saying that *ficaria verna* would be a good name for a nerdcore hip-hop crew that only raps in Latin, and so on. I can picture the whole damned thing, actually, and it almost makes me desperate enough to complain to Mom about the situation, but that will only mean questions about Jane for the next seven to ten years. My parents get so few details about my private life that whenever they do stumble upon some morsel, they cling to it for eons. I wish they'd do a better job of hiding their desire for me to have tons of friends and girlfriends.

Sobutand Tiny calls, and I say, "Hey," and then I get up and go to my room and close the door behind me, and in all that time, Tiny doesn't say anything, so I say, "Hello?"

And he says, "Yeah, hi," distractedly. I hear typing.

"Tiny, are you typing?"

After a moment he says, "Hold on. Let me finish this sentence."

"Tiny, *you* called *me*."

Silence. Typing. And then, "Yeah, I know. But I'm, uh, I gotta change the last song. Can't be about me. Has to be about love."

"I wish I hadn't kissed her. The whole boyfriend thing kind of like gnaws at my brain."

And then I'm quiet for a while, and finally he says, "Sorry, I just got an IM from Will. He's telling me about lunch with this new gay friend he's got. I know it's not a date if it's in the cafeteria, but still. Gideon. He *sounds* hot. It is pretty awesome that Will's so out, though. He like came out to everyone in the entire world. I swear to God I think he wrote the president of the United States and was like, 'Dear Mr. President, I am gay. Yours truly, Will Grayson.' It's fucking beautiful, Grayson."

"Did you even hear what I said?"

"Jane and her boyfriend ate your brain," he answers disinterestedly.

"I swear, Tiny, sometimes . . ." I stop myself from saying something pathetic and start over. "Do you want to do something after school tomorrow? Darts or something at your house?"

"Rehearsal then rewrites then Will on the phone then bed. You can sit in on rehearsal if you want."

"Nah," I say. "It's cool."

After I hang up, I try to read *Hamlet* for a while, but I

don't understand it that well, and I have to keep looking over to the right margin where they define the words, and it just makes me feel like an idiot.

Not that smart. Not that hot. Not that nice. Not that funny. That's me: I'm not that.

I'm lying on top of the covers with my clothes still on, the play still on my chest, eyes closed, mind racing. I'm thinking about Tiny. The pathetic thing I wanted to say to him on the phone—but didn't—was this: When you're a little kid, you have something. Maybe it's a blanket or a stuffed animal or whatever. For me, it was this stuffed prairie dog that I got one Christmas when I was like three. I don't even know where they found a stuffed prairie dog, but whatever, it sat up on its hind legs and I called him Marvin, and I dragged Marvin around by his prairie dog ears until I was about ten.

And then at some point, it was nothing personal against Marvin, but he started spending more time in the closet with my other toys, and then more time, until finally Marvin became a full-time resident of the closet.

But for many years afterward, sometimes I would get Marvin out of the closet and just hang out with him for a while—not for me, but for Marvin. I realized it was crazy, but I still did it.

And the thing I wanted to say to Tiny is that sometimes, I feel like his Marvin.

I remember us together: Tiny and me in gym in middle school, how the athletic wear company didn't make gym shorts big enough to fit him, so he looked like he was wearing a skintight bathing suit. Tiny dominating at dodgeball despite his width, and always letting me finish second just by virtue of putting me in his shadow and not spiking me until the end. Tiny and me at the gay pride parade in Boys Town, ninth grade, him saying, "Grayson, I'm gay," and me being like, "Oh, really? Is the sky blue? Does the sun rise in the east? Is the Pope Catholic?" and him being like, "Is Tiny Cooper fabulous? Do birds weep from the beauty when they hear Tiny Cooper sing?"

I think about how much depends upon a best friend. When you wake up in the morning you swing your legs out of bed and you put your feet on the ground and you stand up. You don't scoot to the edge of the bed and look down to make sure the floor is there. The floor is always there. Until it's not.

It's stupid to blame the other Will Grayson for something that was happening before the other Will Grayson existed. And yet.

And yet I keep thinking about him, and thinking about his eyes unblinking in Frenchy's, waiting for someone who didn't exist. In my memory, his eyes get bigger and bigger, almost like he's a manga character. And then I'm thinking about that guy, Isaac, who was a girl. But the things that were said that made Will go to Frenchy's to meet that guy—those things *were* said. They were real.

All at once I grab my phone from off my bedside table and call Jane. Voice mail. I look at the clock on the phone: it's 9:42. I call Gary. He picks up on the fifth ring.

"Will?"

"Hey, Gary. Do you know Jane's address?"

"Um, yes?"

"Can you give it to me?"

He pauses. "Are you going all stalker on me, Will?"

"No, I swear, I have a question about science," I say.

"You have a Tuesday night at nine forty-two question about science?"

"Correct."

"Seventeen twelve Wesley."

"And where is her bedroom?"

"I have to tell you, man, that my stalker meter is kind of registering in the red zone right now." I say nothing, waiting. And then finally he says, "If you're facing the house, it's front and left."

"Awesome, thanks."

I grab the keys off the kitchen counter on my way out, and Dad asks where I'm going, and I try just getting by with, "Out," but that just results in the pausing of the TV. He comes up close as if to remind me he is just a little bit taller than I am, and sternly asks, "Out with *whom* and to *where*?"

"Tiny wants my help with his stupid play."

"Back by eleven," Mom says from the couch.

"Okay," I say.

I walk down the street to the car. I can see my breath, but I don't feel cold except on my gloveless hands, and I stand outside the car for a second, looking at the sky, the orange light coming from the city to the south, the leafless streetside trees quiet in the breeze. I open the door, which cracks the silence, and drive the mile to Jane's house. I find a spot half a block down and walk back up the street to an old, two-story house with a big porch. Those houses don't come cheap. There's a light on in the front-left room, but as soon as I get there, I don't want to walk up. What if she's changing? What if she's lying in bed and she sees a creepy guy face pressed against the glass? What if she's making out with Randall McBitchsquealer? So I send her a text: "Take this in the least stalkery way possible: Im outside ur house." It's 9:47. I figure I'll wait until the clock turns over to 9:50 and then leave. I shove one hand into my jeans and hold the phone with the other, pressing the volume up button each time the screen goes blank. It's been 9:49 for at least ten seconds when the front door opens and Jane peers outside.

I wave very slightly, my hand not even rising above my head. Jane puts a finger to her lips, and then dramatically tiptoes out of the house and very slowly closes the door behind her. She walks down the steps of the porch, and in the porch light I can see that she's wearing the same green hoodie but now with red flannel pajama pants and socks. No shoes.

She walks up to me and whisper-says, "It's a slightly creepy delight to see you."

And I say, "I have a science question."

She smiles and nods. "Of course you do. You're wondering how it's scientifically possible that you're paying oh-so-much attention to me now that I have a boyfriend when you were totally uninterested in me before. Sadly, science is baffled by the mysteries of boy psychology."

But I do have a science question—about Tiny and me, and about her, and about cats. "Can you explain to me about Schrödinger's cat?"

"Come on," she says, and reaches out for my coat and pulls me down the sidewalk. I'm walking beside her, not saying anything, and she's mumbling, "God God God God God God God," and I say, "What's wrong?" and she says, "You. You, Grayson. You're what's wrong," and I say, "What?" and she says, "You know," and I say, "No I don't," and she—still walking and not looking at me—says, "There are probably some girls who don't want guys to show up at their house randomly on a Tuesday night with questions about Edwin Schrödinger. I am sure such girls exist. But they don't live at my house."

We get five or six houses past Jane's, near to where my car is parked, and then she turns toward a house with a FOR SALE sign and walks up the stairs to a porch swing. She sits down and pats a place next to her.

"Nobody lives here?" I ask.

"No. It's been for sale for, like, a year."

"You've probably made out with the Douche on this swing."

"I probably have," she answers. "Schrödinger was doing a thought experiment. Okay, so, this paper had just come out arguing that if, like, an electron might be in any one of four different places, it is sort of in all four places at the same time until the moment someone determines which of the four places it's in. Does that make sense?"

"No," I say. She's wearing little white socks, and I can see her ankle when she kicks up her feet to keep the swing swinging.

"Right, it totally doesn't make sense. It's mind-bendingly weird. So Schrödinger tries to point this out. He says: put a cat inside a sealed box with a little bit of radioactive stuff that might or might not—depending on the location of its sub-atomic particles—cause a radiation detector to trip a hammer that releases poison into the box and kills the cat. Got it?"

"I think so," I say.

"So, according to the theory that electrons are in all-possible-positions until they are measured, the cat is both alive and dead until we open the box and find out if it is alive or dead. He was not endorsing cat-killing or anything. He was just saying that it seemed a little improbable that a cat could be simultaneously alive and dead."

But it doesn't seem that improbable to me. It seems to me that all the things we keep in sealed boxes *are* both alive and dead until we open the box, that the unobserved is both there and not. Maybe that's why I can't stop thinking about the other Will Grayson's huge eyes in Frenchy's: because he had just rendered the dead-and-alive cat dead. I realize that's why I never put myself in a situation where I really *need* Tiny, and why I followed the rules instead of kissing her when she was available: I chose the closed box. "Okay," I say. I don't look at her. "I think I get it."

"Well, that's not all, actually. It turns out to be some-what more complicated."

"I don't think I'm smart enough to handle more compli-cated," I say.

"Don't underestimate yourself," she says.

The porch swing creaks as I try to think everything through. I look over at her.

"Eventually, they figured out that keeping the box closed doesn't actually keep the cat alive-and-dead. Even if *you* don't observe the cat in whatever state it's in, the air in the box does. So keeping the box closed just keeps *you* in the dark, not the universe."

"Got it," I say. "But failing to open the box doesn't *kill* the cat." We aren't talking about physics anymore.

"No," she says. "The cat was already dead—or alive, as the case may be."

"Well, the cat has a boyfriend," I say.

"Maybe the physicist likes that the cat has a boyfriend."

"Possible," I say.

"Friends," she says.

"Friends," I say. We shake on it.

chapter fourteen

mom insists that before i go anywhere with tiny, he has to come over for dinner. i'm sure she checks all the sex predator websites beforehand. she doesn't trust that i met him over the internet. and, given the circumstances, i can't really blame her. she's a little surprised when i go along with the plan, even if i do tell her

> me: just don't ask about his forty-three ex-boyfriends, okay? or ask him about why he's carrying around an axe.
> mom: . . .
> me: i'm kidding about the axe part.

but really, nothing i can say can calm the woman down. it's insane. she puts on those yellow rubber gloves and starts scrubbing with the intensity you usually reserve for when someone's thrown up all over the furniture. i tell her she really doesn't have to do that, because it's not like tiny's going to be eating off the floor. but she just waves me away and tells me to clean up my room.

i mean to clean up my room. really, i do. but all i manage to do is wipe the history from my web browser, and then i'm totally exhausted. it's not like i don't wipe the snot flakes from my bed in the morning. i'm a pretty clean guy. all the dirty clothes are shoved in the bottom of my closet. he's not going to see them.

finally, it's time for him to get here. at school, gideon asks me if i'm nervous about tiny coming over, and i tell him i'm totally not. but, yeah, that's a lie. mostly i'm nervous about my mom and how she's going to act.

i'm waiting for him in the kitchen, and mom's running around like a madwoman.

mom: i should fix the salad.
me: why should you fix the salad?
mom: doesn't tiny like salad?
me: i told you, i think tiny would eat baby seals if we
gave them to him. but i mean, why do you have
to fix the salad? who broke it? i didn't touch it.
did you break the salad, mom? if you did, YOU'D
BETTER FIX IT!

i'm joking, but she's not really finding it funny. and i'm thinking, *aren't i supposed to be the one who's freaking out here?* tiny is going to be the first b-b-b- (i can't do it) boy-f-f-f (c'mon, will) boyf-boyf (here we go) boyfriend of mine that she's ever met. although if she keeps talking about salad, i might have to lock her in her bedroom before he comes over.

mom: you're sure he doesn't have any allergies?
me: calm. down.

like i suddenly have supercanine sound skills, i hear a car pulling into the driveway. before mom can tell me to comb my hair and put on some shoes, i'm out the front door and watching tiny turn off the ignition.

me: run! run!

but the radio's so loud that tiny can't hear me. he just grins. as he opens the door, i get a look at his car.

me: what the—?!?

it's this silver mercedes, the kind of car you'd expect to be driven by a plastic surgeon — and not the kind of plastic surgeon who fixes the fucked-up faces of starving african babies, but the kind of plastic surgeon who convinces women that their lives will be over if they look older than twelve.

tiny: greetings, earthling! i come in peace. take me to your leader!

it should be weird to have him right in front of me for only the second time in our boyfriendship, and it should be really exciting that i'm about to be caught up in those big arms of his, but really i'm still stuck on the car.

me: please tell me you stole that.

he looks a little confused, and holds up the shopping bag he's carrying.

tiny: this?

me: no. the car.

tiny: oh. well, i *did* steal it.

me: you did?

tiny: yeah, from my mother. my car was almost out of
gas.

it's so bizarre. all the times we've been talking or texting
or IMing or whatever, i've always imagined that tiny was in
a house like mine, or a school like mine, or a car like the
one i might get someday — a car almost as old as me, probably bought off an old woman who isn't allowed to drive
anymore. now i'm realizing it's not like that at all.

me: you live in a big house, don't you?

tiny: big enough to fit me!

me: that's not what i mean.

i have no idea what i'm doing. because i've totally slowed
us down, and even though he's right in front of me now, it's
not like it should be.

tiny: come here, you.

and with that, he puts his bag down and opens his arms
to me, and his smile is so wide that i'd be an asshole to do
anything but walk right inside his welcome. once i'm there,
he leans down to kiss me lightly.

tiny: hello.

i kiss him back.

me: hello.

okay, so this is the reality: he is here. he is real. we are real. i shouldn't care about his car.

mom's got her apron off by the time we get inside the house. even though i warned her that he's the shape of utah, there's still a slight moment of astonishment when she first sees tiny in the flesh. he must be used to this, or maybe he just doesn't care, because he glides right over to her and starts saying all the right things, about how excited he is to meet her, and how amazing it is that she cooked dinner, and how wonderful the house looks.

mom gestures him over to the couch and asks him if he wants anything to drink.

mom: we have coke, diet coke, lemonade, orange juice —
tiny: ooh, i love lemonade.
me: it's not real lemonade. it's just lemon-flavored
crystal light.

both mom and tiny look at me like i'm the fucking grinch.

me: i didn't want you to get all excited for real
lemonade!

i can't help it — i'm seeing our apartment through his eyes — our whole lives through his eyes — and it all looks so . . .

shabby. the water stains on the ceiling and the dull-colored rug and the decades-old tv. the whole house smells like debt.

mom: why don't you go sit next to tiny, and i'll get you
a coke?

i took my pills this morning, i swear. but it's like they ended up in my leg instead of my brain, because i just can't get happy. i sit down on the couch, and as soon as mom is out of the room, tiny's hand is on my hand, fingers rubbing over my fingers.

tiny: it's okay, will. i love being here.

i know he's been having a bad week. i know things haven't been going his way, and that he's worried his show is going to bomb. he's rewriting it daily. ('who knew it would be so complicated to fit love into fourteen songs?') i know he's been looking forward to this – and i know that *i've* been looking forward to this. but now i have to stop looking forward and start looking at where i am. it's hard.
i lean into tiny's meaty shoulder.
i can't believe i'm turned on by anything i'd call 'meaty.'

me: this is the rough part, okay? so just stay tuned for
the good part. i promise it'll come soon.

when mom comes back in, i'm still leaning there. she doesn't flinch, doesn't stop, doesn't seem to mind. she puts our drinks down, then runs to the kitchen again. i hear the oven open and close, then the scrape of a spatula against a cookie sheet. a minute later, she's back with a plate of mini hot dogs and mini egg rolls. there are even two little bowls, one with ketchup and one with mustard.

tiny: yum!

we dig in, and tiny starts telling mom about the week he's had, and so many details about *hold me closer* that i can see she's thoroughly confused. as he's talking, she remains hovering above us, until finally i tell her she should join us, sit down. so she pulls over a chair and listens, even having an egg roll or two herself.

it starts to feel more normal. tiny being here. mom seeing the two of us. me sitting so that at least one part of my body is always touching his. it's almost like i'm back in millennium park with him, that we're continuing that first time-bending conversation, and this is where the story is supposed to go. as always, the only question is whether i'll fuck it all up.

when there are no finger foods left to finger, mom clears the dishes and says dinner will be ready in a few minutes. as soon as she's out of the room, tiny turns to me.

tiny: i love her.

yes, i think, he's the type of person who can love someone that easily.

me: she's not bad.

when she comes in to tell us dinner's ready, tiny flies up from the couch.

tiny: ooh! i almost forgot.

he reaches for the shopping bag he brought and hands it to my mother.

tiny: a host gift!

mom looks really surprised. she takes a box out of the bag — it has a ribbon on it and everything. tiny sits back down so she won't feel awkward sitting down to open it. very carefully, she undoes the ribbon. then she gently lifts open the top of the box. there's a black foam cushion, then something surrounded by bubble wrap. With even more care, she undoes the wrapping, and takes out this plain glass bowl.

at first, i don't get it. i mean, it's a glass bowl. but my mother's breath catches. she's blinking back tears. because it's not just a plain glass bowl. it's perfect. i mean, it's so smooth and perfect, we all sit there and stare at it for a moment, as my mother turns it slowly in her hand. even in our shabby living room, it catches the light.

nobody's given her anything like this in ages. maybe ever. nobody ever gives her anything this beautiful.

tiny: i picked it out myself!

he has no idea. he has no clue what he's just done.

mom: oh, tiny . . .

she's lost the words. but i can tell. it's the way she holds
that bowl in her hand. it's the way she's looking at it.

i know what her mind is telling her to do — to say it's
too much, that she couldn't possibly have such a thing. even
if she wants it so badly. even if she loves it that much.

so it's me who says

me: it's beautiful. thank you so much, tiny.

i hug him, really send him my thank you that way,
too. then mom is putting the bowl on the coffee table she
cleaned to a shine. she's standing up, and she's opening her
arms, and then he's hugging her, too.

this is what i never allow myself to need.

and of course i've been needing it all along.

to tell the truth, tiny eats most of the chicken parm
at dinner, and takes up most of the conversation as well.
mostly, we talk about stupid things — why mini hot dogs
taste better than regular-size hot dogs, why dogs are
better than cats, why *cats* was so successful in the eighties
when sondheim was writing rings around lloyd webber
(neither mom or i really contribute much to that one). at
one point, tiny sees the da vinci postcard mom has on the
refrigerator, and he asks her if she's ever been to italy. so
she tells him about the trip she took with three college
friends their junior year, and it's an interesting story for
once. he tells her he likes naples even more than rome,

because the people in naples are so intensely from the place they're from. he says he wrote a song about traveling for his musical, but ultimately it didn't make the cut. he sings us a few lines:

Once you've been to Naples
it's hard to shop at Staples,
And once you've been to Milan
it's hard to eat at Au Bon Pain.

Once you've been to Venice
you turn from iceberg lettuce.
And you learn that baloney's baloney
When Bologna feeds you rigatoni.

Being a transatlantic gay
is a dangerous game to play.
Because once you've been to Rome
it's hard to call a suburb home

for the first time i can recall, mom looks completely tickled. she even hums along a little. when tiny is done, her applause is genuine. i figure it's time to end the lovefest, before tiny and mom run off together and start a band.

i offer to do the dishes, and mom acts like she's completely shocked by this.

me: i do the dishes all the time.

mom looks seriously at tiny.

mom: really, he does.

then she bursts out laughing.

i am not really appreciating this, even though i'm aware there are many worse ways this could've played out.

tiny: i want to see your room!

this is not a hey!-my-zipper's-getting-itchy! request. when tiny says he wants to see your room, it means he wants to see . . . your room.

mom: go ahead. i've got the dishes.
tiny: thanks, mrs. grayson.
mom: anne. call me anne.
tiny: thanks, anne!
me: yeah, thanks, anne.

tiny hits me on the shoulder. i think he means to do it lightly, but i feel like someone's just driven a volkswagen into my arm.

i lead him to my room, and even manage a ta-da! when i open the door. he walks to the center of the room and takes it all in, smiling the whole time.

tiny: goldfish!

he goes right over to the bowl. i explain to him that if goldfish ever take over the world and decide to have a war crimes trial, i am going to be noosebait, because the mortality rate of my little goldfish bowl is much much higher than if they'd lived in the moat at some chinese restaurant.

tiny: what are their names?

oh, lord.

me: samson and delilah.
tiny: really?
me: she's a total slut.

he leans over for a closer look at the fish food.

tiny: you feed them prescription drugs?
me: oh, no. those are mine.

it's the only way i'll remember to feed the fish and take my meds, if i keep them together. still, i'm thinking maybe i should've cleaned a little more. because of course tiny's now blushing and not going to ask anything else, and while i don't want to go into it, i also don't want him to think i'm being treated for scabies or something.

me: it's a depression thing.
tiny: oh, i feel depressed, too. sometimes.

we're coming dangerously close to the conversations i'd have with maura, when she'd say she knew exactly what i was going through, and i'd have to explain that, no, she didn't, because her sadness never went as deep as mine. i had no doubt that tiny *thought* he got depressed, but that was probably because he had nothing to compare it to. still, what could i say? that i didn't just *feel* depressed – instead, it was like the depression was the core of me, of every part of me, from my mind to my bones? that if he got blue, i got black? that i hated those pills so much, because i knew how much i relied on them to live?

no, i couldn't say any of this. because, when it all comes down to it, nobody wants to hear it. no matter how much they like you or love you, they don't want to hear it.

tiny: which one's samson and which one's delilah?
me: honestly? i forget.

tiny scans my bookshelf, runs his hand over my keyboard, spins the globe i got when i graduated fifth grade.

tiny: look! a bed!

for a second, i think he's going to leap onto it, which would kill my bed frame for sure. but with an almost-shy grin, he sits gingerly on its edge.

tiny: comfy!

how have i ended up dating this sprinkled donut of a person? with a not-unfriendly sigh, i sit down next to him. the mattress is definitely canyoning his way.

but before the inevitable next step, my phone vibrates on my desk. i'm going to ignore it, but then it buzzes again and tiny tells me to get it.

i flip open the phone and read what's there.

tiny: who's it from?

me: just gideon. he wants to see how things are
  going.

tiny: gideon, huh?

there's an unmistakable suspicion in tiny's voice. i close
the phone and head back to the bed.

me: you're not jealous of gideon, are you?

tiny: what, that he's cute and young and gay and
  gets to see you every day? what's there to be
  jealous of?

i kiss him.

me: you have nothing to be jealous of. we're just
  friends.

something hits me then, and i start to laugh.

tiny: what?

me: there's a boy in my bed!

it's such a stupid, gay thought. i feel like i have to carve
'I HATE THE WORLD' into my arm about a hundred
times to make up for it.

the bed really isn't big enough for the two of us. twice i
end up on the floor. all our clothes stay on — but it's almost
like that doesn't matter. because we're all over each other.
he's big and strong, but i match him in the push and pull.
soon we're a complete hot mess.

when we've tired ourselves out, we just lie there. his heartbeat is huge.

we hear my mother turn on the tv. the detectives start talking. tiny runs his hand under my shirt.

tiny: where's your dad?

i'm totally not ready for the question. i feel myself tense.

me: i don't know.

tiny's touch tries to soothe me. his voice tries to calm me.

tiny: it's okay.

but i can't take that. i sit up, knocking us right out of our dreamy breathing, making him shift away a little so he can see me clearly. the impulse in me is loud and clear: immediately, i can't do this. not because of my father — i don't really care that much about my father — but because of this whole process of knowing everything.

i argue with myself.

stop.

stay here.

talk.

tiny is waiting. tiny is looking at me. tiny is being kind, because he hasn't realized yet who i am, what i am. i will never be kind back. the best i can do is give him reasons to give up.

tiny: tell me. what do you want to say?

don't ask me, i want to warn him. but then i'm talking.

> me: look, tiny — i'm trying to be on my best behavior,
> but you have to understand — i'm always standing
> on the edge of something bad. and sometimes
> someone like you can make me look the other
> way, so that i don't know how close i am to falling
> over. but i always end up turning my head. always.
> i always walk off that edge. and it's shit i deal with
> every day, and it's shit that's not going away any
> time soon. it's really nice to have you here, but do
> want to know something? do you really want me to
> be honest?

he should take this as the warning it is. but no. he
nods.

> me: it feels like a vacation. i don't think you know what
> that's like. which is good — you don't want to.
> you have no idea how much i hate this. i hate the
> fact that i'm ruining the night right now, ruining
> everything —
> tiny: you're not.
> me: i am.
> tiny: says who?
> me: says me?
> tiny: don't i get any say?
> me: no. i just ruin it. you don't get any say.

tiny touches my ear lightly.

tiny: you know, you get all sexy when you turn
    destructive.

his fingers run down my neck, under my collar.

tiny: i know i can't change your dad or your mom or
    your past. but you know what i can do?

his other hand works its way up my leg.

me: what?
tiny: something else. that's what i can give you.
    something else.

i am so used to bringing out the pain in people. but tiny
refuses to play that game. while we're texting all day, and
even here in person, he's always trying to get to the heart of
it. and that means he always assumes there's a heart to get
to. i think that's ridiculous and admire it at the same time.
i want the something else he has to give me, even though
i know it's never going to be something i can actually take
and have as my own.

i know it's not as easy as tiny says it is. but he's trying so
hard. so i surrender to it. i surrender to something else.

even if my heart isn't totally believing it.

chapter fifteen

The next day, Tiny isn't in precalc. I assume he's hunched over somewhere writing songs into a comically undersized notebook. It doesn't bother me much. I see him between second and third period when I walk past his locker; his hair looks unwashed and his eyes are wide.

"Too much Red Bull?" I ask, walking up to him.

He answers all in a furious rush. "Play opens in nine days, Will Grayson's adorable, everything's cool. Listen, Grayson, I gotta go to the auditorium, I'll see you at lunch."

"The *other* Will Grayson," I say.

"What, huh?" Tiny asks, slamming his locker shut.

"The other Will Grayson's adorable."

"Right, quite right," he answers.

He's not at our table at lunch, and neither is Gary or Nick or Jane or anyone, and I don't want the entire table to myself, so I take my tray to the auditorium, figuring I'll find everyone there. Tiny's standing in the middle of the stage, a notebook in one hand and his cell in the other, gesticulating wildly. Nick's sitting in the first row of seats. Tiny's talking to Gary onstage, and because the acoustics are fantastic in our auditorium, I can hear exactly what he's saying even from the back.

"The thing you've gotta remember about Phil Wrayson is that he is totally freaking terrified. Of everything. He acts like he doesn't care, but he's closer to falling apart than anyone else in the whole freaking play. I want to hear the quiver in his voice when he's singing, the *need* he hopes no one can hear. Because that's gotta be what makes him so annoying, you know? The things he says aren't annoying; it's the *way* he says them. So when Tiny is taping up those Pride posters, and Phil won't shut up about the stupid girl problems he brought on himself, we've gotta *hear* what's annoying. But you can't overdo it, either. It's the slightest little thing, man. It's the pebble in your shoe."

I just stand there for a minute, waiting for him to see me, and then finally he does. "He's a CHARACTER, Grayson," Tiny shouts. "He's a FICTIONAL CHARACTER."

Still holding my tray, I spin around and leave. I sit down outside the auditorium on the tile floor of the hallway, leaning up against a trophy case, and I eat a little.

I'm waiting for him. To come out and apologize. Or else to come out and yell at me for being a pussy. I'm waiting for those dark wood double doors to open and for Tiny to blow through them and start talking.

I know it's immature, but I don't care. Sometimes you need your best friend to walk through the doors. And then, he doesn't. Finally, feeling small and stupid, it's me who gets up and cracks open the door. Tiny is happily singing about Oscar Wilde. I stand there for a moment, still hoping he'll see me, and I don't even know that I'm crying until this crooked sound comes up out of me as I inhale. I close the door. If Tiny ever sees me, he doesn't pause to acknowledge it.

I walk down the hallway, my head down so far that the salt water drips from the tip of my nose. I walk out the main door—the air cold, the sun warm—and down the steps. I follow the sidewalk until I get to the security gate, then I dart into the bushes. Something in my throat feels like it might choke me. I walk through the shrubs just like Tiny and I did freshman year when we skipped to go down to Boys Town for the Pride Parade where he came out to me.

I walk all the way to this Little League field that's halfway between my house and school. It's right by the middle school, and when I was a kid, I used to go there a lot by myself, like after school or whatever, just to think. Sometimes I would bring a sketchbook or something and try to draw, but mostly I just liked to go there. I walk around the backstop fence and sit down on the bench in the dugout, my back against the aluminum wall, warmed by the sunlight, and I cry.

Here's what I like about the dugout: I'm on the third base side, and I can see the diamond of dirt in front of me and the four rows of wooden bleachers on one side; and then on the other side, the outfield and the next diamond over; and then a large park, and then the street. I can see people walking their dogs, and a couple walking into the wind. But with my back to the wall, with this aluminum roof over my head, no one can see me unless I can see them.

The rarity of the situation is the kind of thing that makes you cry.

Tiny and I actually played Little League together—not

in this park, but in one closer to our houses, starting in third grade. That's how we became friends, I guess. Tiny was strong as hell, of course, but not much good with the bat. He did lead the League in getting hit by pitches, though. There was so much to hit.

I played a respectable first base and didn't lead the League in anything.

I put my elbows on my knees like I did back when I was watching games from a dugout like this one. Tiny always sat next to me, and even though he only played because the coach had to play everyone, he was super-enthusiastic. He'd be all, "Hey, batter batter. Hey, batter batter, SWING, batter," and then eventually he'd switch to, "We want a pitcher, not a bellyitcher!"

Then, sixth grade: Tiny was playing third base, and I was at first. It was early in the game, and we were either just barely winning or just barely losing—I don't remember. Honestly, I never even looked at the score when I was playing. Baseball for me was just one of those weird and terrible things parents do for reasons you cannot fathom, like flu shots and church. So the batter hit the ball, and it rolled to Tiny. Tiny gloved it and threw the ball to first with his cannon arm, and I stretched out to make the catch, careful to keep a foot on the bag, and the ball hit me in the glove and then immediately fell out, because I forgot to squeeze the glove shut. The runner was safe, and the mistake cost us a run or something. After the inning ended, I went back to the dugout. The coach—I think his name was Mr. Frye— leaned down toward me. I became aware of the bigness of his head, his cap riding high over his fat face, and he said,

"FOCUS on CATCHING the BALL. CATCH the BALL, okay? Jesus!" My face felt flush, and with that quiver in my voice that Tiny pointed out to Gary, I said, "Suhrry, Coach," and Mr. Frye said, "Me too, Will. Me too."

And then Tiny hauled off and punched Mr. Frye in the nose. Just like that. Thus ended our Little League careers.

It wouldn't hurt if he weren't right—if I hadn't known somewhere that my weakness aggravates him. And maybe he thinks like I do, that you don't pick your friends, and he's stuck with this annoying bitchsquealer who can't handle himself, who can't close his glove around the ball, who can't take a dressing-down from the coach, who regrets writing letters to the editor in defense of his best friend. This is the real story of our friendship: I haven't been stuck with Tiny. He's been stuck with me.

If nothing else, I can relieve him of that burden.

It takes a long time to stop crying. I use my glove as a handkerchief as I watch the shadow of the dugout roof creep down my outstretched legs as the sun rises to the top of the sky. Finally, my ears feel frozen in the shade of the dugout, so I get up and walk across the park and then home. On the way, I scroll through my list of contacts on my phone for a while and then call Jane. I don't know why. I feel like I need to call someone. I feel, weirdly, like I still want *someone* to open the double doors to the auditorium. I get her voice mail.

"Sorry, Tarzan, Jane's unavailable. Leave a message."

"Hey, Jane, it's Will. I just wanted to talk to you. I . . . radical honesty? I just spent like five minutes going through a list of everyone I could call, and you were the only person I wanted to call, because I like you. I just like you a lot. I think you're awesome. You're just . . . er. Smart*er* and funni*er* and prett*ier* and just . . . *er*. Yeah, okay. That's all. Bye."

When I get home, I call my dad. He picks up on the last ring.

"Can you call the school and tell them I'm sick? I had to go home," I say.

"You okay, bud?"

"Yeah. I'm okay," I say, but the quiver is in my voice, and I feel like I might start up with the sobbing again for some reason, and he says, "Okay. Okay. I'll call."

Fifteen minutes later, I'm slumped on the couch in the living room, my feet up on the coffee table. I'm staring at the TV, only the TV isn't on. I've got the remote in my left hand, but I don't even have the energy to push the goddamned power button.

I hear the garage door open. Dad comes in through the kitchen and sits down next to me, pretty close. "Five hundred channels," he says after a moment, "and nothing's on."

"You get the day off?"

"I can always get someone to cover," he says. "Always."

"I'm okay," I say.

"I know you are. I just wanted to be home with you, that's all."

I blink out some tears, but Dad has the decency not to say anything about it. I turn on the TV then, and we find a show called *The World's Most Amazing Yachts*, which is about yachts that have, like, golf courses on them or whatever, and every time they show some fancy feature, Dad says, "It's UH-MAAZING!" all sarcastically, even though it sort of *is* amazing. It is and isn't, I guess.

And then Dad mutes the TV and says, "You know Dr. Porter?"

And I nod. He's this guy who works with Mom.

"They don't have any kids, so they're rich." I laugh. "But they've got this boat they keep at Belmont Harbor, one of these behemoths with cherry-wood cabinets imported from Indonesia and a rotating king-size bed stuffed with the feathers of endangered eagles and everything else. Your mom and I had dinner with the Porters on the boat years ago, and in the span of a single meal—in that two hours— the boat went from feeling like the most extraordinarily luxurious experience to just being a boat."

"I assume there's a moral to this story."

He laughs. "You're our yacht, bud. All that money that would have gone into a yacht, all that time we would have spent traveling the world? Instead, we got you. It turns out that the yacht is a boat. But you—you can't be bought on credit, and you aren't reducible." He turns his face back toward the TV and after a moment says, "I'm so proud of you that it makes me proud of me. I hope you know that." I nod, tight-throated, staring now at a muted commercial for laundry detergent. After a second, he mumbles to himself, "Credit, people, consumerism. . . . There's a pun in there somewhere."

I say, "What if I didn't want to go to that program at Northwestern? Or what if I don't get in?"

"Well, then I would stop loving you," he says. He keeps a straight face for a second, then laughs and unmutes the TV.

• • •

Later in the day, we decide we're going to surprise Mom with turkey chili for dinner. I'm chopping onions when the doorbell rings. Immediately, I know it's Tiny, and I feel this weird relief radiate out from my solar plexus. "I got it," I say. I squeeze past Dad in the kitchen and then run to the door.

It's not Tiny but Jane. She looks up at me, lips pursed.

"What's my locker combination?"

"Twenty-five-two-eleven," I say.

She hits me playfully on the chest. "*I knew it!* Why didn't you tell me?"

"I couldn't figure out which of several true things was the most true," I answer.

"We gotta open the box," she tells me.

"Um," I say. I step forward so I can close the door behind me, but she doesn't step backward, so now we're almost touching. "The cat has a boyfriend," I point out.

"I'm not the cat, actually. The cat is us. I am a physicist. You are a physicist. The cat is us."

"Um, okay," I say. "The physicist has a boyfriend."

"The physicist does not in fact have a boyfriend. The physicist dumped her boyfriend at the botanical gardens because he wouldn't shut up about how he was going to the Olympics in twenty sixteen, and there was this little voice in the physicist's head named Will Grayson, saying, 'And at the Olympics will you be representing the United States or the Kingdom of Douchelandia?' So the physicist broke up with her boyfriend and insists that the box be opened, because she kind of cannot stop thinking about the cat. The physicist won't mind if the cat is dead; she just needs to know."

We kiss. Her hands are freezing on my face, and she tastes like coffee and the smell of the onion is still stuck in my nose, and my lips are all dry from the endless winter. And it's awesome.

"Your professional physicist opinion?" I ask.

She smiles. "I believe the cat to be alive. And what says my esteemed colleague?"

"Alive," I say. And it truly is. Which makes it all the weirder that as I'm talking to her, some small cut inside me feels unstitched. I thought it would be Tiny at the door, brimming with apologies I would slowly accept. But such is life. We grow up. Planets like Tiny get new moons. Moons like me get new planets. Jane pulls away from me for a second and says, "Something smells good. I mean, in addition to you."

I smile. "We're making chili," I say. "Do you want to—. Do you want to come in and meet my dad?"

"I don't want to imp—"

"No," I say. "He's nice. A little weird. Nice, though. You can stay for dinner."

"Um, okay let me call my house." I stand out there shivering for a second while she talks to her mom, saying, "I'm gonna have dinner at Will Grayson's house. . . . Yes, his dad is here. . . .They're doctors. . . . Yeah. . . . Okay, love you."

I come back inside. "Dad," I say, "this is my friend Jane." He emerges from the kitchen wearing his *Surgeons Do It with a Steady Hand* apron over his shirt and tie. "I give peo-

224

ple credit for buying into consumerism!" he says excitedly, having found his pun. I laugh.

Jane extends her hand, the picture of class, saying, "Hello, Dr. Grayson, I'm Jane Turner."

"Ms. Turner, it's a pleasure."

"Is it okay if Jane stays for dinner?"

"Of course, of course. Jane, if you'll excuse us for a moment."

Dad takes me into the kitchen, then leans in and says softly, "This was the cause of your problems?"

"Strangely, no," I say. "But we are sorta yeah."

"You are sorta yeah," he mumbles to himself. "You are sorta yeah." And then quite loudly he says, "Jane?"

"Yes, sir?"

"What is your grade-point average?"

"Um, three point seven, sir?"

He looks at me, his lips scrunched up, and nods slowly. "Acceptable," he says, and then smiles.

"Dad, I don't need your *approval*," I say softly.

"I know," he answers. "But I thought you might like it anyway."

chapter sixteen

four days before his show is supposed to go on, tiny calls
me and tells me he needs to take a mental health day. it's not
just because the show is in chaos. the other will grayson isn't
talking to him. i mean, he's talking to him, but he's not saying
anything. and part of tiny is pissed that o.w.g. is 'pulling this
shit so close to curtain time' and part of him seems really,
really afraid that something is really, really wrong.

> me: what can i do? i'm the wrong will grayson.
> tiny: i just need a will grayson fix. i'll be at your school
> in an hour. i'm already on the road.
> me: you're what?
> tiny: you just have to tell me where your school is. i
> google-mapped it, but those directions always suck.
> and the last thing my mental health day needs is to
> be google-mapped into iowa at ten in the morning.

i think the idea of a 'mental health day' is something
completely invented by people who have no clue what it's
like to have bad mental health. the idea that your mind
can be aired out in twenty-four hours is kind of like say-

ing heart disease can be cured if you eat the right breakfast cereal. mental health days only exist for people who have the luxury of saying 'i don't want to deal with things today' and then can take the whole day off, while the rest of us are stuck fighting the fights we always fight, with no one really caring one way or another, unless we choose to bring a gun to school or ruin the morning announcements with a suicide.

i don't say any of this to tiny. i pretend that i want him here. i don't let him know how freaked out i am about him seeing more of my life. it seems to me that he's cross-wired on his will graysons. i'm not sure i'm the one who can help him.

it's gotten so intense — more intense than it was with isaac. and not just because tiny is real. i don't know what freaks me out more — that i matter to him, or that he matters to me.

i tell gideon right away about tiny's visit, mostly because he's the only person in the school who i've really talked to about tiny.

gideon: wow, it's sweet that he wants to see you.
me: i hadn't even thought of that.
gideon: most guys will drive over an hour for sex. but
    only a few will drive over an hour just to see you.
me: how do you know this?

it's sort of strange that gideon's become my go-to gay guy, since he's told me the most play he's ever gotten was at boy scout camp the summer before ninth grade. but i guess he's been to enough blogs and chat rooms and things. oh, and he watches hbo-on-demand all the time. i am constantly telling him that i'm not sure the laws of *sex and the city* apply when there's no sex and there's no city, but then he looks at me like i'm throwing spiked darts at the heart-shaped helium balloons that populate his mind, so i let it go.

the funny thing is that most of the school — well, the part that cares, which is not that huge — thinks gideon and i are a couple. because, you know, they see gay me walking in the halls with gay him, and they immediately assume.

i will say this, though — i kind-of don't mind it. because gideon is really cute, and really friendly, and the people who don't beat him up seem to like him a lot. so if i'm going to have a hypothetical boyfriend in this school, i could do much worse.

still, it's weird to think of gideon and tiny finally meeting. it's weird to think of tiny walking the halls with me. it's like inviting godzilla to the prom.

i can't picture it . . . but then i get a text that he's two minutes away, and i have to face facts.

i basically just leave mr. jones's physics class in the middle of a lab — he never really notices me, anyway, so as long as my lab partner, lizzie, covers for me, i'm set. i tell lizzie the truth — that my boyfriend is sneaking into the school to meet me — and she becomes my accomplice, because even if she wouldn't ordinarily do it for me, she'll definitely do it for LOVE. (well, LOVE and gay rights — three cheers for straight girls who max out on helping gay guys.)

the only person who gives me grief is maura, who snorts out a black cloud when i explain my story to lizzie. she's been trying to fuck up my silent treatment by eavesdropping on me whenever she can. i don't know whether the snort is because she thinks i'm making it up or because she's disgusted that i'm mistreating my physics lab. or maybe she's just jealous of lizzie, which is funny because lizzie has acne so bad that it looks like bee stings. but whatever. maura can snort until all the brain-mucus has left her head and pooled at her feet. i will not respond.

i find tiny easily enough in front of the school, shifting from foot to foot. i am not about to start making out with him on school grounds, so i give him a guy-hug (two points of contact! only two!) and tell him that if anyone asks, he should say he's moving to town in the fall and is checking out the school ahead of time.

he's a little different than when i last saw him — tired, i guess. otherwise, though, his mental health seems perfectly fine.

> tiny: so this is where the magic happens?
> me: only if you consider blind enslavement to
>   standardized tests and college applications to
>   be a form of magic.
> tiny: it remains to be seen.
> me: how's the play going?
> tiny: what the chorus lacks in voice, it makes up
>   for in energy.
> me: i can't wait to see it.
> tiny: i can't wait for you to see it.

the bell for lunch rings when we're halfway to the

cafeteria. suddenly, there are people all around us, and they're noticing tiny the same way they'd notice someone who decided to go from class to class on horseback. the other day i was joking with gideon that the reason the school made all of our lockers gray was so kids like me could blend in and make it through the hallways safely. but with tiny, that's not an option. heads turn.

> me: do you always get this much attention?
> tiny: not so much. i guess people notice my
>   extraordinary hugeness more here. do you mind
>   if i hold your hand?

the truth is, i do mind. but i know that since he's my boyfriend, the answer should be that i don't mind at all. he'd probably carry me to class in his arms, if i asked him nicely.

i take his hand, which is big and slippery. but i guess i can't hide the worry on my face, because he takes one look and lets go.

> tiny: never mind.
> me: it's not you. i'm just not a hand-holding-in-
>   hallways kind of guy. not even if you were a girl.
>   not even if you were a cheerleader with big tits.
> tiny: but i *was* a cheerleader with big tits.

i stop and look at him.

> me: you're kidding.
> tiny: only for a few days. i totally ruined the pyramid.

we walk a little farther.

tiny: i suppose putting my hand in your back pocket is
    out of the question?
me: *cough*
tiny: that was a joke.
me: can i at least buy you lunch? maybe there's even a
    casserole!

i have to keep reminding myself that this is what i wanted
— this is what everybody is supposed to want. here's a boy
who wants to be affectionate with me. a boy who will get in
his car and drive to see me. a boy who isn't afraid of what
everyone else is going to think when they see us together. a
boy who thinks i can improve his mental health.

one of the lunch ladies actually laughs when tiny gets
all gleeful about the empanadas that they're serving in celebration of latino heritage week (or maybe it's latino heritage
month). she calls him sweetie when she hands it to him,
which is pretty funny, since i've spent the last three years
trying to win her over enough to stop getting the smallest
piece of pizza from the tray.

when we get to the table, derek and simon are already
there — gideon's the only one missing. since i haven't warned
them about our special guest star, they look surprised and
petrified when we walk over.

me: derek and simon, this is tiny. tiny, this is derek and
    simon.
tiny: lovely to meet you!

simon: ermm . . .

derek: nice to meet you, too. who are you?

tiny: i'm will's boyfriend. from evanston.

okay, now they're looking at him like he's a magical beast from world of warcraft. derek's amused, in a friendly way. simon is looking at tiny, then looking at me, then looking at tiny, in a way that can only mean that he's wondering how someone so big and someone so wiry can have sex.

i feel a hand on my shoulder.

gideon: there you are!

gideon seems to be the only person in the school who doesn't seem shocked by tiny's appearance. without missing a beat, he leans his other hand out to shake.

gideon: you must be tiny.

tiny looks at the hand gideon has on my shoulder before shaking the hand that gideon's offered. he doesn't sound too happy when he says

tiny: . . . and you must be gideon.

his handshake has to be a little firmer than usual, since gideon actually winces before it's through. then he leaves to pull up an extra chair to the table, offering tiny the place where he usually sits.

tiny: now, isn't this cozy?

well, no. the smell of his beef empanada makes me feel like i'm locked in a small, warm room full of dog food. simon, i fear, is on the verge of saying something wrong, and derek looks like he's going to blog about the whole thing. gideon starts asking tiny friendly questions, and tiny keeps giving one-word answers.

gideon: how was the traffic getting here?
tiny: fine.
gideon: is this a lot like your school?
tiny: meh.
gideon: i hear you're putting on a musical.
tiny: yup.

finally, gideon gets up to buy a cookie, allowing me to lean over to tiny and ask

me: why are you treating him like someone who
    dumped you?
tiny: i'm not!
me: you don't even know him.
tiny: i know his type.
me: what type?
tiny: the wispy cute type. they're *poison*.

i think he knows he's gone a little too far there, because he immediately adds

tiny: but he seems really nice.

he looks around the cafeteria.

tiny: which one's maura?

me: two tables to the left of the door. sitting by herself,
poor slaughtered lamb. scribbling in her notebook.

as if sensing our glance, she looks up in our direction,
then puts her head down and scribbles more furiously.

derek: how is the beef empanada? in all my years here,
you're the first person i've ever seen finish it.

tiny: not bad, if you don't mind salty. it's like someone
made a pop-tart out of beef jerky.

simon: and how long have the two of you been, like,
together?

tiny: i dunno? four weeks, two days, and eighteen
hours, i think.

simon: so you're the guy.

tiny: what guy?

simon: the guy who almost lost us the mathletic
competition.

tiny: if that's true, then i'm very sorry.

simon: well, you know what they say.

derek: simon?

simon: gay guys always put dicks before math.

me: in the whole history of the world, no one has ever
said that.

derek: you're just upset that the girl from naperville —

simon: don't go there!

derek: — wouldn't sit on your lap when you asked her to.

simon: it was a crowded bus!

gideon comes back with cookies for all of us.

gideon: it's a special occasion. what did i miss?

me: dicks before math.

gideon: that makes no sense.

me: exactly.

tiny is starting to fidget, and he's not even touching his cookie. it's a soft cookie. with chocolate chips. it should be in his digestive system by now.

if tiny's losing his appetite, there's no way we're going to make it through the rest of the school day. it's not like i have any desire to go to class — why would tiny? if he wants to be with me, i should be with him. and this school will never let me.

me: let's leave.

tiny: but i just got here.

me: you have just met the only people i ever interact
    with. you have sampled our fine cuisine. if you'd
    like, i can show you the trophy case on the way
    out so you can bask in the achievements of the
    alumni who are now old enough to be suffering
    from erectile dysfunction, memory loss, and death. i
    am never, ever, going to be able to display affection
    for you here, but if you get me in private, it will be
    another matter entirely.

tiny: dicks before math.

me: yes. dicks before math. even though i already had
    math class today. i'll skip it retroactively to be with
    you.

derek: go! go!

tiny seems very pleased by this turn of events.

tiny: i'll have you all to myself?

this is borderline embarrassing to admit in front of other people, so i just nod.

we gather our trays and say our good-byes. gideon looks a little bummed, but sounds sincere when he tells tiny he hopes we'll all get a chance to hang out later. tiny says he hopes so, too, but not like he means it.

as we're about to leave the cafeteria, tiny says he needs to make one more stop.

tiny: there's something i have to do.
me: the restroom's down that hallway, to the left.

but that's not his destination.
he's heading straight for maura's table.

me: what are you doing? we don't talk to her.
tiny: you might not — but i have a thing or two i'd
    like to say.

she's looking up at us now.

me: stop.
tiny: step aside, grayson. i know what i'm doing.

she makes a big production of putting down her pen and closing her notebook.

me: don't, tiny.

but he steps forward and hovers over her. the mountain has come to maura, and it has something to say.

there's a flash of nervousness across tiny's face before he begins. he takes a deep breath. she looks at him with a studied blankness.

> tiny: i just wanted to come over and thank you. i'm
> tiny cooper, and i've been dating this will grayson
> for four weeks, two days, and eighteen hours now.
> if you hadn't been such an evil, selfish, deceitful,
> vindictive frenemy to him, we would have never
> met. it just goes to show, if you try to ruin
> someone's life, it only gets better. you just don't
> get to be a part of it.
> me: tiny, enough.
> tiny: i think she needs to know what she's missing,
> will. i think she needs to know how happy —
> me: ENOUGH!

a lot of people hear it. tiny certainly does, because he stops. and maura certainly does, because she stops staring blankly at him and starts staring blankly at me. i am so mad at both of them right now. i take tiny by the hand, but this time it's to pull him away. maura smirks at that, then opens her notebook and starts writing again. i make it to the door, then let go of tiny's hand, head back to maura's table, grab the notebook, and rip out the page that she's writing on. i don't even read it. i just rip it out and crumple it up and then throw the notebook back on the table, knocking over her diet coke. i don't say a word. i just leave.

i am so angry i can't speak. tiny is behind me, saying

tiny: what? what did i do?

i wait until we're out of the building. i wait until we're in the parking lot. i wait until he's led me to his car. i wait until we're inside the car. i wait until i feel i can open my mouth without screaming. And then i say:

me: you really shouldn't have done that.
tiny: why?
me: WHY? because i'm not talking to her. because i've managed to avoid her for a month, and now you just dragged me over to her and made her feel like she matters in my life.
tiny: she needed to be taught a lesson.
me: what lesson? that if she tries to ruin someone's life, *it only gets better*? that's a great lesson, tiny. now she can try to ruin more people's lives, because at least she'll have the satisfaction of knowing she's doing them a favor. maybe she can even start a matchmaking service. clearly, it worked for us.
tiny: stop it.
me: stop what?
tiny: stop talking to me like i'm stupid. i'm not stupid.
me: i know you're not stupid. but you sure as hell did a stupid thing.

he hasn't even started the car yet. we're still sitting in the parking lot.

tiny: this isn't how the day was supposed to go.
me: well, you know what? a lot of the time, you have
    no control over how your day goes.
tiny: stop. please. i want this to be a nice day.

he starts the car. it's my turn to take a deep breath. who
the hell wants to be the one to tell a kid that santa claus isn't
real. it's the truth, right? but you're still a jerk for saying it.

tiny: let's go somewhere you like to go. where should
    we go? take me somewhere that matters to you.
me: like what?
tiny: like . . . i don't know. for me, if i need to feel
    better, i go alone to super target. i don't know why,
    but seeing all of those things makes me happy.
    it's probably the design. i don't even have to buy
    anything. just seeing all the people together, seeing
    all the things i *could* buy — all the colors, aisle
    after aisle — sometimes i need that. for jane, it's
    this indie record store we'll go to so she can look
    at old vinyl while i look at all the boy band cds
    in the two-dollar bin and try to figure out which
    one i think is the cutest. or the other will grayson
    — there's this park in our town, where all the little
    league teams play. and he loves the dugout, because
    when no one else is around, it's really quiet there.
    when there's not a game on, you can sit there and
    all that exists are the things that happened in the
    past. i think everyone has a place like that. you
    must have a place like that.

i think hard about it for a second, but i figure if i had a place like that, i'd know it right away. but no place really matters to me. it didn't even occur to me that i was supposed to have a place that mattered to me.

i shake my head.

me: nothing.

tiny: c'mon. there has to be someplace.

me: there isn't, okay? just my house. my room. that's it.

tiny: fine — then where's the nearest swing set?

me: are you kidding me?

tiny: no. there has to be a swing set around here.

me: at the elementary school, i guess. but school isn't out yet. if they catch us there, they'll think we're kidnappers. i'll be okay, but i bet you'd be tried as an adult.

tiny: okay, besides the elementary school.

me: i think my neighbors have one.

tiny: do the parents work?

me: i think so.

tiny: and the kids are still in school. perfect! lead the way.

this is how we end up parking in front of my house and breaking into my next-door neighbor's yard. The swing set is pretty sad, as swing sets go, but at least it's made for older kids, not toddlers.

me: you're not actually going to sit on that, are you?

but he does. and i swear the metal frame bends a little. he gestures to the swing next to his.

tiny: join me.

it's probably been ten years since i sat on a swing. i only do it to shut tiny up for a second. neither of us actually swings — i don't think the frame could take that. we just sit there, dangling over the ground. tiny twists around so he's facing me. i twist, too, putting my feet on the ground to prevent the chain from unwinding me.

tiny: now, isn't this better?

and i can't help it. i say

me: better than what?

tiny laughs and shakes his head.

me: what? why are you shaking your head.
tiny: it's nothing.
me: tell me.
tiny: it's just funny.
me: WHAT'S funny?
tiny: you. and me.
me: i'm glad you find it funny.
tiny: i wish you'd find it funnier.

i don't even know what we're talking about anymore.

tiny: you know what's a great metaphor for love?
me: i have a feeling you're about to tell me.

he turns away and makes an attempt to swing high. the swing set groans so much that he stops and twists back my way.

tiny: sleeping beauty.
me: sleeping beauty?
tiny: yes, because you have to plow through this
    incredible thicket of thorns in order to get to
    beauty, and even then, when you get there, you
    still have to wake her up.
me: so i'm a thicket?
tiny: and the beauty that isn't fully awake yet.

i don't point out that tiny is hardly what little girls think of when you say the words *prince charming*.

me: it figures you'd think that way.
tiny: why?
me: well, your life is a musical. literally.
tiny: do you hear me singing now?

i almost do. i'd love to live in his musical cartoon world, where witches like maura get vanquished with one heroic word, and all the forest creatures are happy when two gay guys walk hand-in-hand through the meadow, and gideon is the himbo suitor you know the princess can't marry, because her heart belongs to the beast. i'm sure it's a lovely world, where these things happen. a rich, spoiled, colorful world. maybe one day i'll get to visit, but i doubt it. worlds like that don't tend to issue visas to fuckups like me.

> me: it puzzles me how someone like you could drive all this way to be with someone like me.
>
> tiny: not that again!
>
> me: excuse me?
>
> tiny: we're always having this conversation. but if you keep focusing on why you have it so bad, you'll never realize how you could have it so good.
>
> me: easy for you to say!
>
> tiny: what do you mean?
>
> me: pretty much exactly that. i'll break it down for you. *easy* — with no difficulty whatsoever. *for you* — the opposite of 'for me.' *to say* — to vocalize, sometimes ad nauseam. you have it so good that you don't realize that when you have it bad, it's not a choice you're making.
>
> tiny: i know that. i wasn't saying . . .
>
> me: yes?
>
> tiny: i do understand.
>
> me: you DON'T understand. because you have it so easy.

now i've riled him up. he steps out of the swing and stands right in front of me. there's a vein in his neck that's actually pulsing. he can't look angry without also looking sad.

> tiny: STOP TELLING ME I HAVE IT SO EASY! do you have any idea what you're talking about?

because i'm a person, too. and i have problems, too. and even though they might not be your problems, they're still problems.

me: like what?

tiny: you may not have noticed, but i'm not what you'd call conventionally beautiful. in fact, you might say that i'm the opposite of that. *say,* you know — to vocalize, sometimes ad nauseam? do you think that there's any minute in any day when i'm not aware of how big i am? do you think there's a single minute that goes by when i'm not thinking about how other people see me? even though i have no control whatsoever over that? don't get me wrong — i love my body. but i'm not so much of an idiot to think that everybody else loves it. what really gets to me — what *really* bothers me — is that it's all people see. ever since i was a not-so-little kid. *hey, tiny, want to play football? hey, tiny, how many burgers did you eat today? hey, tiny, you ever lose your dick down there? hey, tiny, you're going to join the basketball team whether you like it or not. just don't try to look at us in the locker room!* does that sound easy to you, will?

i'm about to say something, but he holds up his hand.

tiny: you know what? i'm totally at peace with being big-boned. and i was gay long before i knew what sex was. it's just who i am, and that's great. i don't want to be thin or conventionally beautiful or straight or brilliant. no, what i really want — and what i never get — is to be *appreciated*. do you know what it's like to work so hard to make sure everyone's happy, and to have not a single person recognize it? i can work my ass off bringing together the other will grayson and jane — no appreciation, only grief. i write this whole musical that's basically about love, and the main character in it — besides me, of course — is phil wrayson, who needs to figure some things out, but is all-in-all a pretty wonderful guy. and does will get that? no. he freaks out. i do everything i can to be a good boyfriend with you — no appreciation, only grief. i try to make this musical so it can create something, to show that we all have something to sing — no appreciation, only grief. this musical is a gift, will. my gift to the world. it's not about me. it's about what i have to share. there's a difference — i see it, but i am worried that i am the only frickin' one who sees it. you think i have it easy, will? are you really dying to try on these size fifteens? because every morning when i wake up, i have to convince myself that, yes, by the end of the day, i will be able to do something good. that's all i ask — to be able to do something good. not for myself, you whiny shithead bastard complainer who, incidentally, i really, really like. but for my friends. for other people.

me: but why me? i mean, what do you see in me?

tiny: you have a heart, will. you even let it slip out every now and then. i see that in you. and i see that you need me.

i shake my head.

me: don't you get it? i don't need anyone.
tiny: that only means you need me more.

it's so clear to me.

me: you're not in love with me. you're in love with my need.
tiny: who said i was in love with anything? i said 'really, really like.'

he stops now. pauses.

tiny: this always happens. some variation of this always happens.
me: i'm sorry.
tiny: they always say 'i'm sorry,' too.
me: i can't do this, tiny.
tiny: you can, but you won't. you just won't.

it's like i don't have to break up with him, because he's already had the conversation in his head. i should feel relieved that i don't have to say anything. but instead, i only feel worse.

me: it's not your fault. i just can't feel anything.

tiny: really? are you really feeling nothing right now? nothing at all?

i want to tell him: nobody ever told me how to deal with things like this. shouldn't letting go be painless if you've never learned how to hold on?

tiny: i'm going to go now.

and i'm going to stay. i'm going to stay on this swing as he walks away. i'm going to stay silent as he gets in his car. i'm going to stay still as i hear the car start, then drive away. i'm going to stay in the wrong, because i don't know how to get through the thicket of my own mind in order to reach whatever it is that i'm supposed to do. i'm going to stay the same, and the same, and the same, until i die of it.

minutes have to pass before i can admit that, yes, even though i tell myself i'm feeling nothing, it's a lie. i want to say i'm feeling remorse or regret or even guilt. but none of those words seem like enough. what i'm feeling is shame. raw, loathing shame. i don't want to be the person i am. i don't want to be the person who just did what i did.

it's not even about tiny, really.

i am awful.

i am heartless.

i am scared that these things are actually true.

i run back to my house. i am starting to sob — i'm not even thinking about it, but my body is falling to pieces. my hand is shaking so much that i drop the keys before i finally get them in the door. the house is empty. i am empty. i try to eat. i try to crawl into bed. nothing works. i do feel things. i feel everything. and i need to know i'm not alone. so i'm getting out the phone. i'm not even thinking about it. i'm pressing the number and i'm hearing the ring and as soon as it's answered, i'm shouting into the phone:

me: I LOVE YOU. DO YOU HEAR ME, I LOVE YOU?

i'm screaming it, and it sounds so angry and so frightened and so pathetic and desperate. on the other end of the phone, my mother is asking me what's wrong, where am i, what's happening, and i'm telling her that i'm at home and that everything's a mess, and she's saying she'll be home in ten minutes, will i be okay for ten minutes? and i want to tell her i'll be okay, because that's what she wants to hear, but then i realize that maybe what she wants to hear is the actual truth, so i tell her that i feel things, i really do, and she tells me of course i do, i always have had these feelings, and that's what makes life hard for me sometimes.

just hearing her voice makes me feel a little better, and i realize that, yes, i appreciate what she's saying, and i appreciate what she's doing, and that i need to let her know that. although i don't say it right away, since i think that will only worry her more, but when she gets home i say it to her, and she says she knows.

i tell her a little about tiny, and she says it sounds like we were putting too much pressure on ourselves, and that it doesn't have to be love immediately, or even love eventually. i want to ask her which it was with my father, and when it was that everything turned into hate and sadness. but maybe i don't really want to know. not right now.

> mom: need is never a good basis for any relationship. it
> has to be much more than that.

it's good to talk to her, but it's also strange, because she's my mom, and i don't want to be one of these kids who thinks his mom's his best friend. by the time i've recovered enough, school is long over, and i figure i can go online and see if gideon's there. then i realize i can text him instead. then i realize that i can actually call him. finally, i realize i can actually call him and see if he wants to do something. because he's my friend, and that's what friends do.

i call, he answers. i need him, he answers. i go over to his house and tell him what's happened, and he answers. it's not like it was with maura, who always wanted to take the dark road. it's not like it was with tiny, because with him i was feeling all these expectations to be a good boyfriend, whatever that is. no, gideon's ready to believe both the best and the worst in me. in other words: the truth.

when we're done talking, he asks me if i'm going to call tiny. i tell him i don't know.

it's not until later that i decide. i'm on IM, and i see he's on, too.

i don't really think i can salvage us being boyfriends, but at the very least i want to tell him that even if he was wrong about me, he wasn't wrong about himself. i mean, someone should be trying to do good in the world.

so i try.

8:15pm
willupleasebequiet: bluejeanbaby?
willupleasebequiet: tiny?

8:18pm
willupleasebequiet: are you there?

9:33pm
willupleasebequiet: are you there?

10:10pm
willupleasebequiet: please?

11:45pm
willupleasebequiet: are you there?

1:03am
willupleasebequiet: are you there?
willupleasebequiet: are you there?
willupleasebequiet: are you there?
willupleasebequiet: are you there?
willupleasebequiet: are you there?

chapter seventeen

Three days before the play, Tiny and I are talking again as we wait for precalc to start, but there's nothing inside our words. He sits down next to me and says, "Hey, Grayson," and I say, "Hey," and he says, "What's new?" and I say, "Not much, you?" and he says, "Not much. The play is kicking my ass, man," and I say, "I bet," and he says, "You're dating Jane, huh?" and I say, "Sorta, yeah," and he says, "That's awesome," and I say, "Yeah. How's the other Will Grayson," and he says, "Fine," and that's it. Honestly, talking to him is worse than not. Talking to him makes me feel like I'm drowning in lukewarm water.

Jane's standing by my locker with her hands behind her back when I get there after first period, and when I get to her, there's this awkward but not unpleasant should-we-kiss moment, or at least I think that's what the moment is, but then she says, "Sucks about Tiny, huh?"

"What does?" I ask.

"He and the other Will Grayson. Kaput."

I tilt my head at her, baffled. "No, he just said they were fine. I asked him in precalc."

"Happened yesterday, at least according to Gary and Nick and the twenty-three other people who told me about it. On a swing set, apparently. Oh, the metaphorical resonance."

"Then why didn't he tell me?" I hear my voice catch as I say it.

Jane grabs my hand and stands up to say into my ear, "Hey," and then I look back at her, trying to act like it doesn't matter. "Hey," she says again.

"Hey," I say.

"Just go back to normal with him, huh? Just *talk* to him, Will. I don't know if you've noticed, but everything goes better for you when you talk to people."

"You wanna come over after school?" I ask.

"Absolutely." She smiles, then spins a half-circle in place and walks off. She takes a few steps before turning back and saying, "Talk. To. Tiny."

For a while, I just stand there at my locker. Even after the bell rings. I know why he didn't tell me: it isn't because he feels weird that for the first time in human history, he's single and I'm taken(ish). He said the other Will Grayson was fine because I don't matter.

Tiny might ignore you when he's in love. But when Tiny Cooper lies to you about his heartbreak, the Geiger counter has tripped the hammer. The radiation has been released. The friendship is dead.

That day after school Jane's at my house, sitting across a Scrabble board from me. I spell *hallow*, which is a great word but also opens up a triple-word-score spot for her.

"Oh my God, I love you," she says, and it must be close enough to true, because if she'd said that a week before I wouldn't have thought anything of it, and now it hangs in the air forever until she finally bursts the awkwardness by saying, "That would be a weird thing to say to someone you just started dating! Boy-howdy, is this awkward!" After a moment of silence, she keeps going, "Hey, to extend the weird, are we dating?"

And the word turns my stomach a little and I say, "Can we be not not-dating?"

She smiles and spells *cowed* for thirty-six points. It's absolutely amazing, the whole thing. Her shoulder blades are amazing. Her passionately ironic love for 1980s television dramas is amazing. The way she laughs at my jokes really loudly is amazing—all of which only makes it more amazing that she doesn't fill the Tiny hole left by his absence.

To be perfectly honest, I felt it last semester when he went off to become the GSA president and I fell into the Group of Friends. Probably that's why I wrote the letter to the editor and signed it. Not because I wanted the school to know I'd written it, but because I wanted Tiny to know.

The next day, Mom drops me off early. I go in and slip a note in Jane's locker, which I've gotten in the habit of doing. It's always just a line or two that I found from some poem in the gigantic poetry anthology my sophomore English teacher taught from. I said I wouldn't be the kind of boyfriend who reads her poetry, and I'm not, but I guess I am the kind of cheesy bastard who slips lines of poetry into her mornings.

Today's: I see thee better in the dark / I do not need a
light. —Emily Dickinson

And then I settle into my precalc seat twenty minutes
early. I try to study a little for chem but give up within
twenty seconds. I get out my phone and check my email.
Nothing. I keep looking over at his empty chair, the chair
he fills with a completeness unimaginable to the rest of us.

I decide to write him an email, thumbing it out on my
tiny keyboard. I'm just passing time, really. I keep using un-
necessarily long words because they make the writing soak
up the minutes.

*it's not like i feel some urgent desire to be friends, but
i wish we could be one thing or the other. this, even
though rationally i know that your departure from my
life is a bountiful blessing, that on most days you are
nothing but a 300-pound burden shackled to me, and
that you clearly never liked me. i always complained
about you and your general hugeness, and now i miss
it. typical guy, you'd say. they don't know what they've
got till it's gone. and maybe you're right, tiny. i'm sorry
about will grayson. both of us.*

The first bell finally rings. I save the email as a draft.

Tiny sits down next to me and says, "Hey, Grayson,"
and I say, "Hey, how's it going?" and he says, "Good, man.
Dress rehearsal today," and I say, "Awesome," and he says,
"What's going on with you?" and I say, "This paper for
English is killing me," and he says, "Yeah, my grades are in
the tank," and I say, "Yeah," and the second bell rings and
we turn our attention to Mr. Applebaum.

• • •

Four hours later: I'm in the middle of the line of people rushing out of the physics classroom fifth period when I see Tiny walking past the window. He stops, dramatically pivots toward the door, and waits for me.

"We broke up," he says matter-of-factly.

"So I heard. Thanks for letting me know—after telling everyone else."

"Yeah, well," he says. People weave around us like we're a blood clot in the hallway's artery. "Rehearsal's gonna go late—we're gonna do a run-through after dress—but you wanna get some late-night dinner? Hot Dog Palace or something?"

I consider it a minute, thinking about the unsent email in my drafts folder, and the other Will Grayson, and Tiny up onstage telling me the truth behind my back, and then I say, "I don't think so. I'm tired of being your Plan B, Tiny."

It doesn't faze him, of course. "Well, I guess I'll see you at the play then."

"I don't know if I can make it, but yeah, I'll try."

It's hard to read Tiny's face for some reason, but I think I've gotten a shot in. I don't know exactly why I want to make him feel like crap, but I do.

I'm walking to Jane's locker to find her when she comes up behind me and says, "Can I talk to you for a minute?"

"You can talk to me for billions of minutes." I smile.

We duck into an abandoned Spanish classroom. She spins a chair around and sits, the chair's back like a shield. She's wearing a tight T-shirt underneath a peacoat, which she presently takes off, and she looks awfully good, good enough that I wonder aloud if we can't talk at home.

"I get distracted at your house." She raises her eyebrows and smiles, but I see the fake in it. "You said yesterday that we were not not-dating, and like it's not a big deal, and I realize that it has been one week and one week only, but I actually don't want to not not-date you; I want to be your girlfriend or not, and I would think by now you're qualified to make at least a temporary decision on the topic, because I know I am."

She looks down for a second, and I notice her hair parted in the middle has an accidental zigzag at the top of her head, and I inhale to talk, but then she says, "Also, I'm not going to be *devastated* or anything either way. I'm not that kind of person. I just think if you don't *say* the honest thing, sometimes the honest thing never becomes true, you know, and I—" she says, but then I hold up my finger, because I need to hear the thing she just said, and she talks too fast for me to keep up. I keep holding up my hand, thinking *if you don't say the honest thing, it never becomes true.*

I put my hands on her shoulders. "I just realized something. I really really like you. You're amazing, and I so want to be your boyfriend, because of what you just said, and also because that shirt makes me want to take you home now and do unspeakable things while we watch live-action Sailor Moon videos. But but but you're totally right about saying the honest thing. I think if you keep the box closed long enough you do kill the cat, actually. And—God, I hope you won't take this personally—but I love my best friend more than anyone in the world."

She's looking at me now, squinting confusion.

"I do. I fucking love Tiny Cooper."

Jane says, "Um, okay. Are you asking me to be your girl-friend, or are you telling me that you're gay?"

"The first one. The girlfriend one. I gotta go find Tiny."

I stand up and kiss her on the zigzag and then bolt.

I call him while running across the soccer field, holding down 1 to speed dial. He doesn't pick up, but I think I know where he thinks I'm going, so I go there.

Once I see the park to my left, I slow to a fast-walk, heaving breaths, my shoulders burning beneath the backpack straps. Everything depends upon him being in the dugout, and it's so unlikely that he would go there, three days before the opening of the play, and as I walk, I start to feel like an idiot: His phone is off because he's in rehearsal, and I ran *here* instead of running to the auditorium, which means that now I am going to have to run *back* to the auditorium, and my lungs were not designed for such rigorous use.

I slow further when I hit the park, half because I'm out of breath and half because so long as I can't see into the dugout, he's there and he isn't. I watch this couple walking on the lawn, knowing that they can see into the dugout, trying to tell from their eyes whether they see a gigantic someone sitting in the visitors' dugout of this Little League field. But their eyes give me nothing, and I just watch them as they hold hands and walk.

Finally, the dugout comes into view. And damned if he isn't sitting right in the middle of that wooden bench.

I walk over. "Don't you have dress rehearsal?" He doesn't say anything until I sit down next to him on the cold wooden bench.

"They need a run-through without me. Otherwise, they may mutiny. We'll do the dress a little later tonight."

"So, what brings you to the visitors' dugout?"

"You remember after I first came out, you used to say, instead of like saying, 'Tiny plays for the other team,' you'd say, 'Tiny plays for the White Sox.'"

"Yeah. Is that homophobic?" I ask.

"Nah," he says. "Well, probably it is, but it didn't bother me. Anyway, I want to apologize."

"For what?"

Apparently, I've uttered the magic words, because Tiny takes a deep breath before he starts talking, as if—fancy this—he has a lot to say. "For not saying to your face what I said to Gary. I'm not gonna apologize for saying it, because it's true. You and your damn rules. And you do get tag-alongy sometimes, and there's something a little Drama Queeny about your anti-Drama Queenyness, and I know I'm difficult but so are you and your whole put-upon act gets really old, and also you are so self-involved."

"Said the pot to the kettle," I say, trying not to get pissed. Tiny is awfully talented at puncturing the love bubble I felt for him. Perhaps, I think, this is why he gets dumped so much.

"Ha! True. True. I'm not saying I'm innocent. I'm saying you're guilty, too."

The couple walks out of my view. And then finally I feel ready to banish the quiver Tiny apparently thinks is weakness. I stand up so he has to look at me, and so I have to look at him, and for once, I'm taller. "I love you," I say.

He tilts his fat lovable head like a confused puppy.

"You are a terrible best friend," I tell him. "Terrible!

You totally ditch me every time you have a boyfriend, and then you come crawling back when you're heartbroken. You don't listen to me. You don't even seem to *like* me. You get obsessed with the play and totally ignore me except to insult me to our friend behind my back, and you exploit your life and the people you say you care about so that your little play can make people love you and think how awesome you are and how liberated you are and how wondrously gay you are, but you know what? Being gay is not an excuse for being a dick.

"But you're one on my speed dial and I want you to stay there and I'm sorry I'm a terrible best friend, too, and I love you."

He won't stop it with the turned head. "Grayson, are you coming out to me? Because I'm, I mean, don't take this personally, but I would sooner go straight than go gay with you."

"NO. No no no. I don't want to *screw* you. I just *love* you. When did who you want to screw become the whole game? Since when is the person you want to screw the only person you get to love? It's so stupid, Tiny! I mean, Jesus, who even gives a fuck about sex?! People act like it's the most important thing humans do, but come on. How can our sentient fucking lives revolve around something *slugs* can do. I mean, who you want to screw and whether you screw them? Those are important questions, I guess. But they're not *that* important. You know what's important? Who would you *die* for? Who do you wake up at five forty-five in the morning for even though you don't even know why he needs you? Whose drunken nose would you pick?!"

I'm shouting, my arms whirling with gesticulations, and I don't even notice until I run out of important questions that Tiny is crying. And then softly, the softest I've ever heard Tiny say anything, he says, "If you could write a play about anybody . . ." and then his voice trails off.

I sit down next to him, put my arm around him. "Are you okay?"

Somehow, Tiny Cooper manages to contort himself so that his massive head cries on my narrow shoulder. And after a while he says, "Long week. Long month. Long life."

He recovers quickly, wiping his eyes with the popped collar of the polo shirt he's wearing beneath a striped sweater. "When you date someone, you have the markers along the way, right: You kiss, you have The Talk, you say the Three Little Words, you sit on a swing set and break up. You can plot the points on a graph. And you check up with each other along the way: Can I do this? If I say this, will you say it back?

"But with friendship, there's nothing like that. Being in a relationship, that's something you choose. Being friends, that's just something you are."

I just stare out at the ball field for a minute. Tiny sniffles. "I'd pick you," I say. "Fuck it, I *do* pick you. I want you to come over to my house in twenty years with your dude and your adopted kids and I want our fucking kids to hang out and I want to, like, drink wine and talk about the Middle East or whatever the fuck we're gonna want to do when we're old. We've been friends too long to pick, but if we could pick, I'd pick you."

"Yeah, okay. You're getting a little feelingsy, Grayson," he says. "It's kinda freaking me out."

"Got it."

"Like, don't ever say you love me again."

"But I do love you. I'm not embarrassed about it."

"Seriously, Grayson, stop it. You're making me throw up in the back of my mouth a little."

I laugh. "Can I help with the play?"

Tiny reaches into his pocket and produces a neatly folded piece of notebook paper and hands it to me. "I thought you'd never ask," he says, smirking.

Will (and to a lesser extent Jane),

Thank you for your interest in assisting me in the run-up to *Hold Me Closer*. I would greatly appreciate it if you would both be backstage opening night to assist with costume changes and to generally calm cast members (okay, let's just say it: me). Also, you'll have an excellent view of the play.

Also, the Phil Wrayson costume is excellent as is, but it'd be even better if we had some Will Grayson-ish clothes for Gary to wear.

Furthermore, I thought I would have time to make a preshow mix in which the odd-numbered tracks are punk rock and the even-numbered tracks are from musicals. I will not, in fact, have time to do this; if you do, it would be truly fabulous.

You are a cute couple, and it was my distinct pleasure to set you up, and I do not in any way resent either of you for failing to have thanked me for making your love possible.

I remain . . .

Your faithful matchmaker and servant . . .

Toiling alone and newly single in an ocean of pain
so that some light may be brought into your lives . . .
Tiny Cooper

I laugh while I read it, and Tiny laughs, too, nodding his head, appreciating his own awesome.

"I'm sorry about the other Will Grayson," I say.

His smile folds in upon itself. His response seems directed more toward my namesake than me. "There's never been anybody like him."

I don't trust the words as he says them, but then he exhales through pursed lips, his sad eyes squinting at the distance, and I believe him.

"I should probably get started on this, eh? Thanks for the backstage invite."

He gets up and starts nodding like he sometimes does, the repetitive nodding that tells me he's convincing himself of something. "Yeah, I should get back to infuriating the cast and crew with my tyrannical direction."

"I'll see you tomorrow then," I say.

"And all the other days," he says, patting me too hard between the shoulder blades.

chapter eighteen

i start holding my breath. not like you do when you pass a graveyard or something like that. no. i'm trying to see how long i can do it before i pass out or die. it's a really convenient pastime — you can do it pretty much anywhere. class. lunch. at the urinal. in the discomfort of your own room.

the sucky part is that the moment always comes when i take the next breath. i can only push myself so far.

i've given up on hearing from tiny. i hurt him, he hates me — it's as simple as that. and now that he's not texting me, i realize that no one else texts me. or messages me. or cares.

now that he isn't into me, i realize that no one else is all that into me, either.

okay, so there's gideon. he's not much of a texter or a messager, but when we're at school, he's always asking me how things are going. and i always stop not-breathing in order to answer him. sometimes i even tell the truth.

> me: seriously, is this what the rest of my life is going to be? i don't think i signed up for this.

i know it sounds like teenage idiocy — the needles! in my heart! and my eyes! — but the pattern seems inescapable. i am never going to get better at being a good person. i am always going to be the blood and shit of things.

gideon: just breathe.

and i wonder how he knows to say that.

the only time that i pretend i have it all together is when maura's around. i don't want her to see me falling apart. worst case scenario: she stomps on all the pieces. worse-than-that case scenario: she tries to put them together again. i realize: i am now where she was with me. on the other side of the silence. you'd think that silence would be peaceful. but really, it's painful.

at home, mom is keeping close watch on me. which makes me feel worse, because now i'm putting her through it, too.

that night — the night i screwed everything up with tiny — she hid the glass bowl he gave her. while i was asleep, she put it away. and the stupid thing was, when i saw it was gone, the first thing i thought was that she was afraid i'd smash it. then i realized she was only trying to protect me from seeing it, from getting upset.

at school, i ask gideon

me: why is it *up*set? shouldn't it be *down*set?
gideon: i will file a lawsuit against the dictionaries first
      thing tomorrow morning. we're going to tear merriam
      a new asshole and throw webster inside of it.

me: you are such a dork.
gideon: only if you catch me on a good day.

i don't tell gideon that i feel guilty being around him.
because what if the threat tiny felt turns out to be true?
what if i was cheating on him without knowing it?

me: can you cheat on someone without knowing it?

i am not asking gideon this. i am asking my mother.
she has been so careful with me. she has been tiptoeing
around my moods, acting like everything's okay. but now
she just freezes.

mom: why are you asking me that? did you cheat on tiny?

and i'm thinking, oh shit, i should not have asked that
question.

me: no. i didn't. why are you so mad?
mom: nothing.
me: no, why? did dad cheat on you?

she shakes her head.

me: did you cheat on dad?

she sighs.

mom: no. it's not that. it's . . . i don't want you to ever be
    a cheater. not on people. sometimes it's okay to cheat

on things – but don't ever cheat on people. because once you start, it's very hard to stop. you find out how easy it is to do.

me: mom?

mom: that's all. why are you asking?

me: no reason. just wondering.

i've been wondering a lot lately. sometimes, when i'm passing the minute mark on holding my breath, besides imagining being dead, i'm also imagining what tiny is doing. sometimes i picture the other will grayson there. most of the time, they're onstage. but i can never understand what they're singing.

and the weird thing is, i'm thinking about isaac again. and maura. and how weird it is that it was a lie that made me happiest.

tiny doesn't respond to any of my instant messages. then, the night before the musical, i decide to type in the other will grayson's screenname. and there he is. it's not like i think he'll completely understand. yeah, we have the same name, but it's not like we're psychic twins. it's not like he'll wince in pain if i burn myself or anything. but that one night in chicago, i felt he understood a little of it. and, yeah, i also want to see if tiny's okay.

willupleasebequiet: hey

willupleasebequiet: it's will grayson.

willupleasebequiet: the other one.

WGrayson7: wow. hello.

willupleasebequiet: is this okay? me talking to you.

WGrayson7: yeah. what are you doing up at 1:33:48?

willupleasebequiet: waiting to see if 1:33:49 is any
    better. you?

WGrayson7: if i'm not mistaken, i just saw, via webcam,
    a revised musical number that involved oscar wilde's
    ghost, live from the bedroom of the musical's

WGrayson7: director-writer-star-etc-etc

willupleasebequiet: how was it?

willupleasebequiet: no.

willupleasebequiet: i mean, how is he?

WGrayson7: truth?

willupleasebequiet: yes.

WGrayson7: i don't think i've ever seen him more
    nervous. and not because he's the director-writer-
    star-etc-etc. but because it means so much to him,
    you know? he really thinks he can change the
    world.

willupleasebequiet: i can imagine.

WGrayson7: sorry, it's late. and i'm not even sure if i
    should be talking about tiny with you.

willupleasebequiet: i just checked the bylaws of the
    international society of will graysons, and i can't
    find anything in there about it. we're in vastly
    uncharted territory.

WGrayson7: exactly. here be dragons.

willupleasebequiet: will?

WGrayson7: yes, will.

willupleasebequiet: does he know i'm sorry?

WGrayson7: dunno. in my recent experience, i'd say
    hurt tends to drown out sorry.

willupleasebequiet: i just couldn't be that person for him.

WGrayson7: that person?

willupleasebequiet: the one he really wants.

willupleasebequiet: i just wish it wasn't all trial and error.

willupleasebequiet: because that's what it is, isn't it?

willupleasebequiet: trial and error.

willupleasebequiet: i guess there's a reason they don't call it 'trial and success'

willupleasebequiet: it's just try-error

willupleasebequiet: try-error

willupleasebequiet: try-error

willupleasebequiet: i'm sorry. are you still here?

WGrayson7: yes.

WGrayson7: if you'd caught me two weeks ago, i would have had to agree with you fullheartedly.

WGrayson7: now i'm not so sure.

willupleasebequiet: why?

WGrayson7: well, i agree that 'trial and error' is a pretty pessimistic name for it. and maybe that's what it is most of the time.

WGrayson7: but i think the point is that it's not just try-error.

WGrayson7: most of the time it's try-error-try

WGrayson7: try-error-try

WGrayson7: try-error-try

WGrayson7: and that's how you find it.

willupleasebequiet: it?

WGrayson7: you know. *it.*

willupleasebequiet: yeah, *it.*

willupleasebequiet: try-error-try-*it*

WGrayson7: well . . . i haven't become *that* optimistic.

WGrayson7: it's more like try-error-try-error-try-error-
try-error-try-error-try . . . at least fifteen more
rounds . . . then try-error-try-*it*
willupleasebequiet: i miss him. but not in the way he
would want me to miss him.
WGrayson7: are you coming tomorrow?
willupleasebequiet: i don't think that would be a good
idea. do you?
WGrayson7: it's up to you. it could be another error. or
it could be *it*. just do me a favor and give me a call
first so i can warn him.

that seems fair. he gives me his phone number and i give
him mine. i type it into my phone before i forget. when it asks
for the name to go with the number, i just type *will grayson.*

willupleasebequiet: what's the secret to your wisdom,
will grayson?
WGrayson7: i think it's that i hang out with the right
people, will grayson.
willupleasebequiet: well, thank you for your help.
WGrayson7: i like to be on call for all of my best
friend's ex-boyfriends.
willupleasebequiet: it takes a village to date tiny cooper.
WGrayson7: exactly.
willupleasebequiet: good night, will grayson.
WGrayson7: good night, will grayson.

i want to say this calms me. i want to say i fall immediately to sleep. but the whole night my mind goes
try-error-?

try-error-?
try-error-?

by the morning, i am wreckage. i wake up and i think, *today's the day.* and then i think, *it has nothing to do with me.* it's not like i even helped him with it. it's just that now i'm not getting to see it. i know that's fair, but it doesn't feel fair. it feels like i've screwed myself over.

mom notices my unparalleled self-hatred at breakfast. it's probably the way i drown the cocoa puffs until the milk overflows that tips her off.

mom: will, what's wrong?
me: what isn't?
mom: will . . .
me: it's okay.
mom: no, it's not.
me: how can you tell me it's not? isn't that my choice?

she sits down across from me, puts her hand on my hand even though there's now a puddle of cocoa-colored milk under her wrist.

mom: do you know how much i used to scream?

i have no idea what she's talking about.

me: you don't scream. you fall silent.
mom (shaking her head): even when you were little,

but mostly when your father and i were going through what we went through — there were times when i had to go outside, get in the car, drive around the corner, and scream my head off. i would scream and scream and scream. sometimes just noise. and sometimes curses — every curse you can think of.

me: i can think of a lot of them. did you ever scream 'shitmonger!'

mom: no, but . . .

me: 'fuckweasel!'

mom: will —

me: you should try 'fuckweasel.' it's kinda satisfying.

mom: my point is that there are times when you just have to let it all out. all of the anger, all of the pain.

me: have you thought of talking to someone about this? i mean, i have some pills that might interest you, but i think you're supposed to have a prescription. it's okay — it only takes up an hour of your time for them to diagnose it.

mom: will.

me: sorry. it's just that it's not really anger or pain i'm feeling. just anger at myself.

mom: that's still anger.

me: but don't you feel like that shouldn't count? i mean, not the same as being angry at someone else.

mom: why this morning?

me: what do you mean?

mom: why are you especially angry at yourself this morning?

it's not like i'd been planning on advertising the fact that i'm angry. she kinda traps me into it. i of all people can respect that. so i tell her that today's the day of tiny's musical.

mom: you should go.

now it's my turn to shake my head.

me: no way.
mom: way. and will?
me: yes?
mom: you should also talk to maura.

i bolt down the cocoa puffs before there's any way for her to persuade me. when i get to school, i sail past maura at her perch and try to use the day as a distraction. i try to pay attention in classes, but they are so boring that it's like the teachers are trying to drive me back to my own thoughts. i am afraid of what gideon will say to me if i confide in him, so i try to pretend like it's just an ordinary day, and that i'm not cataloging all of the things i've done wrong over the past few weeks. did i really give tiny a chance? did i give maura a chance? shouldn't i have let him calm me down? shouldn't i have let her explain why she did what she did?

finally, at the end of the day, i can't deal with it on my own anymore, and gideon's the one i want to turn to. part of me is hoping that he'll tell me i have nothing to be ashamed of, that i've done nothing wrong. i find him at his locker and say

me: can you believe it? my mom said i should crash
   tiny's show *and* talk to maura.
gideon: you should.
me: did your sister use your mouth as a crack pipe last
   night? are you insane?
gideon: i don't have a sister.
me: whatever. you know what i'm saying.
gideon: i'll go with you.
me: what?
gideon: i'll borrow my mom's car. do you know where
   tiny's school is?
me: you're joking.

and that's when it happens. it's almost astonishing, really.
gideon becomes a little — just a little — more like me.

gideon: can we just say 'fuck you' to the 'you're joking'
   part? all right? i'm not saying you and tiny should
   be together forever and have huge, depressed
   babies that have periods of manic thinness, but
   i do think the way the two of you left it is pretty
   unhelpful, and i'd bet twenty dollars if i had
   twenty dollars that he is suffering from the same
   waves of crappiness that you're suffering from. or
   he's found a new boyfriend. maybe also named will
   grayson. whatever the case, you are going to be
   this walking, talking *splinter* unless someone takes
   your ass to wherever he is, and in this particular
   case, and in any other particular case where you
   need me, i am that someone. i am the knight with

a shining jetta. i am your fucking steed.

me: gideon, i had no idea . . .

gideon: shut the fuck up.

me: say it again!

gideon (laughing): shut the fuck up!

me: but why?

gideon: why should you shut the fuck up?

me: no — why are you my *fucking steed*?

gideon: because you're my friend, wingnut. because
    underneath all that denial, you're someone who's
    deeply, deeply nice. and because ever since you
    first mentioned it to me, i've been dying to see this
    musical.

me: okay, okay, okay.

gideon: and the second part?

me: what second part?

gideon: talking to maura.

me: you're kidding.

gideon: not one bit. you have fifteen minutes while i
    get the car.

me: i don't want to.

gideon gives me a hard look.

gideon: what are you, three years old?

me: but why should i?

gideon: i bet you can answer that one yourself.

i tell him he's totally out of line. he waves me off and
says i need to do it, and that he'll honk when he gets here
to pick me up.

the sick thing is, i know he's right. this whole time, i've thought the silent treatment was working. because it's not like i miss her. then i realize that missing her or not missing her isn't the point. the point is that i'm still carrying around what happened as much as she is. and i need to get rid of it. because both of us poured the toxins into our toxic friendship. and while i didn't exactly invent an imaginary boyfriend trap, i certainly contributed enough errors to our trials. there's no way we're ever going to find an ideal state of *it*. but i guess i'm seeing that we have to at least make it to an *it* we can bear.

i walk outside and she's right there in the same place at the end of the day that she is at the start of the day. perching on a wall, notebook out. staring at the other kids as they walk by, no doubt looking down at each and every one of them, including me.

i feel like i should've prepared a speech. but that would require me to know what i'm going to say. i have no idea, really. the best i can come up with is

me: hey

to which she says

maura: hey

she gives me that blank stare. i look at my shoes.

maura: to what do i owe this pleasure?

this is the way we talked to each other. always. and i

don't have the energy for it anymore. that's not how i want to talk with friends. not always.

> me: maura, stop.
> maura: stop? you're kidding, right? you don't talk to me for a month, and when you do, it's to tell me to stop?
> me: that's not why i came over here. . . .
> maura: then why did you come over here?
> me: i don't know, okay?
> maura: what does that mean? of course you know.
> me: look. i just want you to know that while i still think what you did was completely shitty, i realize that i was shitty to you, too. not in the elaborately shitty way that you were to me, but still pretty shitty. i should have just been honest with you and told you i didn't want to talk to you or be your boyfriend or be your best friend or anything like that. i tried — i swear i tried. but you didn't want to hear what i was saying, and i used that as an excuse to let it go on.
> maura: you didn't mind me when i was isaac. when we would chat every night.
> me: but that was a lie! a complete lie!

now maura looked me right in the eye.

> maura: c'mon, will — you know there's no such thing as a complete lie. there's always some truth in there.

i don't know how to react to that. i just say the next thing that comes to my mind.

me: it wasn't you i liked. it was isaac. i liked isaac.

the blankness has disappeared now. there's sadness instead.

maura: . . . and isaac liked you.

i want to say to her: i just want to be myself. and i want to be with someone who's just himself. that's all. i want to see through all the performance and all the pretending and get right to the truth. and maybe this is the most truth that maura and i will ever find — an acknowledgment of the lie, and of the feelings that fell behind it.

me: i'm sorry, maura.
maura: i'm sorry, too.

this is why we call people exes, i guess — because the paths that cross in the middle end up separating at the end. it's too easy to see an X as a cross-out. it's not, because there's no way to cross out something like that. the X is a diagram of two paths.
i hear a honk and turn to see gideon pulling up in his mom's car.

me: i gotta go.
maura: so go.

i leave her and get in the car with gideon and tell him everything that just happened. he says he's proud of me, and i don't know what to do with that. i ask him me: why?

and he says

gideon: for saying you were sorry. i wasn't sure if you'd
   be able to do that.

i tell him i wasn't sure, either. but it's how i felt. and i
wanted to be honest.

suddenly — it's like the next thing i know — we're on the
road. i'm not even sure if we're going to make it to tiny's
show on time. i'm not even sure i should be there. i'm not
even sure that i want to see tiny. i just want to see how the
play turned out.

gideon is whistling along to the radio beside me. normally that kind of shit annoys me, but this time it doesn't.

me: i wish i could show him the truth.
gideon: tiny?
me: yeah. you don't have to date someone to think
   they're great, right?

we drive some more. gideon starts whistling again. i
picture tiny running around backstage. then gideon stops
whistling. he smiles and hits the steering wheel.

gideon: by jove, i think i've got it!
me: did you really just say that?
gideon: admit it. you love it.
me: strangely, i do.

gideon: i think i have an idea.

so he tells me. and i can't believe i have such a sick and twisted and brilliant individual sitting at my side.

even more than that, though, i can't believe i'm about to do what he's suggesting.

chapter nineteen

Jane and I spend the hours before Opening Night constructing the perfect preshow playlist, which comprises—as requested—odd-numbered pop punk songs and even-numbered tunes from musicals. "Annus Miribalis" makes an appearance; we even include the punkest song from the resolutely unpunk Neutral Milk Hotel. As for the songs from musicals, we choose nine distinct renditions of "Over the Rainbow," including a reggae one.

Once we're finished debating and downloading, Jane heads home to change. I'm anxious to get to the auditorium, but it seems unfair to Tiny merely to wear jeans and a Willy the Wildkit T-shirt to the most important event of his life. So I put one of Dad's sports coats over the Wildkit shirt, fix my hair, and feel ready.

I wait at home until Mom pulls in, take the keys from her before she can even get the door all the way open, and drive to school.

I walk into the mostly empty auditorium—curtain time is still more than an hour away—and I'm met by Gary, whose hair is dyed lighter, and chopped short and messy like mine.

Also, he's wearing my clothes, which I delivered to him yesterday: khakis; a short-sleeve, plaid button-down I love; and my black Chucks. The entire effect would be surreal except the clothes are ridiculously wrinkled.

"What, Tiny couldn't find an iron?" I ask.

"Grayson," Gary says, "look at your pants, man."

I do. Huh. I didn't even know that jeans *could* wrinkle. He puts his arm around me and says, "I always thought it was part of your look."

"It is now," I say. "How's it going? Are you nervous?"

"I'm a little nervous, but I'm not Tiny nervous. Actually, could you go back there and, um, try to help? This," he says, gesturing at the outfit, "was for dress rehearsal. I gotta put on my White Sox garb."

"Done and done," I say. "Where is he?"

"Bathroom backstage," Gary answers. I hand him the preshow CD, jog down the aisle, and snake behind the heavy red curtain. I'm met by a gaggle of cast and crew in various stages of costume, and for once they are quiet, working away on each other's makeup. All the guys in the cast wear White Sox uniforms, complete with cleats and high socks pulled up over their tight pants. I say hi to Ethan, the only one I really know, and then I'm about to look for the bathroom when I notice the set. It's a very realistic baseball field dugout, which surprises me. "This is the set for the whole play?" I ask Ethan.

"God no," he says. "There's a different one for each act."

I hear in the distance a thunderous roar followed by a horrifying series of splashes, and my first thought is, *Tiny has written an elephant into the play, and the elephant has just vomited*, but then I realize that Tiny is the elephant.

Against my better judgment, I follow the sound to a bathroom, whereupon it promptly happens again. I can see his feet peeking out the bottom of the stall. "Tiny," I say.

"BLLLLAAARRRRGGGGH," he answers, and then sucks in a desperate wheezing breath before more pours forth. The smell is overpowering, but I step forward and push the door open a bit. Tiny, wearing the world's largest Sox uniform, hugs the toilet. "Nerves or sickness?" I ask.

"BLLLLLAAAAAAOOOO." One cannot help but be surprised by the sheer volume of what pours forth from Tiny's distended mouth. I notice some lettuce and wish I hadn't, because then I begin to wonder: Tacos? Turkey sandwich? I start to feel like I may join him.

"Okay, bud, just get it all up and you'll be fine."

Nick bursts into the bathroom then, moaning, "The smell, the smell," and then says, "Do not fuck your hair up, Cooper! Keep that head out of the toilet. We spent hours on that hair!"

Tiny sputters and coughs a bit and then croaks, "My throat. So raw." He and I realize simultaneously: the central voice of the show is shot.

I take one armpit and Nick takes another and we pull him up and away. I flush, trying not to look into the unspeakable horror in the toilet. "What did you *eat*?"

"A chicken burrito and a steak burrito from Burrito Palace," he answers. His voice sounds all weird, and he knows it, so he tries to sing. "What's second base for a—shit shit shit shit shit I wrecked my voice. Shit."

With Nick still beneath one Tiny arm and me beneath the other, we walk back toward the crew, and I shout, "I need some warm tea with a lot of honey and some Pepto-Bismol immediately, people!"

Jane runs up wearing a white, men's v-neck T-shirt, Sharpie-scrawled with the words *I'm with Phil Wrayson*.

"I'm on it," she says. "Tiny, you need anything else?"
He holds up a hand to quiet us and then groans, "What is that?"

"What is what?" I ask.

"That noise. In the distance. Is that—is that—goddamn it, Grayson, did you put 'Over the Rainbow' on the preshow CD?"

"Oh yes," I say. "Repeatedly."

"TINY COOPER HATES 'OVER THE RAINBOW'!" His voice cracks as he screams. "Shit, my voice is so gone. Shit."

"Stay quiet," I say. "We're gonna fix this, dude. Just don't puke anymore."

"I am bereft of burrito to puke," he answers.

"STAY QUIET," I insist.

He nods. And for a few minutes, while everyone runs around fanning their pancake faces and whispering to one another how great they'll be, I'm alone with a silent Tiny Cooper. "I didn't know you could get nervous. Do you get nervous before football games?" He shakes his head no. "Okay, just nod if I'm right. You're scared the play isn't actually that good." He nods. "Worried about your voice." Nod. "What else? Is that it?" He shakes his head no. "Um, you're worried it won't change homophobic minds." No. "You're worried you'll hurl onstage." No. "I don't know, Tiny, but whatever you're worried about, you're bigger than the worries. You're gonna *kill* out there. The ovation will last for *hours*. Longer than the play itself."

"*Will*," he whispers.

"Dude, save the voice."

"Will," he says again.

"Yeah?"

"No. *Will*."

"You mean the other Will," I say, and he just raises his eyebrows at me and smirks.

"I'll go look," I say. Twenty minutes to curtain, and the auditorium is now damn near full. I stand on the edge of the stage looking out for a second, feeling a little bit famous. Then I jog down the stairs and slowly walk up the stage-right aisle. I want him here, too. I want it possible for people like Will and Tiny to be friends, not just tried errors.

Even though I feel like I know Will, I barely remember what he looks like. I try to exclude each face in each row. A thousand people texting and laughing and squirming in their seats. A thousand people reading the program in which, I later learn, Jane and I are specially thanked for "being awesome." A thousand people waiting to see Gary pretend to be me for a couple hours, with no idea what they're about to see. And I don't know, either, of course—I know the play has changed in the months since I read it, but I don't know how.

All these people, and I try to look at every last one of them. I see Mr. Fortson, the GSA advisor, sitting with his partner. I see two of our assistant principals. And then as I get into the middle, my eyes scanning faces looking for Will Graysony ones, I see two older faces staring back at me on the aisle. My parents.

"What are you doing here?"

My father shrugs. "You will be surprised to learn it was not my idea."

Mom nudges him. "Tiny wrote me a very nice Facebook message inviting us *personally*, and I just thought that was so sweet."

"You're Facebook friends with Tiny?"

"Yes. He request-friended me," Mom says, epically failing to speak Facebook.

"Well, thanks for coming. I'm gonna be backstage but I'll, um, see you after."

"Say hi to Jane for us," Mom says, all smiley and conspiratorial.

"Will do."

I finish making my way up the aisle and then walk back the stage-left aisle. No Will Grayson. When I get backstage, I see Jane holding a supersize bottle of Pepto-Bismol.

She turns it upside down and says, "He drank it all."

Tiny jumps out from behind the set and sings, "And now I feel GrrrrrEAT!" His voice sounds fine for the moment.

"Rock 'n' roll," I tell him. He walks up to me and looks at me askingly. "There's like twelve hundred people in the audience, Tiny," I say.

"You didn't see him," he says, nodding softly. "Okay. Yeah. Okay. That's okay. Thanks for making me shut up."

"And flushing your ten thousand gallons of vomit."

"Sure, also that." He takes a big breath and puffs out his cheeks, rendering his face almost perfectly circular. "I guess it's time."

Tiny gathers the cast and crew around him. He kneels

in the center of a thick mass of people, everyone touching everyone because one of the laws of nature is that theater people love to be touchy. The cast is in the first circle around Tiny, everyone—guy and girl—dressed like White Sox. Then the chorus, dressed all in black for the moment. Jane and I lean in, too. Tiny says, "I just want to say thank you and you're all amazing and it's all about falling. Also I'm sorry I hurled earlier. I was hurling because I actually got awesome-poisoning from being around so many awesome people." That gets a bit of nervous laughter. "I know you're freaked out but just trust me: you're fabulous. And anyway, it's not about you. Let's go make some dreams come true."

Everyone kind of shouts and does this thing where we raise up one hand to the ceiling, and then there are a lot of jazz fingers. The light beneath the curtain is extinguished. Three football players push the set forward into its place. I step off to the side, standing in cave-darkness next to Jane, whose fingers interlace with mine. My heart pounds, and I can only imagine what it's like to be Tiny now, praying that a quart of Pepto-Bismol will coat his vocal cords, that he won't forget a line or fall or pass out or hurl. It's bad enough in the wings, and I realize the courage it actually takes to get onstage and tell the truth. Worse, to *sing* the truth.

A disembodied voice says, "To prevent interruptions of the fabulousness, please turn off your cell phones." I reach into a pocket with my free hand and click mine over to vibrate. I whisper to Jane, "*I might puke,*" and she says, "*Shh,*" and I whisper, "Hey, are my clothes always superwrinkly?" and she whispers, "Yes. *Shh,*" and squeezes my hand. The curtain parts. The applause is polite.

Everyone in the cast sits on the dugout bench except for Tiny, who walks nervously back and forth in front of the players. "Come on, Billy. Be patient, Billy. Wait for your pitch." I realize that Tiny isn't playing Tiny; he's playing the coach.

Some pudgy freshman plays Tiny instead. He can't stop moving his legs around; I can't tell if he's acting or nervous. He says, all exaggeratedly effeminate, "Hey, Batta Batta THWING batta." It sounds like he's flirting with the batter.

"Idiot," someone on the bench says. "*Our guy* is batting."

Gary says, "Tiny's rubber. You're glue. Whatever you say bounces off him and sticks to you." I can tell from his sloping shoulders and meek look that Gary's me.

"Tiny's gay," adds someone else.

The coach wheels around to the bench and shouts. "Hey! HEY! No insulting teammates."

"It's not an insult," Gary says. But he isn't Gary anymore. It isn't Gary talking. It's me. "It's just a thing. Like, some people are gay. Some people have blue eyes."

"Shut up, Wrayson," the coach says.

The kid playing Tiny glances gratefully at the kid playing me, and then one of the bullies stage-whispers, "You're so gay for each other."

And I say, "We're not *gay*. We're *eight*." This happened. I'd forgotten it, but seeing the moment resurrected, I remember.

And the kid says, "You want to go to second base . . . WITH TINY."

The me onstage just rolls his eyes. And then the pudgy kid playing Tiny stands up and takes a step forward, in front of the coach and sings, "What's second base for a gay man?" And then Tiny takes a step forward and joins him, harmonizing, and they launch into the greatest musical song I've ever heard. The chorus goes:

What's second base for a gay man?
Is it tuning in Tokyo?
I can't see how that would feel good
But maybe that's how it should go?

Behind the two Tinys singing arm in arm, the guys in the chorus—including Ethan—pull off a hilariously elaborate old-fashioned, high-stepping, highly choreographed dance, their bats used as canes and their ball caps as top hats. Midway through, half the guys swing their bats toward the heads of half the others, and even though from my side view I can see it's totally faked, when the other boys fall backward dramatically and the music cuts out, I gasp with the audience. Moments later, they all jump up in a single motion and the song starts up again. When it's done, Tiny and the kid dance offstage to thunderous shouts from the crowd, and as the lights cut, Tiny damn near lands in my arms, bathed in sweat.

"Not bad," he says.

I just shake my head, amazed. Jane helps him out of his shoes and says, "Tiny, you're kind of a *genius*." He rips off his baseball uniform to reveal a very Tiny purple polo shirt and chino shorts.

"I know, right?" he says. "Okay, time to come out to the folks," he says, and hustles out onto the stage. Jane grabs my hand and kisses me on the neck.

It's a quiet scene, as Tiny tells his parents he's "probably kinda gay." His dad is sitting silent while his mom sings about unconditional love. The song is only funny because Tiny keeps cutting in with other comings-out each time his mom sings, "We'll always love our Tiny," like, "Also, I cheated in algebra," and, "There's a reason your vodka tastes watered down," and "I feed my peas to the dog."

When the song ends, the lights go down again, but Tiny doesn't leave the stage. When the lights go back up, there's no set, but judging from the elaborately costumed cast, I gather we're at a Gay Pride Parade. Tiny and Phil Wrayson stand center stage as people march past, chanting their chants, waving dramatically. Gary looks so much like me it's weird. He looks more like freshman-year me than Tiny looks like freshman-year Tiny.

They talk for a minute and then Tiny says, "Phil, I'm gay."

Stunned, I say, "No."

And he says, "It's true."

I shake my head. "You mean, like, you're happy?"

"No, I mean, like, that guy," he points at Ethan, who's wearing a skintight yellow wifebeater, "is hot and if I talked to him for a while and he had a good personality and respected me as a person I would let him kiss me on the mouth."

"You're gay?" I say, seemingly uncomprehending.

"Yeah. I know. I know it's a shock. But I wanted you to be the first to know. Other than my parents, I mean."

And then Phil Wrayson breaks out into song, singing more or less exactly what I said when this really happened:

"Next you're gonna tell me the sky is blue, that you use girl shampoo, that critics don't appreciate Blink 182. Oh, next you're gonna tell me the Pope is Catholic, that hookers turn tricks, that Elton John sucks HEY."

And then the song turns into a call and response, with Tiny singing his surprise that I knew he was gay and me singing that it was obvious.

"But I'm a football player."

"Dude, you couldn't be gayer."

"I thought my straight-acting deserved a Tony."

"But, Tiny, you own a thousand My Little Ponies!"

And so on. I can't stop laughing, but more than that, I can't believe how well he remembers it all, how good— for all of our bad—we've always been to each other. And I sing, "You don't want me, do you?" And he answers, "I would prefer a kangaroo," and behind us the chorus high-kicks like the Rockettes.

Jane puts her hands on a shoulder to bend me down and whispers, "See? He loves you, too," and I turn to her and kiss her in the quick dark moment between the end of the song and the beginning of the applause.

As the curtain closes for a set change, I can't *see* the standing ovation, but I can hear it.

Tiny runs offstage, shouting "WOOOOOOOOOOT!"

"It could actually go to Broadway," I tell him.

"It got a lot better when I made it about love." He looks at me, smiling with half his mouth, and I know that's as close as he'll ever come. Tiny's the gay one, but I'm the sentimentalist. I nod and whisper *thanks*.

"Sorry if you come across a little annoying in this next

part." Tiny reaches up to touch his hair and Nick appears out of nowhere, diving over an amp to grab Tiny's arm, screaming, "DO NOT TOUCH YOUR PERFECT HAIR." The curtain rises, and the set is a hallway in our school. Tiny's putting up posters. I'm annoying him, that catch in my voice. I don't mind it, or at least I don't mind it much—love is bound up in truth, after all. Just after that scene, there's one with Tiny drunk at a party in which the character Janey gets her only time onstage—a duet with Phil Wrayson sung on opposite sides of a passed-out Tiny, the song culminating in Gary's voice suddenly toughening into confidence and then Janey and me leaning over Tiny's mumbling half-conscious body and kissing. I can only half watch the scene, because I keep wanting to see Jane's smile as she watches.

The songs get better and better from there, until, in the last song before intermission, the whole audience is singing along as Oscar Wilde sings over a sleeping Tiny,

> *The pure and simple truth*
> *Is rarely pure and never simple.*
> *What's a boy to do*
> *When lies and truth are both sinful?*

As that song ends, the curtain closes and the house lights come up for intermission. Tiny runs up to us and puts a paw on each of our shoulders and lets forth a yawp of joy. "It's hilarious," I tell him. "Really. It's just . . . awesome."

"Woot! The second half's a lot darker, though. It's the romantic part. Okay okay okay okay, see you after!" he says, and then races off to congratulate, and probably chastise, his cast. Jane takes me off into a corner backstage, secluded behind the set, and says, "You really did all that? You looked after him in Little League?"

"Eh, he looked after me, too," I say.

"Compassion is hot," she says as we kiss. After a while, I see the houselights dim and then come back up. Jane and I head back to our stage-side vantage point. The houselights go down again, signaling the end of intermission. And after a moment, a voice from on high says, "Love is the most common miracle."

At first I think God is, like, talking to us, but I quickly realize it's Tiny coming in over the speakers. The second half is beginning.

Tiny sits on the front edge of the stage in the dark, saying, "Love is always a miracle, everywhere, every time. But for us, it's a little different. I don't want to say it's *more* miraculous," he says, and people laugh a little. "It is, though." The lights come up slowly, and only now do I see that behind Tiny is an actual honest-to-God swing set that seems to have been possibly literally dug out of a playground and transported to the stage. "Our miracle is different because people say it's impossible. As it sayeth in Leviticus, 'Dude shall not lie with dude.'" He looks down, and then out into the audience, and I can tell he is looking for the other Will and not finding him. He stands up.

"But it doesn't say that dude shall not fall in love with dude, because that's just impossible, right? The gays are animals, answering their animal desires. It's impossible for animals to fall in love. And yet—"

Suddenly, Tiny's knees buckle and he collapses in a

heap. I jolt up and start to run onstage to pick him up, but Jane grabs a fistful of my shirt as Tiny raises his head toward the audience and says, "I fall and I fall and I fall and I fall and I fall."

And at that very moment, my phone buzzes in my pocket. I dig it out of my pocket. The caller ID reads *Will Grayson*.

chapter twenty

what's in front of me is the trippiest thing i've ever seen. by far.

i honestly didn't think gideon and i would make it on time. chicago traffic is unkind to begin with, but in this case it was moving slower than a stoner's thoughts. gideon and i had to have a swearing contest in order to calm ourselves down.

now that we've made it, i'm guessing there's no way our plan is going to work. it's both insane and genius, which is what tiny deserves. and it required me to do a lot of things i don't usually do, including:

- talking to strangers
- asking strangers for favors
- being willing to make a complete fool of myself
- letting someone else (gideon) help me

it also relies on a number of things beyond my control, including:

- the kindness of strangers

- the ability of strangers to be spontaneous
- the ability of strangers to drive quickly
- tiny's musical lasting more than one act

i'm sure it's going to be a total disaster. but i guess the point is that i'm going to do it anyway.

i know i've cut it real close, because when gideon and i walk into the auditorium, they're carrying a swing set onto the stage. and not just any swing set. i recognize that swing set. that *exact same* swing set. and that's when the trippiness kicks in, big-time.

gideon: holy shit.

at this point, gideon knows everything that went on. not just with me and tiny, but with me and maura, and me and my mom, and basically me and the whole world. and not once has he told me i was stupid, or mean, or awful, or beyond help. in other words, he hasn't said any of the things i've been saying to myself. instead, in the car ride over, he said

gideon: it all makes sense.
me: it does?
gideon: completely. i would've done the same things
    you did.
me: liar.
gideon: no lie.

then, completely out of nowhere, he held out his pinkie.

gideon: pinkie swear, no lie.

and i hooked my pinkie in his. we drove that way for a little bit, with my little finger curled into his little finger.

me: next thing you know, we'll be blood brothers.
gideon: and we'll be having sleepovers.
me: in the backyard.
gideon: we won't invite the girls.
me: what girls?
gideon: the hypothetical girls that we won't invite.
me: will there be s'mores?
gideon: what do you think?

i knew there would be s'mores.

gideon: you know you're insane, right?
me: this is news?
gideon: for doing what you're about to do.
me: it was your idea.
gideon: but you did it, not me. i mean, you're doing it.
me: we'll see.

and it was strange, because as we drove on, it wasn't gideon or tiny i was thinking about, but maura. as i was in that car with gideon, so completely comfortable with myself, i couldn't help but think that this was what she wanted from me. this is what she always wanted from me. and it was never going to be like this. but i guess for the first time i saw why she would try so hard for it. and why tiny tried so hard for it.

now gideon and i are standing in the back of the theater. i'm looking around to see who else is here, but i can't
really tell in the darkness.

the swing set stays in the back of the stage as a chorus
line of boys dressed as boys and girls dressed as boys lines
up in front of it. i can tell this is meant to be a parade of tiny's ex-boyfriends because as they line up, they are singing,

chorus: we are the parade of ex-boyfriends!

i have no doubt the kid at the end is supposed to be me.
(he's dressed all in black and looks really moody.)

they all start singing their breakup lines:

ex-boyfriend 1: you're too clingy
ex-boyfriend 2: you're too singy
ex-boyfriend 3: you're so massive
ex-boyfriend 4: i'm too passive.
ex-boyfriend 5: i'd rather be friends.
ex-boyfriend 6: i don't date tight ends.
ex-boyfriend 7: i found another guy.
ex-boyfriend 8: i don't have to tell you why.
ex-boyfriend 9: i don't feel the spark.
ex-boyfriend 10: it was only a lark.
ex-boyfriend 11: you mean you won't put out?
ex-boyfriend 12: i can't conquer my doubt.
ex-boyfriend 13: i have other things to do.
ex-boyfriend 14: i have other guys to screw.
ex-boyfriend 15: our love has all been in your head.
ex-boyfriend 16: i'm worried that you'll break my bed.

ex-boyfriend 17: i think I'll just stay home and read.
ex-boyfriend 18: i think you're in love with my need.

that's it — hundreds of texts and conversations, thousands upon thousands of words spoken and sent, all boiled down into a single line. is that what relationships become? a reduced version of the hurt, nothing else let in. it was more than that. i know it was more than that.

and maybe tiny knows, too. because all the other boyfriends leave the stage except for boyfriend #1, and i realize that we're going to go through them all, and maybe each one will have a new lesson for tiny and the audience.

since it's going to be a while before we get to ex-boyfriend #18, i figure it's a good time for me to call the other will grayson. i'm worried he'll have his phone off, but when i go out to the lobby to call (leaving gideon to save me a seat), he picks up and says he'll meet me in a minute.

i recognize him right away, even though there's something different about him, too.

me: hey
o.w.g.: hey
me: one helluva show in there.
o.w.g.: i'll say. i'm glad you came.
me: me too. because, you see, i had this idea. well,
    actually, it was my friend's idea. but here's
    what we're doing. . . .

i explain it to him.

o.w.g.: that's insane.

me: i know.

o.w.g.: do you think they're really here?

me: they said they would be. but even if they're not, at least there's you and me.

the other will grayson looks terrified.

o.w.g.: you're going to have to go first. i'll back you up, but i don't think i could go first.

me: you have a deal.

o.w.g.: this is totally crazy.

me: but tiny's worth it.

o.w.g.: yeah, tiny's worth it.

i know we should go back to the play. but there's something i want to ask him, now that he's in front of me.

me: can i ask you something personal, will grayson to will grayson?

o.w.g.: um . . . sure.

me: do you feel things are different? i mean, since the first time we met?

o.w.g. thinks about it for a second, then nods.

o.w.g.: yeah. i guess i'm not the will grayson i used to be.

me: me neither.

i open the door to the auditorium and peek in again. they're already on ex-boyfriend #5.

> o.w.g.: i better return backstage. jane's going to wonder
> where i went.
> me: jane, eh?
> o.w.g.: yeah, jane.

it's so cute — there are like two hundred different emotions that flash across his face when he says her name — everything from extreme anxiety to utter bliss.

> me: well, let's take our places.
> o.w.g.: good luck, will grayson.
> me: good luck to us all.

i sneak back in and find gideon, who fills me in on what's going on.

> gideon (whispering): ex-boyfriend six was all about the
> jockstraps. to the point of fetish, i'd say.

almost all the ex-boyfriends are like this — never really three-dimensional, but it soon becomes apparent that this is deliberate, that tiny's showing how he never got to know all of their dimensions, that he was so caught up in being in love that he didn't really take the time to think about what he was in love with. it's agonizingly truthful, at least for exes like me. (i see a few more boys shifting in their seats, so i'm probably not the only ex in the audience.) we make it through the first seventeen exes, and then there's a blackout and the swing set is moved to the center of the stage. suddenly, tiny's in the spotlight, on the swing, and it's like my life has rewound and is playing back to me, only in musical form. it's exactly as i remember it . . . until it's not, and tiny's inventing this new dialogue for us.

me-on-stage: i'm really sorry.
tiny: don't be. i fell for you. i know what happens at the end of falling – landing.
me-on-stage: i just get so pissed off at myself. i'm the worst thing in the world for you. i'm your pinless hand grenade.
tiny: i like my pinless hand grenade.

it's funny – i wonder if i'd said that, and if he'd said that, then maybe things would have played out differently. because i would have known that he understood, at least a little. but i guess he needed to be writing it as a musical to see it. or say it.

me-on-stage: well, i don't like being your pinless hand grenade. or anybody's.

but the weird thing is, for once i feel the pin is in.

tiny's looking out into the audience right now. there's no way for him to know i'm here. but maybe he's looking for me anyway.

tiny: i just want you to be happy. if that's with me or
       with someone else or with nobody. i just want you
       to be happy. i just want you to be okay with life.
       with life as it is. and me, too. it is so hard to accept
       that life is falling. falling and landing and falling
       and landing. i agree it's not ideal. i agree.

he's talking to me. he's talking to himself. maybe there's
no difference.
  i get it. i understand it.
  and then he loses me.

tiny: but there is the word, this word phil wrayson
       taught me once: *weltschmerz*. it's the depression you
       feel when the world as it is does not line up with
       the world as you think it should be. i live in a big
       goddamned *weltzschermz* ocean, you know? and so
       do you. and so does everyone. because everyone
       thinks it should be possible just to keep falling
       and falling forever, to feel the rush of the air on
       your face as you fall, that air pulling your face into
       a brilliant goddamned smile. and that *should* be
       possible. you *should* be able to fall forever.

and i think: no.
  seriously. no.
  because i have spent my life falling. not the kind that
tiny's talking about. he's talking about love. i'm talking
about life. in my kind of falling, there's no landing. there's
only hitting the ground. hard. dead, or wanting to be dead.
so the whole time you're falling, it's the worst feeling in the

302

world. because you feel you have no control over it. because you know how it ends.

i don't want to fall. all i want to do is stand on solid ground.

and the weird thing is, i feel like i'm doing that now. because i am trying to do something good. in the same way that tiny is trying to do something good.

tiny: you're still a pinless grenade over the world not being perfect.

no, i am a pinless grenade over the world being cruel. but every time i'm proven wrong, that pin goes in a little more.

tiny: and i'm still — every time this happens to me, everytime i land, it still hurts like it has never happened before.

he's swinging higher now, kicking his legs hard, the swing set groaning. it looks like he's going to bring the whole contraption down, but he just keeps pumping his legs and pulling against the chain with his arms and talking.

tiny: because we can't stop the *weltschmerz*. we can't stop imagining the world as it might be. which is awesome! it is my favorite thing about us!

when he gets to the top of his arc now, he's above the reach of the lights, screaming down at the audience from the darkness. then he swings back into view, his back and ass rushing toward us in the audience.

tiny: and if you're gonna have that, you're gonna have
    falling. they don't call it *rising* in love. that's why i
    love us!

at the top of the arc, above the lights, he kicks out of the
swing. he is so goddamned nimble and quick about it, i can
barely see it, but he lifts himself up by the arms and pulls
his legs up and then just lets go and grabs onto a rafter. the
swing falls before he does, and everyone — the audience,
the chorus — gasps.

tiny: because we know what will happen when we fall!

the answer to this is, of course, that we will crash
right on our ass. which is exactly what tiny does. he lets
go of the rafters, crashes down right in front of the swing
set, and collapses in a heap. i flinch, and gideon grabs my
hand.
    i can't tell whether the kid playing me is supposed to be
in character or out of character when he asks tiny if he's all
right. whatever the case, tiny waves the imitation me away,
motions to the conductor, and a moment later, it starts — a
quiet song, all piano keys spaced far apart. tiny recovers his
breath during the intro and starts to sing again.

tiny:
    it's all about falling
    you land and get up so you can fall again
    it's all about falling
    i won't be afraid to hit that wall again

it's chaos up there. the chorus is desperately clinging to the chorus. they keep singing how it's about the falling, and then tiny steps forward and says his lines over them.

> tiny: maybe tonight you're scared of falling, and maybe there's somebody here or somewhere else you're thinking about, worrying over, fretting over, trying to figure out if you want to fall, or how and when you're gonna land, and i gotta tell you friends that to stop thinking about the landing, because it's all about falling.

it's incredible. it's like he's lifting off the stage, he believes in his words so strongly. and i realize what it is that i have to do. i have to help him realize that it's the belief, not the words, that mean everything. i have to make him realize the point isn't the falling. it's the floating.

tiny calls for them to bring up the houselights. he's looking around, but he doesn't see me.

i gulp.

gideon: ready?

the answer to this question is always going to be no. but i have to do it anyway.

> tiny: maybe there is something you're afraid to say, or someone you're afraid to love, or somewhere you're afraid to go. it's gonna hurt. it's gonna hurt because it matters.

no, i think. NO.

it doesn't have to hurt.

i stand up. and then i almost sit down again. it is taking all of my strength to stand up.

i look at gideon.

tiny: but i just fell and landed and i am still standing
     here to tell you that you've gotta learn to love the
     falling, because it's all about falling.

i reach out my pinkie. gideon takes it in his.

tiny: just fall for once. let yourself fall!

the whole cast is on the stage now. i see that the other will grayson has snuck on, too, and he's wearing these wrinkled jeans and a plaid shirt. right next to him is a girl who must be jane, wearing this shirt that says *I'm with Phil Wrayson*.

tiny makes a gesture, and suddenly everyone onstage is singing.

chorus: hold me closer, hold me closer

and i'm still standing. i'm making eye contact with the other will grayson, who looks nervous but smiles anyway. and i'm seeing a few people nod in my direction. god, i hope they're who i want them to be.

suddenly, with a grand wave of his arms, tiny stops the music. he moves to the front of the stage and the rest of the stage goes dark. it's just him in a spotlight, looking out into the audience. he just stands there for a moment, taking it all in. and then he closes the show by saying:

tiny: my name is tiny cooper. and this is my story.

there's a silence then. people are waiting for the curtain to go down, for the show to definitely be over, for the ovations to start. i have less than a second. i squeeze gideon's pinkie tight, then let go. i raise my hand.
tiny sees me.
other people in the audience see me.
i yell

me: TINY COOPER!

and that's it.
i really hope this is going to work.

me: my name is will grayson. and i appreciate you, tiny cooper!

now everyone's looking at me, and many of them are confused. they have no idea whether this is still part of the show.
what can i say? i'm giving it a new ending.
now this twentysomething-year-old man in a hipster vest stands up. he looks to me for a second, smiles, then turns to tiny and says

man: my name is also will grayson. i live in wilmette.
and i also appreciate you, tiny cooper.

cue the seventy-nine-year-old in the back row.

old guy: my name is william t. grayson, but you can
     call me will. and i sure as heck appreciate you, tiny
     cooper.

thank you, google. thank you, internet telephone direc-
tories. thank you, keepers of the name.

fortysomething woman: hi! i'm wilma grayson, from
     hyde park. and i appreciate you, tiny cooper.

ten-year-old boy: hey. i'm will grayson. the fourth. my
     dad couldn't be here, but we both appreciate you,
     tiny cooper.

there should be one other. a sophomore at northwestern.
there's a dramatic pause. everyone's looking around.
and then HE stands up. if frenchy's could bottle him up
and sell him as porn, they'd probably own half of chicago
within a year. he's what would happen after nine months if
abercrombie fucked fitch. he's like a movie star, an olympic
swimmer, and america's next top male model all at once.
he's wearing a silver shirt and pink pants. everything about
him sparkles.
     not my type at all. but . . .

Gay God: my name is will grayson. and i *love* you, tiny
     cooper.

finally, tiny, who's been uncharacteristically speechless the whole time, gets out some words.

tiny: 847-555-3982
Gay God: 847-555-7363
tiny: WILL SOMEONE PLEASE WRITE THAT
    DOWN FOR ME?

half the audience nods.

and then it's quiet again. in fact, it's a little awkward. i don't know whether to sit down or what.

then there's a rustling from the dark part of the stage. the other will grayson walks out of the chorus. he walks right up to tiny and looks him in the eye.

o.w.g.: you know my name. and i love you, tiny cooper.
    although not in the same way that the guy in the
    pink pants might love you.

and then the girl who must be jane chimes in.

girl: my name is not will grayson, and i appreciate you
    a helluva lot, tiny cooper.

it's the strangest thing ever. one by one, everyone on-stage tells tiny cooper they appreciate him. (even the guy named phil wrayson — what are the odds?) then the audience gets into the act. row by row. some say it. some sing it. tiny's crying. i'm crying. everyone's crying.

i lose track of how long it takes. then, when it's all over, the applause starts. the loudest applause you've ever heard.

tiny steps to the front of the stage. people throw flowers.

he's brought us all together. we all feel that.

gideon: you did good.

i link our pinkies again.

me: yeah, we did good.

i nod to the other will grayson, up onstage. he nods to me. we have something between us, him and me.

but the truth?

everybody has it.

that's our curse and our blessing. that's our trial and our error and our *it*.

the applause continues. i look up at tiny cooper.

he may be heavy, but right now he floats.

ACKNOWLEDGMENTS:

We acknowledge that Jodi Reamer is a kickass agent, and furthermore acknowledge that she could beat both of us at once at arm-wrestling.

We acknowledge that picking your friend's nose is a personal choice, and may not be suitable with all personalities.

We acknowledge that this book probably wouldn't exist if Sarah Urist Green hadn't laughed out loud when we read the first two chapters to her a long time ago in an apartment far, far away.

We acknowledge that we were a little disappointed to learn that the Penguin clothing brand is in no way related to the Penguin publishing company, because we were hoping for a discount on smart polo shirts.

We acknowledge the unadulterated fabulousness of Bill Ott, Steffie Zvirin, and John's fairy godmother, Ilene Cooper.

We acknowledge that in the same way that you could never see the moon if it wasn't for the sun, there's no way you'd ever get to see us if it wasn't for the magnificent and continual brightness of our author friends.

We acknowledge that one of us cheated on the SATs, but he didn't mean to.

We acknowledge that nerdfighters are made of awesome.

We acknowledge that being the person God made you cannot separate you from God's love.

We acknowledge that we timed the completion of this book in order to persuade our masterful editor, Julie Strauss-Gabel, to name her child Will Grayson, even if it's a girl. Which is somewhat disingenuous, because we should probably be the ones naming babies after her. Even if they're boys.

A Conversation between
John Green and David Levithan

John Green: Okay, so admittedly I've heard the story before, but I never tire of it: How'd you come up with the idea for this book?

David Levithan: Funny you should ask. The idea of doing a book about two boys with the same name came from the fact that one of my best friends is named David Leventhal. Not the same name, but close enough. We both went to Brown, and were mistaken for each other a lot. Not only in the normal ways (mixed-up mail and phone calls) but also in some rather awkward, ultimately laughable ways. You see, David Leventhal is an extraordinary dancer. I, David Levithan, am not. So people would come up to me and say, "I saw you onstage last night—you seem to be such an oafish, clumsy guy; but when you dance, you're so graceful!" And I'd have to reply, "Um, that wasn't me onstage last night." It was like my alter ego was walking around campus; and eventually, right before I graduated, I called him up and we met up and became great friends. I wouldn't say our book is about How to Love Your Alter Ego, but it is about how another person can unlock—often inadvertently—the potential of your personality. Oh! And the punch line (which I often forget) is that one of David Leventhal's roommates/best friends in college was named . . . Jon Green. Totally coincidental. But that's a nice lead-in to my question: What has your experience been with other John Greens?

JG: There are, of course, hundreds of us—from real estate brokers in Mississippi to Australian botanists. I've met several John Greens, and they've all been delightful; but I did have one unpleasant run-in a few years ago. There is a John Green in Canada who is a Very Big Deal in the field of Bigfoot research, also known as Sasquatch-ery. (He is the author of such books as *Sasquatch: The Apes Among Us*.) A few years ago, I wrote an article for a magazine in which I casually mentioned that Bigfoot is, you know, fictional. A week after the story was published, I received a very angry letter from John Green, noted Sasquatologist, accusing me of having besmirched the good name of John Greens everywhere.

Fortunately, my reputation survived enough for you to want to write this book with me. So we wrote our first chapters with no idea of what the other person was writing and no idea whether the story would work. What were you thinking when I read my first chapter to you and you were introduced to Will and Tiny and Jane and the problem of picking one's friends and/or their noses?

DL: I don't want to sound easy, but you pretty much had me at the opening line. I mean, the minute you read it, I knew your chapter was going to start the book. And then when Tiny appeared . . . well, I certainly thought, "Oh, I can use this character." What I love is that it's a character everyone would have expected from me; but it's actually you who invented him, and in such an amazing way in relation to your Will. I was also surprised when Neutral Milk Hotel popped up. Because, you know, I'm supposed to be the music obsessive in this relationship. Had I known that I would suddenly be spending five or so years with "Holland, 1945" stuck in my head, I might have reacted differently. (Look, there it is again.)

Most of all, though, I was struck by how you and I had created two very different Wills but at the same time decided to grapple with some very similar ideas. (Note: I don't say "themes" here, because neither of us writes with "themes" in mind.) What was your reaction when you heard my first chapter?

JG: I loved it. I was shocked how immediately and completely I was inside your Will's head. Your half of the novel is very funny but also roaringly angry. One of the things I still love, even rereading your chapters for the millionth time, is how completely you're able to inhabit the mind of someone living with major depression. This is not a question; I just want you to say something about that.

DL: I wanted my will to be very much in the middle of things, because I don't feel there are enough books written about teens caught in the middle of things. I didn't want him to be full of self-loathing about being gay—he's fine with being gay but wants to keep it to himself, not out of fear, but out of a feeling that it's nobody else's business. He's lost a dad, and he's not completely over it; but he's not hung up on it either. And, most important, he lives with depression, but he's at the stage where he's living with it, not discovering it. So many novels—many of them excellent—are written about teens who first grapple with their depression and get help. There are very few about what happens next, when you have to live the rest of your life.

JG: I wonder if you can talk about the lower casedness of your will grayson.

DL: Oh, you noticed that, did you? The reason my will writes in lowercase is simple—that's how he sees himself. He is a lowercase person. He is used to communicating online, where people are encouraged to be lowercase people. His whole self-image is what he projects in that space, and his one comfortable form of communication is when he's anonymous and sending instant messages. It's not even something he thinks about. It's how his self-expression has formed. Is it stunted in some way? Absolutely. But at the same time, it's a true expression; and by the end of the book, I'd bet you don't even notice it. It's only jarring at first. But then you enter his world completely, get used to the rhythms of his life; and hopefully it makes sense.

I'm curious how Schrödinger's cat came into play in your chapters. If I remember correctly, it wasn't in the first draft. What sparked you to add it into the mix with Will and Jane?

JG: I think initially I was looking for another way to think about my Will's aversion to attachment; i.e., so long as you don't open the box, the cat is still alive. (Of course, the cat is also dead.) But I think a lot of the novel is about the weird relationship between identity and existence: In some ways, you are who you are because other people observe you; but in some ways, you are who you are in spite of other people's observations of you. One of the reasons nonphysicists have latched on to Schrödinger's thought experiment is because we all feel that tension between observed identity and interior identity.

DL: When we started talking about the book, neither of us had very many fans—my second book had just come out, and your first book was about to be published. Now we have more fans. And you have nerdfighters. What influence do you think that has on your work and your life?

JG: Well, my half of *Will Grayson, Will Grayson* is dedicated to a particular nerdfighter, but it could have been dedicated to all of nerdfighteria, because I am deeply inspired by their intellectual engagement and also their celebration of all things nerdy. (For those of you who don't know what a nerdfighter is, I make videos with my brother on YouTube; our fans are called nerdfighters because they fight for nerds and nerdiness.) I also learn a lot from them. It's really only because of nerdfighters that I am even aware that teenagers still like musicals.

DL: I couldn't have been more thrilled to marry into the nerdfighter family. Perhaps especially because so many of them like musicals. When you first wrote about Tiny and his musical, did you have any idea how much of it we would end up having in the book? And perhaps can you speak a little about the genesis of "The Nose Tackle (Likes Tight Ends)"?

JG: I had no idea we would ever see the musical in the book when the thought of it first occurred to me; but then as we moved forward, it seemed a good fit for the story we were telling. As to the genesis of "The Nose Tackle (Likes Tight Ends)," it's an old homophobic locker-room joke that I wanted to twist into a proud and celebratory observation. By the way, shouldn't there be an IRL musical?

DL: I'm working on it! Now, it may never, ever see the light of day. But slowly I've been putting on my enormously gay, gaily enormous thinking cap and have been composing some further show tunes. For example, the opening number. Now, I don't know if this will end up being it. But what I have right now is:

Act One, Scene One

It's a dark stage, and at first all you hear are murmurs, a heart-beat, and heavy breathing. Like, serious Lamaze. Then we see, in the middle of the stage, a large piece of paper showing two bare, spread legs, discreetly covered with a hospital sheet. The heartbeat gets louder. The breathing gets heavier. Lamaze on crack. And finally, as it all crescendos, TINY COOPER enters the world, crashing through the piece of paper and entering spectacularly onto the stage.

We are not going for realism here. He should not be naked and covered with amniotic fluid. That's gross. He should not be wearing a diaper. He's not into that. Instead, the person who emerges should be the large, stylish Tiny Cooper who you will see for the rest of the musical. If you want to delineate him from Tiny at other ages, you can have him wearing a button that says AGE: 0.

Most babies come into the world crying or gasping or snotting.

Not Tiny Cooper.

He comes into the world singing.

Cue: Opening chords of "I WAS BORN THIS WAY." This is a big, lively, belty number—because, let's face it, if Elphaba got to sing "Defying Gravity" at the start of *Wicked*, she would have been much, much happier throughout the whole show. Tiny has just crashed into the world—some would say he was pushed—and already he has a sense of who he is and what he's going to do. The music and the production value must reflect that. Sparkles, people. Think sparkles. Do not get stingy about the sparkles. The reason drag queens love them so much is that you can get them for cheap.

TINY (spoken):
Hello, my name is Tiny Cooper . . . what's yours? I've just been born; and, man, it feels good!

[Cue music.]

["I WAS BORN THIS WAY"]

TINY (singing):

> I was born this way
> Big-boned and happily gay
> I was born this way.
> Right here in the U.S. of A
>
> It's pointless to wonder why
> I ended up so G-A-Y
> From the very first day
> The rainbow's come my way
>
> I've got brown hair,
> big hips,
> blue blue eyes.
> And one day
> I'm gonna make out
> with guys,
> guys,
> guys!
>
> Why try to hide it?
> What good would that do?
> I was born this way
> And if you don't like it
> That says more about you
>
> If you find it odd
> Take it up with God
> Because who else do you think
> Could make me this way?
>
> All God's children wear traveling shoes whether you've got
> flat feet or twinkle toes. I'm going to dance right into this
> life And keep dancing as it goes
>
> I've got genes that fit me well
> And a spirit all my own

I was born this way
The rest is the great unknown

[really belting now]

I.
was.
born.
this.
way.

And I love.
the.
way.
I.
was.
born.

The rest
is the great unknown.
But I'm ready
Oh yes I'm ready
for it
to
begin!

DL: Now, I have to admit, this was written in August 2010. In September of this same year, at the MTV Video Music Awards, Lady Gaga (also enormously gay) announced that the title of her new album would be *Born This Way*. Coincidence? I think not. (Okay, I think so.) As of this writing, in November 2010, I have yet to hear her version. We'll see how it goes.

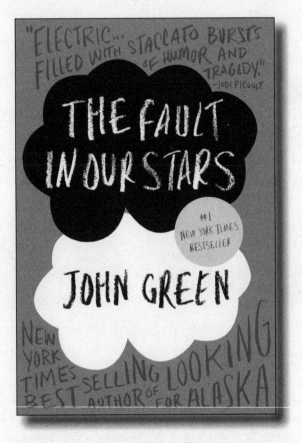

#1 *NEW YORK TIMES* BESTSELLER

Winner of the MICHAEL L. PRINTZ AWARD

A Michael L. Printz Honor book

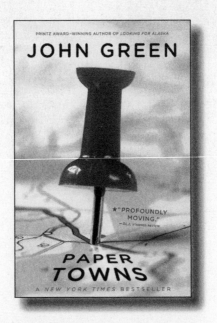

A *New York Times* Bestseller

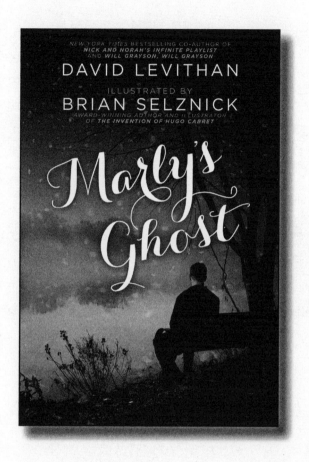

DAVID LEVITHAN

ILLUSTRATED BY

BRIAN SELZNICK

Marly's Ghost

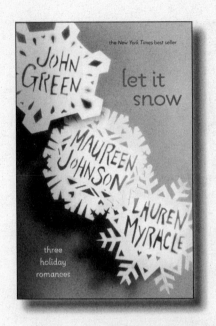

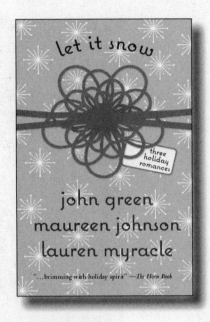

A *NEW YORK TIMES* BESTSELLER